Lawyers Gone Bad

by Vincent L. Scarsella

DIGITAL CRIME FICTION

Lawyers Gone Bad

by Vincent L. Scarsella

To Brooks!
Happy Reading!
Vin C. Scarsella

DIGITAL FICTION
P U B L I S H I N G   C O R P

Edition 2.01 Copyright © 2016 Digital Fiction Publishing Corp.
Story Copyright © 2016 Vincent Scarsella
All rights reserved.

ISBN-13 (paperback): 978-1-927598-24-5
ISBN-13 (e-book): 978-1-927598-25-2

Dedication

This book is dedicated to the many good lawyers out there.

— Vincent Scarsella

Part One
A Grand Mistake

Vincent Scarsella

Chapter One
Resignation

The Lawyer was crying.

His name was Frank Martin and he was slumped forward on a chair facing the desk of Dean Alessi, Deputy Director of the state's Lawyer Discipline Office. Dean had slid a resignation affirmation to the front of his desk so that Frank Martin could read and sign it. After staring blankly with red swollen eyes at the affirmation for a time, Martin slid it away, then leaned forward, put his face into his hands and started crying again.

Dean leaned back in his chair and waited. He'd seen lawyers cry before.

"Jesus, Dean," Frank said, finally looking up. "My life is over. Fucking ruined."

"It's not over, Frank," Dean said. "Your life as a lawyer is over. You're a talented guy. You'll find something else to do. It's either this, resign your license, or we file a disciplinary petition and the world gets to know what a scumbag thing you did. And you certainly don't want that, all the messy details coming out. Right? By resigning, that can't happen. Nobody will know why. Only you."

Dean sighed and waited as Frank drooped forward and seemed about ready to start sobbing again.

"And, best thing about it," Dean added, "you won't have to tell Jackie a thing." He frowned and asked, "She doesn't know, does she?"

"Course not," Frank said, looking up. Dean noticed that his eyes were genuinely red and swollen and there were large, dark circles under them. He hadn't been faking his remorse as some lawyers did. The guy probably hadn't slept very well since learning that the LDO was on to his grotesque love affair. "How could I tell her something like that?"

The "something like that" was what he had been caught doing—screwing the wife of his own divorce client, the husband, during the divorce proceedings. During. And, he'd given some questionable legal advice to the husband that he'd been secretly cuckolding that would have resulted in a substantial financial gain for the soon to be ex-wife—had he not gotten caught.

Frank Martin took a long deep breath.

"You want to hear something ridiculous," he said to Dean, "I still love that bitch. Can you appreciate that?"

All Dean could do was shrug and look away.

"But she doesn't love me," Frank went on. "That's for sure. She laughed in my face the last time I called her. Laughed. The bitch used me. She's the one who should be resigning, resigning from life. I should kill the bitch. Strangle the fucking life out of her."

"Look, Frank, don't make this worse than it already is,"

Dean said and nodded to the resignation form. "You start making death threats, I have to call the police. Just sign the affirmation. Move on with your life. Forgot about that woman. Re-kindle whatever you once had with Jackie. As far as I can tell, she's a fine woman."

"You haven't seen Jackie in a long time, Dean," Frank said. "Since law school, right? She's let herself go. They all do, in some way or another."

Dean sighed. Thinking of his own situation with Laura, he couldn't disagree with that.

He sat back in his chair and watched as Frank picked up the resignation affirmation and appeared to be reading through it.

"Doesn't say much, does it?"

"That's the beauty of it," Dean said. "What it doesn't say. What won't become part of the public record. All the world will know is that on this date, you handed in your law license, became a civilian. The why of it is forever secret."

Just as Frank Martin again started reviewing the resignation affirmation, the door to Dean's office opened and the LDO's long-time Chief Investigator, Stu Foley, stepped in. In his early sixties, Foley was a short, solidly built bullish man, a product of ten years in the Marine Corps including two tours in Viet Nam. He kept his hair buzz-cut short and reminded Dean of the drill sergeant from all the army movies he had ever seen, a tough, loyal, no bullshit kind of guy. Foley had left the Marines after ten years, came back home and after a brief stint as a cop, became a private investigator. He still ran a couple miles every other morning, tried to eat right, and never smoked. Except for good booze of various kinds, he kept drugs of any kind, even the prescription variety, out of his body. In this regard, he never drank coffee and laughed at anyone who took Viagra or blood pressure pills.

Foley had developed over the years a decidedly cynical view of the world, often telling Dean that the saying, "what goes around, comes around," was "pure unadulterated bullshit." He once added that justice was solely a chance proposition in this world that God, if there was one, exercised no priority in doling out.

As usual, Foley was scowling that morning as he edged forward into Dean's office. The local morning newspaper was lodged under his right arm as he sat down in a chair against the side wall. When Frank Martin looked across at him, Foley nodded and said, "Hi, Frank."

"Hi, Stu," Frank said, then shook the resignation affirmation. "Giving my fucking life away this morning."

"I know," Foley said with an uncaring shrug. "Can't be helped."

Foley didn't have much use for Frank Martin or any man who'd break his marriage and professional vows in one fell swoop. "Any guy who thinks with his pecker that bad doesn't deserve to be a lawyer or have a marriage license for that matter," he had told Dean when his ethical and marital breaches had been conclusively demonstrated during the investigation.

Martin turned his attention back to the resignation affirmation and after a minute or so, looked up at Dean.

"That's it? Six lousy paragraphs?"

"Didn't you look it over last night like I told you?" Dean asked.

"No," Frank said. "I wasn't up to it. I drank myself to sleep instead."

"Well, that's it," Dean said. "Short and sweet."

As Martin started re-reading the affirmation, Dean slid a pen across the desk to him and asked, "So I guess you didn't talk to a lawyer either, as I advised, did you?"

"What the fuck good is that going to do?" Frank asked as he picked up the pen and looked at Dean. "He'd tell me to resign, right?"

"Either that or be disbarred," Foley chimed in. "And the disbarment would come after we file charges, and the whole sordid mess becomes public."

"I know, I know," Martin said. "Your boss here has made abundantly clear the benefits of resigning."

Martin sighed, held up the pen and read the resignation affirmation for the third time. As he read through it, he mumbled the words softly to himself.

I, Franklin Richard Martin, upon careful review of the facts found during a disciplinary investigation pending against me regarding allegations of professional misconduct under the Rules of Professional Conduct of this State, as set forth in State Supreme Court Rules and Regulations, do hereby agree and affirm:

1. That this resignation is voluntarily made without duress and with full awareness of the consequences, that is, that my name will be removed from the roll of attorneys in this State;

2. That I admit the charges or allegations of misconduct involving violations of Rules 1.6, Breaching Confidentiality of a Client, and Rule 1.7, Engaging in a Conflict of Interest, of the Rules of Professional Misconduct;

3. That I acknowledge and agree that I have no defense to these

7

charges and allegations;

4. That I have had the opportunity to consult with counsel and am submitting this resignation after doing so or waiving that right.

5. I agree and affirm that I will take all steps as required in Court Rule 1001.27 to notify my clients that I am no longer licensed as an attorney in this state and take steps to protect their interests;

6. I acknowledge that I will not be able to apply for reinstatement to the practice of law in this State for seven (7) years from the date of the issuance of the Court's order removing my name from the roll of attorneys in this State.

Frank Martin looked up from the resignation form at Dean and blinked.

"That's it?" he asked.

"Yep, that's it," Dean said. "Like I said, short and sweet."

Frank Martin sighed and closed his eyes. After a moment, he opened them and with one swift motion, scribbled his name across the signature line, followed by the date, and then slid the form abruptly across the desk back to Dean.

"You did the right thing, Frank," Dean said.

"Fuck you, Dean," he said. After a moment, he sighed. "I'm sorry. That fucking skank ruined my life."

"Don't they all," Foley said.

"Now what?" Frank asked.

"Now, I fax it over to the Court with the investigative report," Dean said. "And, provided the Chief Judge approves, which I can't see why he wouldn't, an order will be issued, like the form says, removing your name from the roll of attorneys." Dean shrugged. "They don't even call it a disbarment."

"Which is what it is," Foley added.

"So I cease being a lawyer," Frank said. "Just like that."

Dean shrugged, nodded.

"And what gets in the papers?" Frank asked.

"Like I said, nothing," Dean said. "We don't do a press release or anything. And the news guys never look at disciplinary orders. If by some quirk one of the local reporters picks up on it, all I can legally tell them is that under the Court's rules, you resigned. Not why. If they call you, you tell them the order speaks for itself and that'll be the end of it."

"And, as you know, the skank, as you call her, and her lawyer, and your former client and his new lawyer," Foley added, "have also agreed to keep quiet about it."

Indeed, that had been part of the deal to get Frank Martin to resign.

"What are you telling Jackie?" Dean asked.

"That I messed up my trust account," he said. "That I used some of my clients' money to pay bills. I handle all the personal and law firm finances, the credit cards and all that. I can tell her a big fee that I thought was coming in didn't, and so I couldn't pay the money back. Jackie knows what a big sin it is for a lawyer to mess around with clients' money. She might even be sympathetic, supportive. She might even go back to her old accounting firm. Now that the kid is out of diapers, I been bugging her to do that anyway."

"See," Foley said, "a silver lining." Then, he frowned and asked, "You didn't, did you, Frank, mess with your clients' money?"

Frank shot him a sideways glance.

"No, Stu," Frank said. "What a shitty thing to ask. And what if I did, you gonna make me resign twice?"

"No, better than that, Frankie," Stu said. "Help put you in jail."

"Fuck you, Stu. You really like to kick a man when he's down, don't you?" Frank said.

Dean scowled at Foley, a signal to keep quiet, let this conversation end.

"I can't believe my asshole client hired an investigator and had me followed," Frank said and sighed. "Know what tipped him off that I was screwing his beloved soon to be ex?"

Dean shook his head.

"He could smell her on me," Frank said. "That's what he said the moment before he spit in my face." Frank laughed. "Fucking bastard spit in my face."

"Can't say as I blame him, Frank," Foley said.

A few days after the spitting incident, Dean received a one paragraph letter from Frank's cuckold client. Enclosed with it was a DVD showing a series of meetings between Frank and the cuckold's wife during the divorce proceedings, mostly going into a room at a cheap motel.

"Well, what's done is done, Frank," Dean said. "You just have to move on. And at least you still have Jackie to move on with."

Frank sighed. He seemed to be wanting to prolong the inevitable.

"Thanks for all you've done, Dean," he said. "I bet you never thought I'd end up this way in law school."

Actually, Dean was not surprised. They had been in several classes and study groups together during their three years in law school. From that experience, Dean had always felt there may be a deficit in Frank's character. He drank too much, he chased women incessantly, and he didn't seem to have a definitive goal in life. And that had led to this, his lawyer's license lost.

"You're sure that nothing can be done?" Frank asked. "A suspension instead of this?"

Dean sighed. Now he was getting angry. There was no way he wanted Frank Martin to be a member of the same club to which he belonged. That was the whole point of what he did, getting rid of lawyers gone bad.

"Don't you understand the gravity of what you've done, Frank?" Dean asked. "While you were representing a husband in a divorce proceeding, you screwed his wife then did some things that appear to have financially favored her in the divorce. Why should something like that deserve clemency?"

"You always were on a high horse," Frank said. "Well, fuck you."

"Time for you to go, Frank," Foley said from the side wall.

Frank glared over at Foley. Finally, he stood but didn't move for a time. It seemed as his body had locked and was about ready to explode.

"Look, Frank," Dean said. "I'm sorry, that's all I can say. There was nothing else that could be done."

"You get a cheap thrill out of this, don't you, Dean," Frank went on. "Ruining lawyers' lives."

"Only the bad ones," Foley said and now, he stood.

"You signed the form," he added, "now it's time for you to go."

Frank turned to Foley and they stood glaring at each other for a time.

"Well, fuck you both," Frank said. Then he turned and walked out of Dean's office, slamming the door behind him.

"Want me to go after him?" Foley asked. "Make sure he leaves peacefully?"

"No, he'll be fine," Dean said. "He'll end up making a million dollars in shady real estate deals."

Foley smiled, then moved to the seat directly in front of Dean's desk where Frank Martin had just been sitting.

Dean waved the resignation affirmation at Foley.

"See, there is justice in the world, Stuey," Dean said.

"Yeah," Foley said. "If you can call that justice. But justice for fools like Frankie Martin is one thing and justice for lawyers truly gone bad is quite another."

Chapter Two
Death of a Prosecution

"And speaking of lawyers truly gone bad," Foley said, "take a look at this."

Foley got out of his chair and set the morning newspaper onto Dean's desk. Dean unfolded it, leaned forward and scanned the front page.

"Far left column," Foley said. "Half way down."

Dean soon found the story. The headline blared:

DA Won't Charge 1st Assistant

Squinting, Dean read out loud, "Erie County District Attorney Sam Marcum announced late yesterday afternoon that his office will not pursue criminal charges against his first assistant district attorney, Susan Hines-Laurence, related to the shooting death of her husband of five years, local builder, Kent J. Laurence, calling it a tragic accident. Laurence was allegedly shot and killed with his own revolver while demonstrating how it worked for Mrs. Hines-Laurence in the bedroom of their Wellington Boulevard mansion."

Dean looked up from the newspaper at Foley with a

curious frown.

"Holy shit," he said.

"Yeah," Foley said with a laugh. "Holy shit. Talk about justice."

"He really thinks he can get away with this?" Dean asked as he resumed reading the story.

"Figures people won't understand or care," Foley said. "Rich bastard shot by his dumb-ass trophy wife. The fact that she's an assistant district attorney working for Marcum, his second in command, will somehow get lost in translation."

"But we know better, don't we," Dean said, looking up. "I mean, he can't make a decision like that."

"Yeah, huge conflict," Foley said. "A violation of Rule 1.7, right?"

"Hey, that's good, Stuey," Dean said with a nod and a smile. "Only took you seventeen years to memorize the Rules of Professional Conduct."

"Eighteen," he said and laughed. "Well, I know that one."

Dean lifted the paper, re-read the story, then looked over at Foley and shook his head.

"Unbelievable," Dean said. "Why didn't Marcum just get a special prosecutor appointed? If it was an accident, it was an accident. If it wasn't, he loses his first assistant. So what?"

"Maybe the proof in regard to it being an accident isn't all that strong," Foley said. "Maybe the proof indicates it wasn't an accident."

"So? Why protect Mrs. Hines-Laurence?"

"Lots of reasons," Foley said. "Politically, it would make

him look bad to have appointed as his trusted first assistant someone who turned out to be a cold-blooded murderer. Who needs the aggravation of a long-drawn out criminal investigation that can be nipped in the bud?" Foley sighed. "Or…"

"Or? Or what, Stuey?"

"Or, Marcum's got a closer relationship with Mrs. Hines-Laurence than boss and worker bee."

"They're lovers," Dean asked, "is that what you're saying?"

"Been known to happen," Foley said. "She's one good-looking woman. And he's got mid-life crisis written all over him."

"What about Laurence's family?" Dean asked. "How are they taking this decision?"

"Not sure about that," Foley said. "As I remember it, when Kent Laurence went off and married Miss Hines, who's what, twenty-five years younger than him, the family wasn't all too pleased. His older brother, Don, quit the company right after and moved to Florida. He's got a sister, too. Forget her name."

Foley waited for a time while Dean continued reading the article.

"Listen to this," Dean said. "The District Attorney stated that all evidence points to a tragic accident." He looked up. "What evidence is that? What Miss Hines-Laurence told the homicide detectives? What did he expect her to say, I shot the bastard in cold blood?"

"Appears that's it," Foley said. "That's the investigation – her statement. So, you gonna open a file."

Dean sighed. He swiveled around and reached back to the book containing the latest Rules of Professional Conduct, dog-worn after several months of cracking it open at least ten times a day. He quickly leafed through it and found what he was looking for.

"Rule 1.7 reads as follows," he said to Foley. "A lawyer shall not represent a client if a reasonable lawyer would conclude that there is a significant risk that the lawyer's professional judgment on behalf of a client will be adversely affected by the lawyer's own financial, business, property or other personal interests."

Dean squinted as he thought about the present case.

"Here, the lawyer, our illustrious county District Attorney," he said, "represented the People of the State in assessing the viability of a criminal prosecution, with a significant risk that his professional judgment, that is, the exercise of prosecutorial discretion, would be adversely affected by his own business or personal interests – that is, his interest in protecting his own office from adverse publicity and a close subordinate, and presumably, at very least, a friend – with how close a friendship to be determined - from criminal prosecution."

He shrugged and looked at Foley.

"Yeah, I'd say it's pretty damned arguable," Dean said. "Enough so, at least, to open a file and get some answers." He sighed. "Of course, if there was something more than an employment and professional relationship between Marcum and Mrs. Hines-Laurence, then that would make the conflict all the more juicy."

"That they were what I think they were?" Foley said.

"Bonafide lovers."

"Yes," Dean said. "That." He sighed. "Of course, proving that, that the DA and his first assistant were more than just colleagues and friends, is another matter. I have no idea how we prove that."

"I never heard any rumors about them," Foley said. "And you would think something like that, you would."

Dean nodded and thought about it for a time.

Finally, he said, "No way I'm going to open a file. Not until the Court appoints a new Director. That'll be his decision."

"Well, that's gonna be you, right?" Foley said. "Or it better be."

"Well, we'll see," Dean said. "My interview went well last week..."

"It's bullshit that they conducted interviews in the first place," Foley said, "and it's bullshit it's taken so long to do them. They should have given you job outright, boss. It's a damn slap in the face that they didn't, you ask me. Based on your experience, your performance, your integrity. You certainly earned it."

Dean raised a hand. It was a speech he'd heard Foley make numerous times before. Frankly, he was not at all surprised at having to undergo the formality of an interview. What surprised him was that the Court's three-member panel of justices appointed as the selection committee had interviewed so many candidates.

"We'll see," Dean repeated. "The decision should be announced any time now. Soon as today, in fact. They can't leave the job vacant too much longer, and the interviews concluded last Tuesday."

"Well, all I gotta say, it better be you, boss," Foley said. "It just better be you."

Again, Dean shrugged.

"I got no control over what the Court does," he said.

"Still, it should be you," Foley said.

"Point is about this DA mess," Dean said, "I have to leave the decision whether to open a conflict file against him to the next Director. If it's me, we'll be looking into it."

"Who'll handle it?" Foley asked. "Kat?"

"No, me," Dean said. "And you."

Just then, Dean's telephone buzzed. He picked up the receiver and the long-time LDO receptionist, Kathy Barnes, told him that the Chief Judge's Law Clerk was on the phone.

"Well, here it comes," Dean said to Foley.

"Yeah," Foley said, and hoped, on this occasion anyway, that what comes around, goes around.

Chapter Three
A New Director

The Chief Judge's confidential law clerk, Margo Anson-Clark, was an irritable, arrogant woman around Dean's age. She was a short, about four foot eleven, with a layer of brown kink brillo-pad hair and a swarthy complexion.

Margo had been clerk for Chief Justice Ernest Alexander "Chip" Krane, the "CJ" to everyone—colleagues, subordinates and even to Mrs. Krane—since his appointment ten years ago as Associate Justice to the Supreme Court, the highest court in the state. Before that, the CJ had spent twenty years as a moderately successful litigator in the blueblood firm, Dow, Morgan, and Cole. Indeed, after marrying the unattractive and mostly unspoiled Clarissa Cole, daughter of founding partner, J. Preston Cole, the CJ had used his father-in-law's political connections to finagle a spot on the Supreme Court despite having held no prior judicial office. Cole and his fellow partners knew that having one of their own on the court would not only further enhance the prestige of the firm, but it would get their often abrasive and overly ambitious, and some said, sinister, rising junior partner out of their collective hair.

"Hello, Margo," Dean said. "What can I do for you?"

Dean knew that if she was calling about the Director job, his goose was cooked. It was going to be someone else. If he'd been selected, the CJ would have been the one breaking it to him. Therefore, Dean hoped that Margo was calling about something entirely unrelated to the job, a disciplinary case up at the Court about which she had an annoying question.

"Well, the CJ asked I call you," Margo began. She cleared her throat, coughed, then hesitated a moment longer. "He wanted me to let you know they're hired ah, Brad Gunther, ah, for the Director position." She paused a few moments. "You know him?"

"Ah, no, not personally, I mean," Dean said. His throat had gone dry and he was suddenly angrier than he supposed he'd be for being rejected for the job.

"I know of him," he finally added.

He looked across at Foley with a smirk, lifted his right hand and stuck his thumb upside down.

"Bastards," Foley whispered.

"Well, the CJ wanted to express his appreciation for your application," Margo said and added, almost as an afterthought, "and your years of dedicated service."

"Sixteen," Dean said.

"What?"

"Sixteen years," Dean said. "That's how long I've been here."

Margo fell silent. There was nothing else to say.

"Well, have a great day," Margo said. "Oh, and Mister Gunther will start tomorrow morning. The CJ wants him to get off and running. An official email will be coming around some time later today."

Dean hesitated a moment, thought of asking her why he'd been passed over. What possible reason except asshole politics could anyone have for not hiring someone with sixteen years' experience?

Instead, he said, "Very well."

Margo hung up without saying goodbye. Dean stared into the receiver for a moment before hanging up. He looked over at Foley with a blank expression.

"So who got it?" Foley asked.

"Brad Gunther," Dean said. "Justice Millwood's clerk. Before that, he was with Solomon and Moore for a few years. His father, Ed Gunther, was a state legislator, years back. I think he died in office. Heart attack."

"This's bullshit," Foley said. "Last thing we needed is a political hire."

"Well, that's the way of the world," Dean said and stood.

"Where you going?"

"I have to get this resignation affirmation faxed to the CJ," he said.

"Fuck the CJ," Foley said. "Let's go to The Pub and get smashed."

"It's ten-thirty in the morning," Dean said. "I've got work to do. Plus, I need to meet with the staff and tell them about Gunther."

Foley sighed and looked away.

"You know what, Dean," he said.

"No, what Stuey."

"Sometimes your skin is too thick for your own good," he said.

"What do you want me to do, Stuey?"

"Yell and scream," Foley said. "Blow a gasket. Be good for you. Don't you understand you just been royally screwed over?"

"But I have no control over that," Dean said. "To be honest, Stu. I never really thought I would get the job. I got no political juice. You know that."

Foley sighed and shook his head.

"So now what?" he asked.

"I have no idea, Stu."

Foley shook his head and thought a minute. He looked disheartened, as if he'd been passed over for the job. Finally, he turned to Dean.

"What do you think our new Director is going to do about the DA case?"

"Not a clue," Dean said. "They might know each other. I think they graduated the same year from UB Law School."

"Well that's just dandy," Foley said. "Politics on top of politics." He sighed and looked away. "And I'm fucking sure Liza Hartman will love this development."

"I wouldn't doubt that," Dean said with a shrug as he buzzed Kathy Barnes.

"Hi, Kathy," he said. "Send an email around to everyone announcing a mandatory meeting. Make it for Noon."

Chapter Four
The CJ

While some boys grow up dreaming of becoming major league baseball stars, NFL quarterbacks, NBA point guards, or NHL goal scorers, Chip Krane had always aspired to the highest judicial office in the land, the major leagues of judges, so to speak, that is, a spot on the United States Supreme Court, or SCOTUS, as he fondly referred to it. This aspiration was heightened during law school in the early nineteen eighties as he realized the first step in the long and winding road toward the achievement of that goal. During long hours studying in the law school library, and even after he became an associate attorney for Dow, Morgan and Cole, the CJ would often daydream about the day he'd be seated in one of two rows of chairs among his fellow justices on the Supreme Court, staring out at the photographer charged with unenviable task of taking their annual official photograph. Like each of them, he'd wear a smug and serene expression that comes with the consistent recognition of one's honor, privilege, and respect.

Of course, the CJ's ultimate aim was to be appointed by the President of the United States as Chief Justice of the Supreme Court. Like Chief Justice Rehnquist years earlier, he might wear sets of golden bars along the sleeves of his black judicial robe signifying his supreme status among his supreme colleagues.

In law school, the CJ's grades were nothing special, slightly above-average. But he fought and politicked his way onto the law review, writing articles mostly on criminal law that were deemed competent and somewhat insightful if not brilliant. Throughout law school and then upon his admission to the state bar, the CJ cultivated a reputation for hard work, tough-minded fairness and intellectual superiority. That he was in truth none of those didn't matter. He knew that the appearance of being tough, fair and smart was all that mattered.

Politically, he promoted himself as a moderate to conservative Democrat, a regular, law-and-order guy when it came to law-and-order questions, but solidly in the middle on most of the hot-button social issues of the day. He was careful never to announce his opinions or beliefs, orally, or especially in writing, about such things as abortion, gay rights, women's rights, immigration reform, or any of the many and varied controversial subjects of the hour. The idea was that no politician, executive or legislator, examining his credentials for the highest judicial office would be able to point to some obscure statement on one side or another of a hot-button issue that might slow down, or worse, scuttle his ultimate aspiration.

Only two years after his appointment by a Republican

Governor as an Associate Justice to the Supreme Court, following some bare-knuckle lobbying on the part of his father-in-law, J. Preston Cole, he again relied on the old man's influence and "friends" to convince the now Democratic Governor to appoint him as Chief Judge when the office was vacated by the sudden, unexpected death, by heart attack, of his predecessor, Chief Judge Elliot Baxter.

Thus, Krane became the leading jurist in the State at the relatively young age of fifty-two, putting him on the fast track, so he thought, to realizing his dream of becoming a Supreme Court justice and ultimately, Chief Justice. The frosting on that cake, of course, was that his appointment as CJ had put him in charge of a significant administrative and political machine, enabling him to set the court's agenda, and its general tone and philosophy in deciding the important cases of the day affecting every man, woman, and child in this large and populous state. As Chief Judge, Krane would preside over the most important and notorious cases of the day, and the decisions that were issued by the Supreme Court based upon them would bear his name.

Indeed, several "Krane decisions," as they soon came to be called, on such varied issues as privacy interests and civil rights, criminal law, divorce, and business and commercial duties, were marked by a certain gravitas, and were soon talked about with the same respect and reverence, if not awe, of a "Cardozo decision" of decades past. "Krane decisions" were soon being cited and dissected in law review articles, bar journals, and discussed and debated at lawyer seminars and in law school classrooms around the nation. And better yet, as far as the CJ was concerned, in some legal and bar association circles, his name was being bandied about as a possible appointment for the next vacancy on the United States Supreme Court.

A major problem, the CJ felt, for realizing his lofty ambitions, was his lack of physical stature. He was a "small" man, only five feet six. Thus, he was fastidious about exercising and eating right and took great pride in maintaining a lean, athletic frame. He would go out of his way, almost obsessively so, to lecture a subordinate, or even a colleague, about his or her eating habits to everyone's general, secret annoyance.

Not surprisingly, it was whispered behind the CJ's back that he had a serious case of "short man's complex," that other short men in positions of authority, like Napoleon, for instance, made him so overbearing, controlling, micro-managing, abrupt and generally difficult. Proof of his complex was supported by the fact that he wore lifters in his shoes that made him look around five foot eight. In addition to that, it became obvious to his closest subordinates and friends (though never brought to his attention) that he avoided speaking with anyone so tall that he had to bend his neck at a forty-five-degree angle to look up at the speaker during a conversation and subject him to that person's downward gaze. Indeed, he almost completely shunned one-on-one conversations with his colleague on the Supreme Court, Associate Justice Sidney Dexter, who stood six feet six. For the longest time, Justice Dexter truly believed that the CJ had some sort of mysterious personal animus toward him until Margo Anson-Clarke whispered into his ear what the problem was. After that, Justice Dexter avoided approaching the CJ out in the open to discuss a matter but instead visited the CJ's chambers so he could sit down before him to address it.

The CJ had served in the Navy Judge Advocate General Corps for a three-year stint upon his graduation from law school, from 1985-88, and considered briefly making a career of it, thinking that his rise through the judicial ranks as a Special Courts-Martial and then General Courts-Martial judge, followed by an appointment as an associate justice to the Court of Appeals for the Armed Forces, as an interesting and unique road to the U. S. Supreme Court. But then, during a trip home on annual leave, he met Elizabeth "Betty" Cole and, after only a three-month courtship, asked for her hand in marriage (after asking permission to do so, of course, from her father, having the displeasure of having to look upward to do so to the robust and tall, J. Preston Cole). Because Betty had no interest in becoming a military wife, and spending a tour or two overseas, away from the life of privilege to which she had grown accustomed, the CJ gave up the "military plan," as he had come to secretly call it, left active duty after his present tour was up, and joined her father's firm to begin his quest for higher judicial office through a more ordinary, political-connection plan.

The CJ maintained his physique, and reputation for athletic prowess, by running daily and competing in several marathons during the course of a year, and by playing competitive racquetball three times a week in the fall, winter and spring at the historic and exclusive Grover Cleveland Alexander Club on Essex Avenue. During Buffalo's too-short summers, from mid-May until mid-September or so, he made time to play tennis and golf on alternating evenings after a purposefully shortened workday and, of course, on most weekends.

The CJ had a square, almost boyishly congenial and handsome face and he always kept his swatch of silver gray hair neatly cut. He was, for unknown reasons, irrationally disdainful of anyone with facial hair or bow-ties. He could be heard to chide his colleagues and subordinates and attorneys appearing before the court to remove that "grass growing on your face" and, except for Ed Chase, to stop wearing that "silly, unseemly bow-tie." He also expressed scorn for eyeglasses though he wore bifocals in the privacy of his judicial chambers.

Getting to know the CJ was not an easy prospect. He kept his distance from most of his fellow justices and subordinates. His inner circle included his wife, Justice Len Peters, who had been appointed to the Supreme Court within a couple months after him, and a couple of law school classmates that had hitched themselves to his wagon. He was cold and abrasive toward his long-suffering confidential law clerk, Margo Anson-Clark. She had been a brilliant though unconfident lawyer fifteen years younger than the CJ, toiling away as a junior associate at Dow, Morgan and Cole, when he asked her to join him as his clerk after being tapped for the associate justice position on the state Supreme Court. Why he had selected her was anyone's guess, though he told Preston Cole that he had recognized in her the kind of talent that would help his tenure on the Court succeed. Cole had shrugged, not seeing much in the girl by way of smarts and looks, but acceded to the request. The CJ could have her.

After hiring Margo, the CJ seemed to take pleasure in badgering the poor girl, and that may have been the real reason behind her hiring—he needed someone who would take his relentless and mostly undeserved needling. The CJ seemed to take especial pleasure chiding her about her rather plain appearance, sometimes going on and on about it that she had to visit the ladies room for a cry within the confines of an empty stall. He often made snide comments to her, or to others within her hearing, and to still others behind her back, that she should somehow find a way to make herself more attractive. Once he called her into his chambers late in the day and asked her point blank if there wasn't anything she could do, some cosmetic procedure, to straighten her "Negro like hair." And on more than one occasion, the CJ even chirped that perhaps she should wear more make-up.

This relentless needling only stopped when overheard over a course of time by Associate Justice Len Peters. Peters at some point took the CJ aside and told him that he could be setting himself up for a sexual harassment complaint by Anson-Clark for making too many comments like that. Indeed, although Peters did not reveal this to the CJ at the time, Margo had recently come to him and confided that she was about to do just that if the CJ didn't cool it.

It was well known that the CJ tolerated and forgave little, was especially impatient and could be intolerably and impulsively cruel no matter how small the mistake or error of judgment. The worst case scenario for anyone, staff subordinate, lawyer or colleague, was to end up within the cross-hairs of his disdain for whatever reason, real or imagined. This propensity for intolerance had come close to scuttling his budding career as a jurist when, during his first year as CJ, several of the junior pool law clerks of the Court had considered filing a grievance against him with the state Inspector General for his abusive tirades. However, at the last minute, the ringleader of the group thought better of making an adversary of such a politically connected man and unilaterally ripped up the letter to the IG's office that he and five other pool clerks had collectively drafted and signed.

But for the few who became objects of his affection, by some formula only he understood, mistakes and errors of judgment, even serious ones, were usually overlooked. Among these "pets" was Bradley Thomas Gunther II. He was a tall man, around six foot two, but as one of the CJ's pets, even this physical trait, or handicap, from the CJ's point of view, was disregarded.

Gunther had been summoned late that morning to the CJ's spacious judicial chambers in the large, rather new, downtown Supreme Court building that, in addition to the judicial chambers of himself and his colleagues on the Court, housed clerks' offices, courtrooms, various other offices and a large, ornately decorated law library. Gunther knew, of course, why he had been summoned. He arrived fifteen minutes early for the appointment and was made to wait twenty minutes after its scheduled time before he was finally called into the CJ's chambers at eleven thirty-five.

As he walked into the CJ's chambers, he stopped a moment and nodded deferentially.

"Congratulations, Bradley," the CJ said and gestured to the chair facing his long, immaculately polished and uncluttered mahogany desk. After Gunther sat and gave the CJ an uncomfortable smile, the CJ continued, "I assume you will accept the Court's appointment as Director of Lawyer Discipline?"

"Of course, your Honor," Gunther said and bowed. "I am greatly honored."

"You were clearly the best candidate," the CJ said. "And you have your work cut out for you after the mess that idiot, Percy Madison, left over there."

"I realize that, your Honor," Gunther said. "And it is my sincere hope that I can live up to the Court's expectations."

"I have no doubt that you will," the CJ said as he sat down.

"What about his Deputy?" asked Gunther. "How's he taking this? He's been over there a long time."

"Dean Alessi?" The CJ shrugged. "Frankly, I don't give a damn what he thinks. He's small potatoes. Let him quit for all I care. He's got absolutely no political capital. In fact, making him quit, or finding cause to fire him, may become one of your top priorities."

"What's he done?" Gunther asked.

Gunther had asked around and he had heard mostly good things about Dean. He was a fair and a hard worker, if not a tad too zealous and over-bearing at times for the tastes of many lawyers and judges.

"I worry about his judgment sometimes," the CJ said. "Some of the cases brought before the Court seem, well, unnecessary."

Gunther nodded. "I – I see."

"Well, the Court, or at least certain members," the CJ went on, "are hoping you are not as rigid as Alessi. That you can be flexible to fit the circumstances of the case. You know, see the larger picture."

The CJ sighed.

"So," he went on, "I won't interfere with your judgment should you need to let Alessi go. But, please, don't do anything about that right away. We need to maintain some semblance of stability over there. And don't get me wrong, Alessi does have some allies on the Court."

The CJ scratched his chin for a time.

"What I'm trying to say is that you need not be such a stickler for the rules, unlike your Deputy," the CJ said. "As I said, that's been Alessi's biggest problem—he is too damned rigid. You need to establish more flexibility over there. Cut the not so bad, bad guys, some slack. As I think you already know, Brad, your job as Director is to protect the honor of the professional club to which we belong. Get rid of the truly dishonorable guys, not everyone who makes a silly mistake, as Alessi seems prone to want to do. You get my drift? What we need is someone who understands the pitfalls and difficulties of practicing law.

"And you know, being rigid, a stickler for the rules is not always a good thing. Sometimes, to preserve the reputation of the club, you have to make the victims of certain wrongdoing whole, but look the other way when it comes to doing anything affecting the lawyer who screwed up his career. What I'm saying is, it's not always such a bad thing to sweep a dirty little secret of the profession under the rug every now and then. Be practical, is what I'm saying. I mean, that man Alessi cannot ever be practical. I'm not suggesting, mind you, that we look the other way if a thief comes along, but even then, we have to be careful who the thief knows and what other means of damage control can be pursued.

"What I'm telling you, Brad, the reason you got the job is that you seem to understand these principles. You, unlike Dean Alessi, are a practical man."

"Thank you, your Honor," Gunther said.

"Well, the Court is putting an enormous amount of trust in you," the CJ said. "And after what that idiot Madison did, we need every ounce of your dedication in that regard."

"And I promise you and the Court will get every last ounce of it, your Honor," Gunther said.

"Good," the CJ said and sighed.

"I spoke with Judge Millwood just a couple minutes ago," the CJ said. "He's sorry to lose you, but I promised to get him a clerk by tomorrow that will take over for you. He'll be fine. He wants to take you to lunch."

The CJ checked his watch.

"And look," he said and smiled. "It's that time already."

But the CJ's smile quickly faded as if he had recalled some unpleasant memory. He looked down and found the newspaper on his desk, unfolded it, turned it around and showed the front page to Gunther.

"See this?" the CJ asked.

"The DA story? Yes, your Honor. Stupid."

"Damn right it's stupid," the CJ said. "What is Sam thinking? Probably been screwing that first assistant for years and now is trying to figure some way to protect her." He slapped down the paper and sighed. "Except what he did—

nothing—looks screwy. It looks wrong, even to the ordinary guy."

"Well, even if that's true," Gunther said. "I know Sam. And if he says he found no evidence of criminality, that the shooting was just a horrible accident, a tragedy, I believe him."

"But what if he was screwing that Hines-Laurence woman when he came to that conclusion?" the CJ asked. "And what if that somehow comes out?"

"Is there an indication that was going on?" Gunther asked. "That he and she were…"

"There's been some rumors flying around they've been having an affair since before his re-election," the CJ said. "I mean how else did she get the First Assistant's job? I mean, Sal Parlatto was way more qualified."

"Didn't he quit because of that?" Gunther asked.

"Yes, that's what I heard," the CJ said. He picked up the newspaper and gazed at the article and focused on the small photograph of Hines-Laurence that was next to it.

"Can't say I would blame Sam if he is doing her. She's one attractive woman."

The CJ looked up from the newspaper and stared off for a time. Finally, he looked back at Gunther.

"But even without that, an affair between them or something," the CJ continued, "it looks horrible, deciding not to pursue a murder investigation against his own trusted subordinate. And it will look even worse if something comes out—that he was screwing her."

The CJ picked up the front page of the paper and examined it for a time, staring at the photograph of Hines-

Laurence again. After a few moments, he put the paper down. "You know him, right?" The CJ asked. "Marcum?"

"Yes," Gunther said. "We were friends in law school. Socialized from time to time, joined some study groups, that sort of thing. But then after graduation, we went our separate ways."

And that was true. After law school, Marcum got a job as an Assistant DA, gained a reputation as a competent if sometimes over-zealous trial attorney. Eventually, he rose through the ranks of the office to Chief of the Felony Trials Bureau. Seeking his ultimate goal of becoming the DA, he involved himself in county politics, made the right allies, and after five years as Bureau Chief, found himself being nominated as the Democratic candidate for County District Attorney. He won the November election in a fairly typical landslide.

As for Gunther, he took a quieter route to the advancement of his legal career. After a short stint with the firm, "Soloman and Moore", he took a position as "pool clerk" for the county judges and that got him noticed by Judge Millwood who plucked him eventually as his confidential law clerk. Six years later, he now found himself named to the prestigious and important position as Director of Lawyer Discipline.

"I want you to meet with Sam soon as you can," the CJ said. "Express my feelings." He sighed. "Suggest a way out of this little dilemma that he's created."

"A way out?"

"Yes."

"Can I ask you something, your Honor—why do we

care?"

"Because he's got connections who have the kind of connections that I—that we both—need," the CJ said. "For example, his Uncle is Fred Marcum. Fred Marcum is a Congressman from downstate who may run for the Senate next year. If he wins, that will be good for someone who wants an appointment to the Supreme Court." The CJ winked at Gunther. "You know, the US Supreme Court. SCOTUS."

"Of course, your Honor," Gunther said with a nod.

"And we also care because Sam Marcum is seen as a shoo-in to get the appointment to this Court when Justice Myers, well, decides to retire."

"I heard he was sick," Gunther said. "Is that…"

"Well, it's rather hush-hush," the CJ said, "but yes, Myers is pretty sick. Bone cancer, and the prognosis for a seventy-one-year-old heavy smoker is not good. So that will leave a vacancy on the Court and I think Marcum's on the Governor's short list to get an appointment, provided this little lapse of judgment," and he waved the newspaper at Gunther, "doesn't muck that up. And if I push for Sam's appointment, that'll help me make friends with his Uncle Fred, the Congressman."

The CJ let all that sink in. After a time, Gunther nodded.

"And then, once Justice Meyers spot is filled," the CJ continued, "that'll leave a vacancy in the DA's job. And the Governor gets to fill that, too. It's likely that Marcum's appointed successor will run unopposed in the special November election since the GOP is in such disarray in this county."

"I still don't…."

"You ever thought of becoming District Attorney, Bradley? Six months or so successfully running the LDO won't hurt you in lobbying for the job. And I will attest that you will have done a stellar job. Which I fully expect anyway. And you could imagine what opportunities might arise from that running that office."

"Yes," Gunther said and a light smile spread across his lips. "I could imagine."

The CJ smiled and nodded at him and Gunther nodded and smiled in return. Somehow, for Brad Gunther, this day was going even better than he had ever imagined. He had come to the CJ's judicial chambers expecting merely to accept the appointment to the rather obscure position as Director of Lawyer Discipline and would leave with the prospect of becoming county DA, and perhaps more after that.

There was justice in the world.

"So what's the DA's way out of this lapse of judgment?" he asked the CJ.

Chapter Five
Staff Meeting

A minute or so before Noon, Dean stood in the LDO's conference room at the head of a long, oval table that was, all agreed, too large for the room. The LDO staff ambled in and took their seats in the dozen or so chairs squeezed around it. Behind Dean was a large window with its blinds drawn in order to block the unpleasant view of a desolate alley six floors below the drab ten story, "Simon L. Forster" state office building, where the LDO offices were located. Its next door neighbor, the luxurious, opaque glass fifteen story Larimer Building housed numerous law firms, CPA practices, advertising agencies, doctors, dentists and optometrists offices, surveyors, title insurance companies, several state agencies, and various other corporate suites.

The LDO's four disciplinary counsel—dis-cons as they had come to be called over the years (or dis-clowns by some unappreciative lawyers in town)—sat at the end of the conference table closest to Dean. The oldest among them, Ed Chase, occupied the chair to Dean's immediate left. He leaned all the way back, with his legs out-stretched and his characteristic carefree smirk of an expression. He was in his late fifties with a shock of thick, white hair covering a seemingly over-sized head. He had a well-developed pouch from eating regularly at fancy restaurants with his equally stout wife of thirty-nine years, Margie. To Dean's envy, Chase's stress meter always seemed to register only a tick or two above zero.

Right out of law school now well over thirty years ago, Chase had landed a series of state jobs. His most recent, five years ago, was with the LDO, a lateral transfer from the Bureau of Mental Hygiene, another auxiliary agency of the Supreme Court. His demand for the transfer had been summarily granted, to Dean's chagrin, after the Court had reluctantly succumbed to the LDO's request, submitted at Dean's suggestion by the former Director, Percy Madison, to finally add a new attorney to the staff. Dean had wanted to fill the new position with a young, aggressive attorney rather than the tired old hack that Ed Chase was rumored to have become.

Unfortunately for the LDO, and Dean, Dean's expectation in regard to Chase was not disappointed. As a long-time, practiced state employee, Chase knew that it was in his own best interest to never, ever rock the boat, and to avoid bringing attention to himself by doing anything above-average or especially controversial or unique, in his quest to slip through the bureaucratic cracks on his way to what promised to be a comfortable six figure retirement. Although it was rumored that Chase drank too much during evenings at home, even long after Margie went to bed, and may have become an unrepentant alcoholic, he always looked fresh and dapper in the morning. After five years of putting up with his cynical and carefree attitude, the singular thing Dean liked about Chase was that he persisted in wearing bow-ties on a daily basis even though it was well known that CJ Krane detested them.

Across from Chase sat the long-legged, short-haired pretty blonde, thirty-year-old Liza Hartman, who for reasons unclear to Dean, had developed a decided dislike for him and had indeed become his almost daily workplace nemesis. She was, for the most part, an arrogant young woman who thought more of her looks and intelligence than reality suggested. Like many fellow lady attorneys, Liza had a definite feminist chip on her shoulder. Soon after being hired, she had constantly questioned or outright challenged Dean's pronouncements on office policy and suggestions regarding her assigned investigations, demanding to know the logic behind his every decision that affected her and others. Sometimes Dean laboriously tried to comply with her requests and at other times, he simply ignored her.

Stu Foley often told Dean that he shouldn't take Liza's bad attitude toward him personally. That it wasn't him, *per se*, that bothered her but men in general, or, at least, a certain type of man that Dean, and Stu, of course, represented.

"That girl," Foley said, summing it up for Dean, "has serious daddy issues."

"What the hell does that mean?" Dean had asked Foley the first time he had said that, during the very first week of her employment, now already five years ago.

"Her daddy left her mommy for another woman when

she was a kid," Foley had explained. "You know, in her formative years. So now she hates most, if not all, men."

"How you know that?" Dean had asked.

"Because a buddy of mine—I'll leave his name out of it," Foley had said, "used to follow her daddy when he took his mistress to a cheap motel. Which was often."

Sometimes, Foley would sigh when he had reason to make another "she has daddy issues" comment about Liza, and add, "but I'd love to be her daddy and have those long, slender legs strapped around my midsection."

"And you're a dirty old man," Dean would respond with a laugh, then add, "though I sometimes think about that, too."

The boyish Pete O'Brien, who'd been with the LDO less than a year, sat next to Liza with an apprehensive frown. He never said much during staff meetings, or any other time for that matter, and seemed content to go about his duties like a good soldier. His father had been a high school chum of the CJ, and it was that relationship that gotten him the job. Dean and the Chief Clerk, Margo Anson-Clarke, had already completed their interviews of four other candidates and had settled on hiring Jack Brewster, a fairly accomplished, thirty-something Assistant District Attorney out of Marcum's office. When Margo called Dean late the same afternoon they had made their decision and in a rushed voice, asked if he had called Brewster yet and offered the job, Dean told her he hadn't. Margo let out a sigh and told him that the CJ had scuttled that hiring and wanted them to hire Pete O'Brien instead.

"What?" Dean asked. "His credentials are nowhere near

Brewster's. He's a pool clerk in City Court. Out of law school all of three years?"

"It's what the CJ wants," was all Margo had said or needed to say.

Dean would later learn that the CJ and Pete's Dad were long-time friends and the Dad was now a committee chairperson on the Executive Committee of the County Democratic Party assigned to an important precinct. So, after a hastily arranged, more-or-less sham interview, Dean offered the open dis-con job to Peter J. O'Brien, Jr, and thought to himself, no wonder they call us "dis-clowns."

"Fucking politics," Foley had said when Dean told him of the CJ's interference. "Brewster would have been a real asset. Plus, he's a good guy."

Despite this bad beginning, Dean tried to keep an open mind, and in truth, Pete had not turned out half-bad. His work ethic was sound and he kept his mouth shut about office politics. He also frequently joined Dean and Foley when they talked sports in the kitchen during morning coffee breaks.

Across from Pete sat the presently grim-faced, Kat Franklin. She was thirty-five and had been with the LDO over ten years, second longest behind Dean. Though Kat seemed content with her plain appearance, Foley had often commented that there was something innately sexy about her, that if you caught her at just the right angle or in just the right light, she could look downright pretty. Her face was angular and sharp, and her body much like it. Foley had added that when Kat wore her hair down to her shoulders, instead of in her usual way, in a tight bun on the top of her head, she could be just about as desirable as Liza Hartman. Every so often, she'd apply some makeup and, with her hair down, those glimpses of sensuality would be enhanced, causing Dean and Foley to do double-takes.

This particular morning, however, was not one of those days.

Kat had been married once, a year or so after she had been hired as an associate dis-con. It had ended badly, almost comically, when the guy, some creep by the name of Ken Soto, himself a lawyer with a sleazy reputation, had cheated on her with her best friend and maid of honor at their wedding. Since then, Kat had fallen into refuge as the scorned woman. She went on dates now and then, and sometimes there would be a brief fling, but each of them fizzled or ended in some other bad way. It had been some time, in fact, since Dean remembered her mentioning a new man in her life.

Only a few weeks ago, Foley had predicted that Dean and Kat could end up together.

"What? I don't think so, Stuey," Dean has scoffed. "For one thing, I'm a happily married man."

Foley had frowned at that.

"That's news to me, boss," Foley had said. "That's not what I hear. And after our last Christmas party, Kat knows maybe you're not either."

The Christmas party, Dean had thought. Not that again. A two-minute span of weakness, kissing and groping Kat, trying to run his hand under her blouse, in the dark hallway leading to the restrooms just outside the Hyatt Hotel banquet hall where the Supreme Court's annual Christmas Party had been held for the fifth straight year. And the fact that Kat had let him do it, or seemed to. And had he imagined that for a brief, blurry moment, she had lowered her right hand to his crotch. Then, as if waking from a dream, they had backed off, breathless, staring at each other for a time. What had just happened?

Dean was sorry he had told Foley about that incident, a drunken admission after work about a month after the Christmas party, after three or four beers at The Pub, their regular watering hole on a dark side street off Allen Street in the northern section of the city.

"Like everything else in Kat Franklin's life, she is obsessed with you and doesn't even know it," Foley had told Dean and then drank down his beer.

"I have no idea what that even means," Dean had said, "like a lot of your rambling lately. And anyway, even if it's true, nothing can come of it. No matter how obsessed she is with me, or me with her, I'm married and that's that."

"No," Foley had said as he put his arm around Dean's shoulder. "Obsession can be a serious problem, maybe even worse than what ails your present bride. Drinking, you can cure, or it'll kill you. Obsessiveness is a lifelong affliction that has no cure."

Dean had shrugged, still not quite sure what the hell Foley was talking about or where he was going with this.

"Well, rest assured then, my old LDO buddy," Dean said, "I promise to keep my distance from Kat Franklin."

The middle seats of the conference table were taken by Stu Foley, who many years ago had been promoted to Chief Investigator of the LDO, and his staff of two junior investigators, the joyless Larry Stevens, and the sour, scatterbrained and mostly ineffectual Dawn Smith.

The LDO's secretaries, or "legal assistants", their official state title, had settled into seats along the far end of the table. Among them was Kathy Barnes, the LDO's senior legal assistant, who over the years, seven, in fact, had become kind of secondary confident for Dean. However, lately, she seemed to have seen the writing on the wall for him that he was not going to become Director, and had begun to distance herself from him. She would be loyal to the new Director, whomever that was, and if that meant betraying him, so be it. Like most people, self-interest was more important than friendship.

Finally, on four split-screens on a wide-screen television set on a high cart in the corner of the room, were the satellite office staff. The LDO satellite offices were based in the leading cities of each of the four judicial departments into which the state had long ago been divided. Each satellite office consisted of at least one disciplinary counsel and investigator, as well as both full-time and part-time dis-cons, investigators and secretaries.

"Where's Carol Pelowski?" Dean asked Kathy Barnes.

"Out sick," Kathy said.

"Again?" Dean sighed.

He looked to the television screen on the corner table.

"Can you people see and hear me alright?" Dean asked.

When none of the offices responded, he shouted, "Bill, Don, Frank, Mark, are you seeing and hearing me?"

After hearing mumbled, seemingly affirmative responses, Dean looked back to faces of the staff members before him around the conference table. They wore expectant or worried expressions wondering why this special meeting had been called.

"Did you see this?" Kat Franklin asked, interrupting momentarily Dean's train of thought. She held up the morning edition of the local newspaper and pointed to the article about the DA.

"Yes, Kat," Dean said. "I've seen it."

"We opening a file?" she asked with some annoyance. "Slight conflict, wouldn't you say?"

Across the table, Dean saw Liza Hartman role her eyes while Ed Chase smiled.

"What did little Sammy boy do now?" Chase asked. "I went to law school with him. A cheater if there ever was one."

"Let the man, speak," Stu Foley chimed in.

"Look," Dean said to Kat, "what is done with the case is not going to be my decision."

Dean sighed and looked out at the staff, trying not to settle his gaze upon Foley's disapproving scowl.

"And that gets us to the point of this meeting," Dean said, and then his gaze did settle on Foley, who grimaced and shook his head. Dean quickly looked away and continued, "I wanted to let all of you know that the Court has selected a new Director. His name is Brad Gunther. Judge Millwood's clerk."

Liza Hartman let out a small yelp, like a cheer. Bad news for Dean it seemed, was good news for her. Dean glanced at her, wondering what he had ever done to have earned such abiding scorn. Probably, nothing, and it was simply as Foley had said, she had "serious daddy issues."

"I've been told that Mister Gunther will start first thing

tomorrow morning," Dean continued.

No one said a word. Dean looked at Foley who held his arms across his chest and seethed. He opened his mouth momentarily, as if to say something, thought better of it, and remained silent.

"And that's it," Dean said. "I just thought all of you should know. And I'd ask that we join together in supporting Mister Gunther as he assumes the Director position so that we can continue to fulfill the important function of this office in protecting the public from dishonest and dysfunctional lawyers and protecting the integrity of the legal profession in this state."

Foley stood, no longer able to restrain himself, and said, "Well, I for one think it's a bunch of crap. You deserved the appointment, Dean. Pure and simple." Then, he stormed out of the room.

"Is that it?" Liza Hartman asked, checking her watch. "We can go?"

"Yes, Liza," Dean said. "That's it. Meeting's over."

And to hell with you, Dean wanted to add but didn't.

Chapter Six
The Anonymous Letter

Kat Franklin lingered behind as her colleagues shuffled out of the conference room on their way to lunch. Finally, with her standing there before him with a befuddled look, Dean asked, "Help you, Kat?"

"I just wanted to say," Kat said, "it really sucks what the Court did. You deserve the job."

"Well, what's done is done," he said with a shrug. "I refuse to get upset over something I can't control." He sighed. "And, you know, I'm not really surprised. I have no political juice, you know that. The only thing I can do, and hopefully you will as well, is live with it."

Kat gave a sideways nod toward the door.

"I bet Liza can live with it," she said.

Dean put his hands in his pockets, suddenly feeling uncomfortable where this conversation was going. The others knew that Kat had stayed behind, and the last thing he needed was for anyone to be wondering what they were talking about or doing alone in the conference room. Only bad rumors could come of it. There had already been some whispering among the LDO staff regarding their little indiscretion during last year's Christmas Party. Dean suspected Dawn Smith was behind it. After all, he had seen her lurking about in the main hallway after he and Kat had emerged from the dark corridor outside the restrooms right after their fleeting tryst back there in the shadows.

"You ready for the McMahon argument?" Dean asked.

"Sure," she said with a shrug. "Nothing to it, really. I wasn't planning on saying much."

"Don't be so flip about it," Dean said. "The CJ's on the panel. And you know what a stickler he can be — no, will be, on that case."

"Pain in the ass is a more apt description," Kat said. "Worse even than Dick O'Leary's gonna be."

Dean laughed.

"O'Leary's O'Leary," Dean said. "Like Tom Morgan told me once, O'Leary's a C plus student with an A plus ego."

"Yep, an A plus pain in the ass," she said.

Dean couldn't deny that. He'd battled O'Leary long enough to know that even the simplest case could become a royal headache. The problem was, O'Leary had a reputation for representing attorneys in trouble, and whether he was good or bad, lawyers who got into trouble reached out to him. In addition to that, he was a contemporary, and very friendly with several justices on the Supreme Court, including the CJ. "I just wish he'd stop with those *ad hominem* attacks all the time," Kat added. "It's frustrating how much the JHOs and Court let him get away with."

"Well, that's our lot in life as dis-cons," Dean said with

a short laugh. "To get crapped on."

"Yeah," she said, "sometimes I feel we dis-cons are treated with less respect than the unethical lawyers we prosecute."

"Investigate," Dean said and laughed again. "Never use the word prosecute in this office."

Kat sighed and rolled her eyes.

"Just be ready for the McMahon case," Dean added. "I have a bad feeling. The CJ's had such a bee in his bonnet over that one."

"Any more recent inappropriate *ex parte* contacts from him about it?" Kat asked.

"No, not lately," Dean said. "I think he's been preoccupied with other matters, like hiring a new Director." He sighed, frowned. "Anything else?"

Kat shrugged, stared up at Dean for a time, sighed, and seemed about to say something, before saying, "No." She hesitated a moment longer before finally walking out of the conference room.

Dean waited a few moments before starting out himself. As he did so, he almost walked into Pete O'Brien who was standing waiting for him with an apprehensive frown in the hall just outside the doorway.

"Mister Alessi," he said.

Although Pete had been with the office just short of a year, he had never gotten over the habit of addressing Dean by his last name, and Dean had months ago stopped asking him to please, just call him, "Dean."

"Yes, Pete," Dean said. "What's up?"

"I – I have the intake duty this week," he said.

"I know," Dean said.

"This came in this morning."

Pete handed Dean a single page, undated, typed letter.

"It's about the DA."

"The DA?" Squinting, Dean read it:

To Whom It May Concern:

Thought you might like to know that the DA's conflict of interest in not conducting a fair and impartial murder investigation into his first assistant's shooting (murder?) of her late husband is much worse than it already looks. Did you know that the DA and Mrs. Hines-Laurence are having an affair, and that is had been going on for quite some time before she shot (murdered?) Mr. Laurence????

A Friend

PS/ More to come!!!!

"Four question marks," Pete said.

"Huh?" Dean asked as he looked up from the note.

"There's four question marks," Pete said.

"Yes, I see that," Dean said, looking down at it. "And four exclamation marks." He looked up at Pete. "And a PS."

"What should I do with it?" Pete asked. "I wasn't sure. You told Kat that we should wait to open a file. Let Mister … I already forgot his name. The new Director."

"Gunther," said Dean. "His name is Gunther."

"Yes," Pete said. "You said let Mister Gunther decide."

"Yes," he said. "We should do that. Let Mister Gunther decide."

Still, it seemed like a no-brainer, with or without the anonymous note, with or without the alleged affair between the DA and his first assistant. They should open a file, commence an investigation, or at least, get the DA to respond to the allegation that he engaged in a conflict of interest by simply exercising his prosecutorial discretion in a case involving his second in command. There was no way for the DA to have been impartial, for his judgment not to have been affected and for him not to have been conflicted personally about conducting a criminal investigation involving one of his own employees, one of his closest advisors in fact.

"What do you think it means, the PS?" Pete asked. "More to come."

"I guess what it says," Dean said. "There's more to come."

Chapter Seven
An Unofficial Investigation

Stu Foley was waiting in Dean's office, sitting on the blue cloth chair with the uncomfortable oak arms in front of his desk. His legs were crossed and he was leaning back reading the sports pages. As Dean came around and sat behind his desk, Foley lowered the paper and said, "See, more proof that there is no justice in the world."

"Not now, Stuey," Dean said, rubbing his eyes. "I'm not in the mood for your negative philosophy."

"Negative?" Foley put the paper down on his lap and sighed. "It's truth."

"Yeah, yeah," Dean said. "There's no justice in the world. Like, who doesn't know that?"

Foley sighed and stared off. After a time, he said, "Look, now that it's officially afternoon, let's blow this popsicle stand and hit The Pub, spend the afternoon drowning our sorrows."

Dean held up the anonymous letter about the DA that Pete O'Brien had given him.

"What's that?" Foley asked. "Your resignation?"

"Course not," Dean said and held the letter out for Foley. "Take a look at this. Just came in the morning mail."

Foley leaned forward, took the letter out of Dean's hand and as Dean leaned back in his chair, started reading it. After a time, he looked up and said, "Interesting. Who do you suppose sent it?"

"Not a clue," Dean said with a shrug. "Who left there recently?"

Foley thought a while.

"I heard Sal Parlatto left under bad terms," he said. "About a month ago."

"Really? Sal's been there forever."

"Twenty-five years," Foley said and snapped his fingers. "Just like that, he walked out. Like I said, a month or so ago. Three years back, he got passed over for first assistant after Ted Maloney retired when Marcum appointed Hines-Laurence. Guess he was finally got sick of the bullshit so he quit. Same thing you ought to do, you had any balls."

"Hey, it's easy to have balls if you have a million dollars in the bank like you," Dean said. "But all I got is bills and a drunken wife to take care of. And, unlike you, I'm still fifteen years from retirement."

"Sometimes it takes a barrage of harassment and frustration for a guy like Parlatto, or you, to quit," Foley said.

"Gee, thanks," Dean said. "Lots to look forward to."

"Just giving you the facts of life, boss," he said. 'It's like I always say…"

"What goes around never comes around, I know, I know." Dean gestured for the anonymous letter and Foley handed it back to him. "What do you think the 'more to come' part means?"

"Exactly what it says," he said. "Proof of the alleged affair between the DA and his first assistant. Photographs maybe, a video would be nice. Something beyond innuendo showing the DA and Mrs. Hines-Laurence were *in corpus delecti*. You know, in each other's arms, smooching shamelessly. And pornographic would be nice – well, at least for her."

"You are a dirty old man," Dean said then frowned as he thought a moment. "You'd think that whoever sent this letter would have included something like that in the envelope. Photographs, videos, a PowerPoint presentation. Some kind of proof. Something. Anything."

"Maybe whomever likes keeping us in suspense," Foley said. "The thrill of playing the game."

"Yeah, maybe," Dean said.

"What we know is that the DA appears to have done something rather questionable," Foley went on. "His decision not to pursue a criminal investigation or, better yet, appoint a special prosecutor in a case that screams out for one, that happens to involve the second in command in his own office, a very attractive young lady, no less. That kind of decision was either based on stupidity, arrogance or worse, deceit."

"I agree," Dean said. "It certainly looks bad. At the very least, whether or not the DA was banging Mrs. Hines-Laurence, he engaged in a serious conflict of interest, failed to avoid the appearance of impropriety. From day one, he should have gotten off that investigation."

"Right, that's obvious," Foley said. "To a second grader,

it's obvious. So obvious, in fact, it begs the question…"

"Why didn't he?" Dean asked.

"Exactly," Foley said.

"And now we have this further information," Dean said, nodding to the letter on his desk, "whatever it's worth. And if there's proof to back up its claims, all the better. The shit will hit the fan, as far as the DA is concerned."

"Right you are," Foley said.

"But the sixty-four thousand dollar question remains," Dean added with a sigh, "is this enough to convince the new LDO Director, Mister Brad Gunther, to commence a disciplinary investigation against Sam Marcum, the DA for the entire county?"

"Yes," Foley said with a shrug. "That is the sixty-four thousand dollar question."

Foley and Dean mulled all this over for a time, worrying over the same thing. Gunther was an unknown and the fact that his appointment was purely political didn't bode well for the continued aggressive (some said over-aggressive) pursuit of attorney disciplinary investigations as they had been under Dean's watch. The prior LDO Director, Percy Madison, had been a hands-off kind of guy, and despite his other obvious foibles, had let Dean run the office the way he saw fit. If Dean was still in charge or had been appointed as the new Director succeeding Madison, there would be no question that the DA's action in closing the criminal case against Susan Hines-Laurence alone would have resulted in an investigation to find out why.

"We need something else," Foley finally said. "An anonymous letter, probably from some bitter ex-ADA like

Parlatto, isn't gonna cut it. And Gunther will know, or you'll have to tell him, that we almost never base the opening of a disciplinary file upon an anonymous complaint."

"Yes, but here we have the conflict," Dean said. "Conflict is the essence of this. No matter if the DA was or wasn't banging his first assistant before she shot her husband, 'accidentally,' as she says, there was a conflict of interest on his part that requires looking into. That requires some kind of adverse comment. Doesn't it?"

"That kind of conflict alone is not going to be enough, boss," Foley said. "You know that. As long as the public is kept in the dark, they'd see it as a technical breach about which who really cares. And Gunther will realize that, too. No, the basic conflict of interest in this case, that the DA should never have exercised prosecutorial discretion when the suspect was his trusted first assistant, is just not going to be enough."

Dean nodded. He saw all that, too.

"And even if Gunther turns out to be honest about this job," Foley went on, "about which I have grave reservations, and even if he comes here thinking you are better than sliced bread, he's still gonna be a little gun-shy at first. Not wanting to screw up, or get involved in something horribly controversial on his first day. Because you know the moment a file is opened, Marcum's going to call Chief Judge Krane."

"So we do nothing?" Dean asked.

"No, we do something," Foley said. "We start an investigation ourselves, on our own. I don't mean we open an official file or anything. But we go ahead and do some investigating. Unofficially. In secret."

"Like what investigating?" Dean asked. "In secret."

"Like I stake-out the DA tonight," he said. "And if need be, the next few nights. And if I find something, like him meeting secretly with his first assistant..."

"You don't think the new Director is going to be pissed that we did this?" Dean asked.

"Not if he doesn't find out," Foley said. "And I don't plan on telling him. Unless, of course, we find out something incriminating."

"Well, what if you do find out something incriminating?" Dean asked. "Then what?"

"Well, then we just gave him a feather to put in his cap," Foley said. "Right? He might want to bring a guy like the DA down. Or maybe he'll be pissed. I don't know."

"You know it's been rumored that Marcum is set to get the next open spot on the Supreme Court," Dean said. "Next January, when Judge Meyers retires, if he doesn't die first."

"Yeah, I heard that?" Foley said.

Dean sighed and stared up at the ceiling. After a minute or so, he looked at Foley.

"I can't authorize overtime for this," Dean said.

"You think I'm in this for the money?" Foley asked.

"No," Dean said. "Like me, you're in it to do what's right."

"Though the money helps," Foley laughed.

From the laptop on a side table came a beeping sound. Dean turned and pecked a key waking the machine from sleep mode. After a moment, he laughed.

"It's from the CJ," he told Foley as he read the email. "The official notice, addressed to all staff. Subject: LDO

Director. And I quote: 'It is with great pleasure that I announce the appointment of Bradley T. Gunther as the new Director of the Lawyer Disciplinary Office, succeeding Percy Madison. Mr. Gunther is a superior attorney with outstanding credentials who I have no doubt will do a wonderful job as the new Director. I want to personally thank all of you for your hard work and dedication to duty during the interim four months following Director Madison's unfortunate resignation. I have no doubt that you will do your utmost to make Mr. Gunther's transition into office a smooth one so that you can continue your important work in safeguarding the public from dishonest lawyers.'"

"What a bunch of bullshit," Foley said. "Now, can we get to The Pub for that beer?"

Chapter Eight
The Pub

Stu Foley and Dean spent the rest of that afternoon at The Pub, a cramped, dark old tavern with a long, mahogany bar that took up most of the place. Located on the corner of a couple nondescript side-streets in an artsy section of the city known as Glenwood Village, it was a quaint old place frequented by oddballs and professionals alike hoping to find respite from wives and girlfriends (or boyfriends) and the job-related and the other stresses that bogged down life while watching a ball game or engaging in heated and exhausting political discussions or downright gossip over several beers. Not to mention that the kitchen served a delicious bowl of creamy potato soup, the hottest chicken wings in town, savory roast beef piled high onto salted Kimmelweck rolls, known simply in these parts as Beef on Weck, and a wide assortment of Canadian and other beers that were always served ice cold.

Around four, after their fourth beer, Foley suggested that they had better order something to eat. Then, he'd go home and catch a couple hours shut-eye before traveling over to Wellington Boulevard and staking out the DA's mansion.

"I don't think you are in any shape to be staking anyone out," Dean said and laughed. "It was a stupid idea anyway, one that could get us both fired."

"No, I'll be fine," Foley said. "A coupla hour's nap, I'll be good as new."

"Ginnie's gonna kill both you and me," Dean laughed.

"Ginnie's a fat old Polack," Foley said. "Should have dumped her twenty years ago, that whiny old bitch."

Foley always talked about Mrs. Foley like that. They had been married thirty-seven years and separated for perhaps ten of them. Still, they had managed to grow old together though Foley told Dean he only stayed with her now because of the grandkids.

"And you're a drunken old Mick," Dean said. "Ginnie's biggest mistake was marrying your dumb ass. Ruined her life for sure."

"Fuck you," Foley said and lifted what little remained in his glass of beer for a toast. "Fuck you and fuck Brad Gunther, too."

Dean raised his empty glass and with a nod, said, "I'll drink to that."

They laughed and ordered a couple Beef on Weck sandwiches with a pile of French fries drenched in beef gravy and a bowl of potato soup along with a couple more beers. When they were almost finished eating, Dean said to Foley, "You're not really gonna try and follow that asshole tonight, are you?"

"Sure," Foley said. "Why not. Like I said, I'll go home,

sleep a couple hours, then get to his place around eight. I'll be sobered up by then."

"Suit yourself," Dean said. "Just don't get caught."

"I will disavow all knowledge of your activities, Mr. Phelps," Foley said.

"What?"

"It's from 'Mission Impossible'," he said. "The original series, not the crap Tom Cruise did. Remember? Didn't you watch that as a kid? 'Good morning, Mr. Phelps.'"

"You are a fucking dinosaur."

Foley shrugged as he took a last bite of his sandwich. Dean pushed his plate away and thought a minute.

"You're probably wasting your time anyway," Dean said. "If they are involved in something, the last thing they'll do is meet. Don't you think?"

"You'd be surprised what dumb things smart people do," Foley said. "I've seen it my whole life. Like that dumb shit Frank Martin." He laughed a moment and shook his head. "Fucking the wife of his divorce client." He took a sip of beer. "How dumb can you get? How did he ever think he could get away with that?

"Or like all the dumb things all the cheating spouses I ever followed over the years did," Foley went on. "It was like they wanted to get caught, or they'd been doing something bad that felt so good so long that they felt immune from being caught doing it. Plus, you are forgetting the power of love, or lust, I should say, because that's all love is but lust turned inside out, or backwards, upside-down, or whatever the fuck."

"I don't know what the fuck you're talking about half

the time, Stuey," Dean said and swallowed the last of his glass of beer. Then, he asked, "And say he is screwing her or has been screwing her for a while? So what? What does that prove?"

"Well, like we said, makes the conflict a whole lot worse," Foley said. "Or interesting. Right?"

"Well, yeah," Dean said. "It's a stronger personal interest – instead of having your judgment affected by some professional relationship, which, in my opinion, is bad enough, you are screwing a lady who shot her husband who you have decided you are not going to criminally investigate for doing just that. Looks real bad."

"But is there more to it than that," Foley said. "Aren't we aiming a bit low here?"

"What do you mean, Stuey?" Dean asked. "Where you heading with this?"

"Well, if they were lovers," Foley said, "maybe they planned the whole thing – kill poor old Kent Laurence to be free of him and in the process, inherit his riches. You can then say it was an accidental shooting, and have the perfect cover. The very DA charged with investigating the crime decides that the perpetrator, who happens to be his mistress, is not guilty. That like she said, the shooting of her poor rich husband was a tragic accident. Only it wasn't really an accident. It was murder."

"That's what you think this is about?" Dean asked and laughed. "Conspiracy to commit murder? Murder? With the DA and his pretty Miss first assistant district attorney as the conspirators?"

"Stranger things have happened, Deanny boy," Foley

said.

After a shrug, Dean said, "Yes, I suppose they have."

Foley swallowed the last of his beer and sighed.

"Look, pay the tab," he said. "I'm off to work."

"Hey," Dean said with a laugh. "I disavow all knowledge of that."

"Well, you already said you're not paying me overtime on this one," Foley said. "Officially, that is."

"Damn straight, I'm not," Dean said.

"Well, you pick up the tab, then, you cheap ass," he said. "Call it an unofficial payment for an unofficial investigation."

Dean laughed and bowed as if to say, touché.

It was close to five when Foley and Dean stood and wobbled slightly out of The Pub, just as the first wave of lawyers and some other professionals just getting out of work were venturing inside. Dean recognized Pete Davis and Larry Mariani and they exchanged brief nods. Both had been subject of disciplinary complaints over the last couple of years and though they had been dismissed without merit, Dean was an unpleasant memory for them, like he had become for a lot of lawyers over the years.

In general, because of his job, it was not surprising that Dean was not all that popular among his brethren in the legal community. His fellow lawyers knew where he worked and wanted to stay clear of him, even when they were on their best behavior. And to make matters worse, Dean had gained a reputation for being aggressive in prosecuting attorneys who couldn't or didn't follow the rules of ethical conduct. Some said he was over-aggressive and bore some in-bred animus toward his own profession. In short, Dean was known as your standard bureaucratic prick. Some lawyers considered him worse than that, a traitor to the profession who took the job of policing the profession only because he couldn't hack it as a real lawyer in the real world. And, to add insult to injury, he had then taken his role all too seriously and never let anything slide. It sometimes seemed to Dean, perhaps paranoidly so, that only a minority of his fellow lawyers appreciated what he did and respected him for doing it aggressively. Dean had often lamented, mostly in silence to himself, that there seemed to be far too few lawyers who accepted or understood that weeding the bad lawyers out of the profession served to make it better for the good guys.

Being considered in a negative light by some of his peers had not and would not ever dissuade Dean from doing what he felt was right, what he felt needed to be done. Whatever the opinions of his fellow lawyers, Dean could fulfill his job in only one way, by being aggressive in identifying those attorneys who shouldn't be in the honest lawyers' only club. It was as simple, and difficult, as that.

Dean slunkered out of The Pub right behind Foley into a chilly spring drizzle that late gray afternoon. Smells like worms, he thought to himself, huddling against a stiff breeze. He patted Foley on the back and said, "I think you should forget that stake-out idea tonight."

Foley waved him off as he split from Dean and staggered slightly to his car parked a considerable distance from The Pub down a dreary side street.

Chapter Nine
Dear Old Dad

Dean did not drive straight home from The Pub. Instead, fueled by the five beers he'd guzzled down that afternoon, he felt guilty for not having seen his seventy-nine-year-old father, Vincent Alessi, in the last three weeks or so. His dad lived at The Orchards, an assisted living facility in the quiet farm village of Asheville, about a half hour's drive. He called Laura to tell her he was going out there and she slurred something inane, like "you gotta do what you gotta do," and hung up.

She's drunk again, Dean thought to himself. It's getting worse.

Six months ago, his dad had fallen in the bathroom stepping out of the shower of his small cape-cod house in a deteriorating neighborhood and fractured his hip. After surgery, and three futile weeks in physical rehabilitation, the old man had been confined to a wheelchair. His doctor had told Dean that he wasn't optimistic that his father would ever get out of that wheelchair and walk again. He simply didn't seem to care enough to try.

"I think he just wants to die," Dean had told the doctor. "Or says he does. Ever since Mom died, he hasn't been interested in doing too much of anything."

The only good that had come out of this incident was that it made the decision to sell his parents' house and put the elder Alessi in an assisted living facility that much easier. Even his Dad finally seemed to accept the wisdom of doing that.

Dean had found The Orchards with the help of his younger sister, Rachel, and none from his older brother, Pete. The monthly cost of the place consumed whatever the old man received in his monthly pension and social security, but it came with a decent sized, relatively clean private room, despite the inevitable smell of urine and Clorox out in the hallways and common areas. A spacious dining room was kept clean enough and offered mostly edible and decent-sized portions of breakfast, lunch and dinner.

After six months of living at The Orchard, old man Alessi seemed to have settled in. He hardly complained anymore about the bad smells and stupid nurses and orderlies, and even seemed to like some of the other residents. He also seemed to have begrudgingly accepted his fate, that this was how he was going to spend what little life he had left, among old folk and piss smells and bad food and diapers, a tranquil if not entirely happy existence.

Mentally, the old man had his good days and bad. The Orchards' resident doctor had assured Dean that there was no indication of Alzheimer's or senile dementia setting in — yet, anyway. The problem was depression, which was not unusual for elderly residents especially after the loss of a spouse (but that was three years ago, Dean had told the doctor); the constant medical problems and aches and pains like those he was experiencing; and, the realization of rapidly approaching mortality. The doctor put the old man on a pill in addition to his other pills to control his high blood pressure and kidney issues that seemed to do nothing.

Upon his arrival around six-thirty, Dean found his father in his room watching the local news on his 32-inch flat screen TV that Dean had bought for him last Father's Day. His sister, Rachel, had pitched in a couple hundred dollars for the eight-hundred-dollar set and his brother, Pete, had promised to chip in another hundred that Dean had yet to receive.

Dean sat in a narrow loveseat in the corner of the room as his father used the remote to shut off the TV.

"You can watch it," Dean said.

"Na, nothing but commercials," the elder Alessi said. He turned to Dean and looked him over for a time. "So how are you? You look tired."

Dean shrugged. The beer buzz had mostly worn off and it was true, he was tired.

"I'm okay," he said. At that moment, however, his kidneys ached from too much beer.

"You get that job?"

Dean sighed and said, "No. They gave it someone else."

The old man shrugged. He regarded his youngest child with a concerned, meditative expression.

"Politics?"

"I guess," Dean said. He met his old man's stare. "Yes."

"Ah, there's politics in everything," the old man said. "Even at the paper. You were friends with the foreman, you got breaks."

"Yeah, I guess," Dean said and shrugged. "I'll be alright."

"What's his name?"

"Who?"

"The guy who got the job?"

"Gunther," Dean said. "Brad Gunther."

"German," his father said.

"What?"

"He's German," his father said. "Gunther. It's a German name."

"Yeah, I guess."

"If he's German, you gotta watch him."

"What are you talking about, Dad?"

"Germans think they're better than everyone else," his father said. "They're cold, calculating pricks. Bastards to work for." He sighed and stared off for a time. Then, he pointed at Dean. "And they hate Italians. We had this foreman, George Kaiser, at the paper. He was a son-of-a-bitch. Hated Italians. Called us dagos, guineas."

"Well, we'll see," Dean said.

"That's from ancient times, you know," the old man said.

"What is, Dad?"

"Their hatred of Italians," he said. "Germans. Stems back to when the Roman legions occupied Germany. They were barbarians then, the Germans. Romans ruled them."

"Really?" Dean said. "I didn't know that."

"No, it's true," the elder Alessi said. "Same thing with the Micks, the Irish, and Brits. Roman legions were up there, too. Kicking ass. Beat the crap out of them."

They fell silent for a time and Dean thought with some dread about meeting his new boss tomorrow morning and having to kowtow and act respectfully subordinate. After sixteen years, he was tired of that, being an underling to guys who knew less than him about how to do the job the right way, how best to discipline bad lawyers.

"How's home?" his father asked.

"Home's home," Dean said.

"She still drinking?"

"Yeah, she still drinks," Dean said, not really feeling like getting into it.

"Too bad," his father said. "She's ruining her life. But you know, what happened…"

His father trailed off.

Though his mother had never liked Laura, for some reason, his father had developed a fondness, a soft spot for her. Maybe it was a father-like-son sort of thing. Fathers and sons were much alike, while mothers were on a different keel. Dean's mother had told him almost every chance after he'd met Laura and brought her home that she wasn't good enough for him, and worse, that she was nothing but trouble. Countless times, even after they were married, she had scolded him that he could have done better, a lot better. Laura wasn't as attractive as any of the other girls he had dated, especially Teresa Fino, and Laura couldn't even give him another child after their firstborn died. Dean had stopped arguing the point with her, especially as Laura's alcoholism flared up to the point requiring an intervention seven years ago. His mother had rolled her eyes when Dean had asked her to sit in on it and contribute.

Laura had recently fallen off the wagon and there seemed no way to get her to stop drinking without another intervention. But he had held off reaching out to her best friend from high school, Kathy Parks, and especially her sister, to set up another one. But with each passing day, it seemed more and more necessary. His mother must be turning over in her grave, Dean often thought. I told you so, she would be saying. Laura turned out to nothing but trouble, just like I said.

"Well, anyway, watch out for that German bastard," his father said.

"I will, Dad," Dean said. "How you feeling? Your hip."

"As usual, like crap," he said. "I miss my house, my own backyard. It stinks like an old folk's home in here. And they treat us like little kids."

"I know Dad, but we talked about that," Dean said.

It had been a long time since the old man had complained about the Orchards and it brought Dean even lower than he'd felt when he walked into the place. He was thinking now he should have gone straight home. He was tired and have a mess to clean up there. Hopefully, Laura had just crashed into a drunken slumber and not done any physical damage to the house or made a mess.

"I wish I'd die already," the elder Alessi added. "Join your mother."

"Dad, not tonight," Dean said. "Please."

The old man fell quiet. He looked away, focusing on the closed blinds along the window on a side wall. They were kept closed most of the time because the window provided a cheerless view of the main parking lot.

Dean excused himself to use the old man's bathroom. When he returned, his father asked, "Catching any more bad ones?"

"What?"

"Lawyers," the old man said. "You used to come here and tell me about your cases. And I know, you can't tell me any real names. Just the facts."

Dean shrugged, not really feeling like discussing anything about his job. Like everything else that evening, he was sick of it.

"So what's the latest?" his father asked. "What's it about?"

Dean thought a minute, sighed.

"I just got this guy to turn in his license," he told his father. "Know what he did?"

His father shook his head.

"He was having sex with the wife of his own divorce client," Dean said.

The old man thought about that for a time, then shook his head and laughed to himself.

"That's rich," he said. "He was screwing his client's wife. In a divorce case."

"Yep," Dean said. "That's about it. Well, now she's the client's ex-wife."

"Well, that's good," the elder Alessi said. After thinking a while, he said, "What you do, the cases, should be a TV show. That would be better than the crappy lawyer shows they put on now, making lawyers look so smart, when most of them are scumbags."

"Well, not most, Dad," Dean said. "Most lawyers are decent, hard-working people. I just see all the bad ones. The ones gone bad."

The elder Alessi snapped his fingers.

"That's it," he said.

"What's it?" Dean asked, happy that his father had suddenly become so full of life.

"That could be the name of the TV show," the old man said, "'Lawyers Gone Bad,'"

"Yeah, Dad," Dean said and smiled, "'Lawyers Gone Bad.'"

Chapter Ten
Laura

It was ten-thirty by the time Dean pulled into the driveway of his modest, three-bedroom Cape Cod in a well-maintained, middle-class suburban neighborhood about fifteen minutes from downtown. He had called Laura from his cell phone in the parking lot of The Orchards after helping an orderly get his already gently snoring father into bed after the old man had fallen asleep in his wheelchair while he and Dean were watching some crime drama on TV.

Laura had not answered his call, probably a good thing. It was likely that she had passed out on the living room couch with the TV blaring an episode of the housewives of this or that city or another new contest show on The Food Network. Hopefully, she had not been on Facebook that evening posting more of her inane, incomprehensible, and sometimes flirtatious or vicious comments to friends and strangers alike.

On the way home, Dean had stopped at Wacky Tacos, a fast food taco place famous for its goofy commercials with a funny jingle that played multiple times a day on local radio stations and occasionally on TV especially during Buffalo Bills football games. He ordered three Wacky Taco Supremes, hot, with a side of Spanish rice, and a cola, and finished eating all that in less than five minutes in a back booth of the place. On his way out, he ordered another couple tacos to take home.

As expected, Laura was sprawled out on her stomach on the living room couch with her hands tucked at her sides and her laptop on the floor. She had always been on the thin side and drinking too much and eating too little had caused her to lose even more weight, to the point where Dean feared that she was becoming anorexic. But she showered or bathed every day, got her hair done regularly and painted her toenails and so had maintained, for now at least, a healthy enough appearance, despite the inner turmoil caused by her chronic depression and raging alcoholism. There was no longer any way around the fact that Laura was an unrepentant and likely incurable drunk. What she drank never varied, starting around mid-afternoon with two or three heaping glasses of bourbon or rum and coke over ice, depending on how low she felt, followed by several glasses of cheap wine until she ultimately passed out.

Her maiden name was Doyle and her mother was also Irish, Joan Sullivan. It was not surprising then that she had inherited a fair complexion with pretty freckles running up her nose to her forehead. Her freckles even spread across her breasts and upper chest to Dean's amusement and appreciation.

His mother's opinion notwithstanding, Laura was not an unattractive woman. She had a small, pretty square face with sharp cheekbones, complete with all those adorable freckles, framed by a thick, long swatch of auburn hair with reddish tints that tumbled down to her shoulders. Although her frame was slender, almost boyish, her breasts were ample enough and, of course, there were those lovable freckles. Lying there helpless on the couch, she looked sexy, ready for the taking and Dean thought a moment of doing exactly that – turning her over, pulling down her jeans, then her panties and fucking her right there on the couch, despite her drunken unconsciousness and not really caring whether or not she liked or objected to it, or even if she wouldn't remember much of it in the morning. But Dean chased that admittedly disturbing fantasy from his mind just as Laura rolled onto her right side and, out of some alcohol-fueled dream, mumbled, "Fuck you, bitch."

Dean spotted the TV remote on the edge of the couch near Laura's right shoulder and went over to retrieve it so he could turn off the blaring TV. But as he was about to reach for it, she collapsed downward and the remote now lay somewhere under her left shoulder. After a sigh, Dean gently dug his right hand under her, found the remote and pulled it out, desperate not to wake her. If that happened, she'd no doubt start calling him names and want to start another of their many booze incited fights.

Thankfully, she stayed asleep, tightening up her face and mumbling some other curses out of some dream landscape that continued to plague her mind and soul. Dean turned and pointed the remote at the TV and silenced it, then picked up the laptop on the carpet next to the couch and set it on the coffee table. He went over and switched off the lamp on the end table next to the couch placing the room under the distant glow of light from kitchen. It was sufficient, despite the long shadows it cast, for Dean to see what he needed to see as he sat on the loveseat across from the couch and Laura and contemplated the day. After a minute or so, Dean got up and went to the kitchen and retrieved a beer from the fridge, returned to the living room with it, and sat back down on the loveseat. Laura was gently snoring now, far from the waking, real world, still apparently experiencing some bizarre sequence of dreams.

Several years ago during one of her rehab phases, a fortyish female counselor had told Dean that although Laura was prone to alcoholism due to a combination of genetics and upbringing, what had pushed her over the edge was her inability to get past the grief over the death of their infant son, Steven.

The baby was only three months old when SIDS claimed him. Laura had come into the nursery while Dean was at work and found Steven. He was dead. She had fallen asleep on the couch in the living room that morning after putting him down, on his stomach, in his crib. She woke up forty-five minutes later and in a premonitory panic, ran to the nursery only to find that she was too late, realizing a young mother's worst nightmare.

She had called Dean at work screaming incoherently. He ran out of the office and rushed home where he found the EMTs wheeling out a gurney. A white sheet covered a small body. With a sad frown, the EMT, a pretty, thin girl in her early twenties, told him with a shrug, SIDS – Sudden Infant Death Syndrome. Instead of lifting the sheet to see his dead baby boy, Dean ran into the house. He found Laura sitting at the kitchen table. Another EMT, a handsome kid about twenty-five, was standing there with a glum expression watching Laura sob into her hands. The kid looked at Dean and shrugged. After a moment, he sighed and left them alone.

That was fifteen years ago.

Dean sipped the beer as he watched Laura sleeping. She had turned her head so he could see her face in the shadows. He again wondered what she was dreaming about. She had told Dean over the years that she sometimes dreamed of Steven. And in some of these dreams, he wasn't a baby, but all grown up. A full grown man with his own family, and a job, and three kids. So she and Dean were grandparents. And on occasion, Steven took his family on vacation to visit them at their nice Florida pool home near Disney World.

Disney, Dean laughed and took another sip of beer. It had been their dream, but now it seemed about as possible for them to get as the moon. And in truth, he no longer wanted to go to the place where dreams come true.

Though Dean had encouraged her after Steven died, Laura resisted having another baby right away. She was afraid for it, she said, blaming herself for Steven's death. Doing that was natural, to be expected, but it never stopped. Still, at first, Dean persisted, telling her it was just the thing that she needed, that they both needed. It would go a long way, he insisted, in helping them alleviate their grief. But she eventually threw the suggestion right back into his face and put an end to it. One night about five months after Steven's death, when he had brought it up again lying in bed next to her, trying to come on to her (they hadn't made love since the tragedy), she had started pummeling his chest. He had tried to calm her down, by bringing her close and hugging her, patting her hair, but finally, she violently pulled away from his grasp and jumped out of bed.

"What do you think he was?" she yelled at Dean. "A dog that you can replace with a new puppy?"

So he had dropped the subject and it was not long after that when Laura started drinking heavily, and only then did she start having sex with him. She was on the pill and always changed the subject, or gave him a cold stare, when he brought up going off it and trying to get pregnant. Having a child was no longer possible for them. Without telling him, she had secretly made an appointment and gotten a tubal ligation. No children, only the memory of a three-month-old boy and the grief about what might have been.

Dean took another long sip of beer and he turned his thoughts to the first time he had ever seen Laura. It was her first day as the receptionist in the entrance foyer of the public defender's office when she attracted his attention. He had been an Assistant Public Defender going on three years by then and it seemed that there was a new front receptionist every other month. Some of his fellow APDs were raving about this new one as he walked back to the kitchen area of the main office. Finally, somebody good looking, even hot, was the general consensus. But it wasn't until the office Christmas Party, four months later, when Dean finally engaged Laura in a meaningful conversation. After the party, she went with him for a couple drinks at a downtown nightclub and he asked her out. But she did not go to bed with him until their third date. Six months later, they were getting married.

By then, Dean had grown tired of being overworked, underpaid and under-appreciated as an assistant public defender representing the helpless dregs of society and was sending out resumes to private firms and government agencies. After several unsuccessful interviews, he landed a job as assistant disciplinary counsel for the LDO. And it was six months after that when Laura had Steven.

Laura's alcoholism reached a crisis phase and became patently evident to family, friends, and co-workers when, about two years after Steven's death, she got arrested for DWI. She and Dean had gone out to dinner and, as usual, she had too many glasses of wine and had started an argument with him over nothing. At some point, she got up, threw a glass of wine in his face and ran out of the restaurant. By the time he got over the shock and got up and ran after her, it was too late. She had driven out of the parking lot, and only six blocks away, going too fast, she had skidded off the road and struck a telephone pole.

Laura had spent the next couple days in the hospital, and three months later, she went to court and pled guilty to DWI. The judge sentenced her to six months' probation, the statutory fine, and revocation of her license for a year. Still, matters didn't progress to a full blown intervention by family and friends until five months after her DWI plea. Laura got drunk and made a fool of herself at her nephew's wedding reception, interrupting the mother-son dance and throwing up in the middle of the dance floor toward the end of the night.

Dean finished his beer and set the empty bottle down on the coffee table. He leaned back on the loveseat and closed his eyes, imagining how life might be if he finally divorced Laura and took up with Kat Franklin. But that might just end up being another can of worms. Kat was neurotic and obsessive, an addictive personality in her own way. As the saying goes, the grass was not always greener on the other side, although when he had mentioned that to Foley, his quick response had been that, in this case, one bad lawn might be better than the other.

Sometime later, Dean dozed off and some indeterminable time later, the annoying chime of his cell phone woke him. Looking around, he was surprised to see the couch empty. His first thought was that Laura had probably gotten up while he dozed and, like she often did, stumbled down the long hall to the master bedroom and crawled, fully clothed, into her side of their king-sized bed. But scanning the room, with the cell phone ringing a second time, Dean noticed that the entrance door in the foyer leading to the front porch was wide open. He pushed himself off the couch and went to the front door. With his cell phone ringing a third time as he entered the foyer, Dean noticed that his keys were no longer dangling from the key holder next to the coat rack. He immediately dug his hands into his pants pockets. They were empty.

"Jesus," he said, as the cell phone rang a fourth and final time before sending the caller to voicemail.

He ran outside and immediately spotted Laura in the driver's seat of his car. He also realized that the car was running.

Dean ran to the driver's side door, yanked it open and reached in as Laura started to stir. With the car door alarm dinging incessantly, he found the keys hanging from the ignition and turned off the car. By now, Laura was up, laughing.

"What are you doing?" Her voice was a continuous slur. "Coping a feel? I just want to get some tacos. Lemme get some fucking tacos."

"I brought you some home," Dean said and pulled the keys from the ignition. "From Wacky Tacos."

"You did," she said dreamily.

"Yeah," he told her and helped lift her out of the car. "They're in the kitchen."

Laura wobbled in his arms along the walkway to the front door and Dean led her to the kitchen. She leaned into him, nuzzled into his neck and said, "You brought me tacos?"

"Two," he said. "All for you."

But now she wasn't moving with him.

"Laura?" He sighed. She had passed out on her feet. "Laura?"

She finally stirred and leaning on him, allowed herself to be pulled by him into the master bedroom

"C'mon," he said, "one step at a time."

"I'm so tired, Steven," she mumbled.

"I know," he said. "I know."

"Steven?"

"No," he said. "It's me, Dean."

"Fuck you," she said and laughed.

Dean finally managed to position her at the edge of their bed and sat her down. He slid back the sheets and blanket and puffed up the pillow. Then, he helped her out of her pants and top and lowered her backwards on her side and covered her.

"Want to fuck me, Dean?" she asked softly.

"Not tonight," he whispered. "Tomorrow."

"You never fuck me," she said with her eyes closed.

He stood and watched her for a time as she dozed off into an alcoholic dream.

A moment later, Dean's cell phone started ringing again. He checked his watch and noted that it was almost midnight. Who could be calling him at this hour?

He pulled his phone from his front pocket and walked out of the master bedroom. By now, Laura was fast asleep, snoring, oblivious to the call. Out in the hall, Dean clicked the answer button of his cell and said, "Yeah? Hello?"

"Where were you?" It was Stu Foley.

"Asleep," Dean said. "You know what time it is? What's up?" Then Dean remembered that Foley was going to stake-out the DA's house, see if he went anywhere and met anyone special. "What happened?"

"What happened?" Foley laughed. "A lot. Look, I'm at The Pub. Why don't you come out here for a nightcap and let me tell you."

"It's midnight, Stuey," Dean said. "I need to get to sleep. Tomorrow, remember, is going to be a long day. The first day of the rest of my life under a new boss. So why don't you tell me what this is about over the phone?"

"Because the tale I got to tell you deserves to be told in person," Foley said. "Over a beer. Or two."

Dean sighed. He looked into the master bedroom. The light was still on but Laura wasn't stirring. She hadn't moved since he had tucked her in. She was down for the night.

"Alright," he said. "But what you have to tell me better be goddamn good."

Chapter Eleven
The Stake-Out

Twenty minutes later, Dean was sitting in a booth in the dark, back corner of The Pub. There were a couple slumped, shabby looking guys sitting along the bar watching game highlights on ESPN Sports Center on a 19-inch flat screen TV up on a shelf behind the bar.

"So what's this about, Stu?" Dean asked and slurped up foam from his glass of draft beer. "It better be good."

"Oh, it's good," Foley said.

He took a long sip of beer from his glass and launched into his tale.

He'd slept longer than he'd planned because Ginny had forgotten to wake him up by seven-thirty and it was almost nine by the time he rushed out of the house cursing her for being such a stupid, fat Polack cow.

"I almost didn't go," Foley said. "Figured, by the time I got there, he'd probably already left to meet Susie Hines-Laurence or was in for the night."

But Foley did go. After five passes, he finally found a

parking spot at around nine-thirty along a shadowy stretch of Wellington Boulevard that gave him a clear view of the DA's one-hundred year old Georgian monstrosity next to the similar, five hundred thousand to million dollar monstrosities in this high-brow city neighborhood of lawyers, doctors, bank vice-presidents, stockbrokers and financial managers. Wellington Boulevard overlooked the scenic and well-maintained Hudson Park with its well-manicured golf course, level tennis courts and meditation paths for upper middle-class power brokers of the city.

Nothing at all happened for forty-five minutes. Foley was aching to pee and was ready to call it a night, when to his surprise, the DA came bounding down the steep front porch steps and trotted among the shadows of the ancient Maple trees on his long front lawn to a black BMW parked in his driveway behind what was likely his wife's silver Lexus. Bingo! Foley thought. After the BMW pulled out of the driveway, he waited a moment before driving off heading in the same direction.

"Guess where he went?" Foley asked Dean.

Dean shrugged. "To meet Susan Hines-Laurence?" he asked.

"No," Foley said and took another sip of beer. "He came here."

"Here?" Dean frowned. "As in The Pub?"

"Yep," Foley said. "The Pub. Our very own drinking hole."

Then, Foley smiled.

"And guess who he met here, sat with, right here in this very booth?"

"I have no idea, Stuey," Dean said. "Enough of the guessing games. Just tell me."

"Our very own boss to be," Foley said. "Brad Gunther."

"What? Who?"

"Yep, Gunther."

"Brad Gunther?"

"That's what I just said." Foley shrugged. "Bradley T. Gunther."

"So they do know each other?" It wasn't so much a question on Dean's part as a statement of surprise.

"I guess so," Foley said.

"You followed him in?" Dean asked. "The DA?"

"Sure," Foley said. "The place had a few more souls at that hour, around ten or so, but not many. I sat at the corner of the bar and tried to blend in. You know, act inconspicuous. Neither the DA or Gunther know me, but I didn't want Gunther connecting any dots tomorrow morning when I meet him officially for the first time. I could have said I was just having a beer, but I don't know." Foley laughed. "And then Mike Dibble almost blew it for me when he came stumbling over and welcomed me with a slap across my back and one of his, 'Hey, Foley, how's the bad lawyer biz?'"

"Oh, geez," Dean said and the next moment, he frowned. "And you're absolutely sure it was Gunther?"

"I've seen him around," Foley said and thought a moment. "Yes, I'm sure. It was our new boss."

"How long did they meet?"

"Long enough for each of them to down a couple beers," Foley said. "Hour or so."

"What the hell could they have been meeting about?"

"Sorry, boss," Foley said. "I couldn't get close enough to eavesdrop on that."

"No, I know," Dean said.

Dean thought things over for a time. So Gunther knows the DA well enough to meet him at some bar late at night. How did he know him and what the hell did they talk about?

"Well what the fuck," Dean finally blurted out.

"Yeah," Foley said. "What the fuck."

In a spacious den on the first floor of a five-bedroom sprawling colonial in a subdivision of similar houses, with long, wide driveways, separated by long, wide lawns cut regularly and meticulously by landscaping crews in the elite suburb of Williamsville just north of the city, Bradley T. Gunther was sitting behind a squat, cherry wood antique desk placing a call to Chief Justice Krane. The Tiffany lamp on the corner of the desk bathed the room in a dim yellow glow. It was eleven-thirty, and due to the late hour, Gunther had hesitated a few moments before dialing the CJ's private cell number.

After the fourth ring, the CJ answered.

"Hello," the CJ answered, his voice gruff, impatient.

"Hello, your Honor," Gunther said and then took a moment to clear his throat. "It's me. Sorry to call you so late."

"You met with him," the CJ said. "How'd it go?"

"As planned," Gunther said. "I told him about your case."

"And?"

"He seemed to understand."

"Alright then," the CJ said. "Very well. Thank you."

"Yes, your Honor."

"You ready for tomorrow? Your first day?"

"Yes, your Honor," Gunther said.

"As we talked about earlier, keep an eye on that Deputy," the CJ said. "He's a loose cannon. And that investigator of his. Old guy. Forgot his name."

"Foley," Gunther said. "Stuart Foley."

"Yes, him."

"He's about due to retire," Gunther said. "Maybe I can push him in that direction."

"Just do it quietly," the CJ said. "The less noise out of the LDO, the better off the profession is. As I told you earlier, Alessi doesn't seem to understand that concept." He sighed. "But don't underestimate him either. He's a pretty good lawyer."

"Yes, your Honor."

"Well, goodnight, Brad," the CJ said. "And thanks for doing that tonight, extending yourself. The last thing we need is the public thinking that the DA is unethical. Or worse." He laughed. "Not to mention it might cost him a seat on a bench up here."

"I agree, your Honor," Gunther said.

"Well, good night," said the CJ.

"And you too, your Honor."

After hanging up, Gunther sat a few minutes in the pale light of his den considering what he was going to do on his first day in charge of the LDO, and what he was going to tell the staff during the morning meeting. He'd start by subtly putting Alessi in his place, and that Chief Investigator, Foley, as well.

At some point in the morning, he'd personally meet with each of the LDO's four disciplinary counsel: the eccentric, bow-tie wearing clown, Ed Chase; the obsessive, Kat Franklin, that new kid, Peter O'Brien, and last but not least, the lovely and sexy Liza Hartman with significant political connections of her own. At least, that was the way the CJ's confidential clerk, Margo Anson-Clarke had described each of them, with an almost bitter twang.

Margo had gone on to inform Gunther that Liza Hartman had confided to her for some time that she was not particularly fond of Dean Alessi though the exact reasons were not all that clear. Therefore, it appeared to Gunther that he and Hartman may have a common adversary in Alessi that might require long, private meetings behind the closed door of his office to discuss what should be done about it.

Yes, he nodded in the silence of his den as he reached over to switch off the lamp on his desk, a series of private, behind-closed-door meetings with Liza Hartman looked like a definite possibility.

Chapter Twelve
The Old Director

Dean had forgotten to set the alarm and overslept that morning. He woke in a panic and pushed himself out of bed. Laura was snoring near the edge of their king-sized bed and she did not stir as Dean got out of the bed.

Despite a mad rush to get ready, Dean didn't pull out of his driveway until ten after nine and it was nine forty-five by the time he found a spot in the parking garage a block away from the LDO's building. Great first impression, he thought, as he hustled from the garage into a gray, morning drizzle, trotted a block then cursed waiting for the crosswalk light to change. He had his usual wait at the lobby elevator and the slow ride to the sixth floor. Upon pushing open the front door and entering the LDO waiting room at nine fifty-five, Dean noticed that the reception kiosk was empty telling him that the new Director, Brad Gunther, had gone ahead and started his introductory staff meeting without him.

With his head hurting a bit from one too many beers and too little sleep last night, Dean sighed as he punched the four-digit code on the keypad enabling him to open the waiting room door leading back to the LDO offices. He walked past the kitchen around the corner and stopped at the main conference room door. From inside, he heard a muffled voice, someone among the staff asking a question. That meant he was so late that he had probably missed Gunther's official introduction of himself and what his intentions were for the office.

After a breath, Dean gently knocked on the door and without waiting for permission, he slowly opened it. Everyone turned to him as he gingerly stepped inside. He smiled and gave brief, apologetic nod to Gunther, a large man, six feet three or so, with short, sandy blonde hair who stood imposingly at the head of the over-sized conference table. As Dean entered the room and found a seat at the far corner of the table, Gunther crossed his fairly thick arms. His head was large with a face that was, at least to Dean, cold and serious and plain. Dean thought that this imposing, stony and unsympathetic man standing before him was the epitome of his father's stereotypical view of a German uber-man.

"Good of you to join us, Mister Alessi," Gunther said without a hint of humor or tolerance in his voice, as if automatically deeming Dean's tardiness an affront to his authority. Not that Dean could blame him. In his shoes, he might have been similarly annoyed. But unlike Gunther, he would not have so expressively demonstrated his displeasure and certainly would have withheld judgment until he heard an excuse or let enough time pass to see that it was an aberration of Dean's work ethic and respect for authority.

"Sorry," Dean said. He thought of providing a

convenient and false excuse. Instead, he shru
late this morning."

"Yes, we see that," said Gunther. "N
we?"

A question had been raised about some procedure, a
minor point of one of the secretaries who may have disagreed
with one of Dean's lesser office policies. But Dean could not
concentrate on the dispute, even when he was called upon to
indicate the basis for the policy. He had too many things on
his mind – the meeting last night between Gunther and the
District Attorney, for one, being stupidly late, for another.

"Do you have anything to add, Mister Alessi, on this
point?" Gunther asked.

"Quite frankly," Dean told Gunther, "I can't recall why
we instituted that particular policy," though, he wasn't even
sure what policy was being discussed.

"Sounds like a lot of things around here," said Liza
Hartman.

Dean glanced at her and frowned.
"Well, then, I suppose we can get rid of it," Gunther said.
"Go back to using *Acco-fasteners* instead of paper clips."

Gunther sighed and looked around the room.

"Is there anything else from anyone?" Gunther asked.
He clearly wanted the meeting to be over, and everyone
shrugged. "Alright then. As I said, I am a quick study and feel
confident I can get up to speed as to procedures and policies
affecting the office. I am also confident that all of us will get
along nicely, and that each of us will have a rewarding
experience in policing the profession. I have an open door
policy. If anything is bothering you, please come to me and

s discuss it. The worst possible thing is for you to let a problem, or perceived problem, fester."

Gunther looked around the table at the now blank faces of the staff.

"Very well, then," he said. "It's been a pleasure meeting all of you. Let's get back to work."

As Dean shuffled out of the conference room with his colleagues, Gunther called after him.

"Mister Alessi," he said. "Would you please join me in my office?"

Dean followed behind Gunther down the long, wide hallway to the Director's spacious corner office. Two windows ran the length of the side walls behind a wide, cherry wood desk, providing an impressive view of the upper end of Main Street bordering the theater district. Gunther entered the office with Dean a couple steps behind. He went around his desk and sat down on his plush, leather swivel chair while Dean sat in one of two chairs facing it.

The office, now belonging to Brad Gunther, had been vacant ever since the previous Director, Percy Madison, had abruptly resigned in disgrace just over six months ago. Madison had served as LDO Director for almost twenty years. He had hired Dean and over the years, had granted his Deputy more and more authority to set policy and run the office.

Dean was not privy to all the juicy details that had resulted in Madison's abrupt resignation as Director. What he eventually learned had come entirely from Stu Foley late one night over several beers at The Pub.

According to Foley, like many men, Madison's shameful demise was caused by his love, or lust, for a beautiful and much younger woman. Her name was Monica Harding, a twenty-eight-year-old leggy, blonde attorney (Madison was fifty-nine when they met). At some point, Monica had taken control over the financial affairs of her parents' neighbor, Nancy Weiss, an eighty-five-year-old widow. The woman and Mr. Weiss, who had died only a couple months earlier, had been childless, and Monica, after a fairly exhaustive search, using two private investigators, could not locate any of the Weiss' next of kin. Mrs. Weiss's older sister, also childless, had died several years earlier. Mr. Weiss had a younger brother, a kind of free spirit who had moved out to California or Oregon years ago.

Within a few days of Mr. Weiss' death, Monica began spending more and more time with the old widow. After a few weeks, she had quit her job as an associate attorney in a medium-sized personal injury firm where she had been assigned doing research, drafting and filing motions, and conducting minor depositions. After quitting, Monica spent virtually all her time at the old woman's house, cleaning it, going food shopping at a local supermarket, taking the old lady to doctors' appointments or for blood work, and doing various other errands. She spent whole afternoons watching soap operas and drinking tea and eating cookies and crackers with Mrs. Weiss while the old lady droned on about her distant and fluttering memories concerning her family and friends, some of whom she had liked, but many more she had despised, with most of them, if not all, now long dead. Her one-sided reminisces included her fond and not so fond memories regarding the late Mr. Weiss. At least once a week, Monica drove Mrs. Weiss out to the cemetery where she visited the graves, if she could remember where they were, of her only sister, Mary, cousins and friends and, of course, Mr. Weiss.

It was not long before Monica had Mrs. Weiss executing a Power of Attorney granting her complete authority over her financial affairs. Within a few weeks, Monica had cashed in over a million dollars of securities, and transferred another one hundred thousand dollars, give or take a few cents, into a joint account in the name of Mrs. Weiss and herself. While Mrs. Weiss had never worked a day in her life, Mr. Weiss had been a CPA with substantial luck at picking stocks and mutual funds. He had also invested substantially in gold. Still, Mr. Weiss never had flaunted their wealth and the Weiss' led a fairly frugal existence. He had bought a new car only every five years or so, and they lived in a relatively modest house in a middle-class neighborhood. They rarely traveled or went out to dinner. Indeed, Mrs. Weiss was in the dark as to the exact value of Mr. Weiss' estate when Monica had first questioned her about it and seemed flabbergasted to learn from Monica that, because of Mr. Weiss's adept financial planning, and general frugality, she was worth well over five million dollars.

One night almost a year and a half after Monica had taken complete control of Mrs. Weiss' financial affairs, and, in the process, had siphoned off thousands of dollars from their joint accounts into several of her own personal checking accounts, Mrs. Weiss died quietly in her sleep. Because all the money obtained from the sale of stocks and other of Mrs. Weiss' assets had been already transferred into joint accounts in Monica's name and the old lady's name, or into Monica's solely owned bank accounts, those securities and funds did not fall within Mrs. Weiss' probate estate, thus giving Monica a substantial and secret windfall. Once the old lady died, all those assets and money became Monica's assets and money and as far as Monica could tell, no one was the wiser. Within a week of Mrs. Weiss' death, Monica transferred all the assets and money siphoned from Mrs. Weiss' estate being maintained in the joint and her own checking accounts, a tidy sum of 3.4 million dollars, into a newly opened personal checking account in a bank down in central Florida, near Disney World, where Monica had already bought a three-hundred thousand dollar home.

After Mrs. Weiss' funeral, Monica took a trip to Antiqua and paid half a million dollars in cash for another house on the beach. She'd also purchased a house back up north for a hundred thousand dollars where she'd spend summers. What remained of Mrs. Weiss' money, almost 2.5 million dollars, she reinvested in mutual funds, gold and Roth accounts. It seemed her life was set. She had no intention of ever working again, let alone engaging in the drudgery of practicing law.

But then, two years after Mrs. Weiss unlamented death, there came the glitch in what had otherwise seemed a flawlessly executed scam. Mr. Weiss's free spirit brother had fathered a child out of wedlock years ago and naturally failed to mention that fact to anyone. And somewhere along the way, the child, a long-haired drug abuser, got interested in his family while in his third rehab stint, and learned that he might have a wealthy, elderly uncle living back east. He quit rehab and went looking.

By now, Monica Harding was alternating spending the winter in her beach home on Antigua or in central Florida. And then, as Foley described it to Dean that night at The Pub, all proverbial hell broke loose.

Mr. Weiss's long-haired nephew hired a local lawyer, an aggressive, beady-eyed, balding shark by the name of Ted Bennett, and Bennett soon discovered that the lovely, though apparently devious, Monica Harding, had gotten all too friendly with old lady Weiss and had allegedly taken serious advantage of her. He filed a complaint with the LDO (a process Bennett had become all too personally familiar with over his somewhat dubious thirty-year career) complete with a series of fairly damning account spreadsheets. Dean remembered thinking when it came in that it was a slam dunk, a likely disbarment for the lovely Miss Harding for breach of fiduciary duty and a rather serious conflict of interest. Dean also remembered being extremely busy at the time, as were Kat Franklin and Liza Hartman, with several serious investigations on their plates, so he thought there'd be no harm in assigning the case to Ed Chase.

"When did Percy take over?" Dean had asked Foley. "How did that come about?"

"Chase brought the lovely Miss Harding into the office one morning for a deposition and was taking it in the conference room," Foley had explained. "She was defending herself at the time and old Percy happened to be walking past the room during a break. I guess it was love, or lust, at first sight. After her depo, Percy spoke with Ed about the case and told Ed he was taking over. Within a couple weeks, the investigation was over. He worked a deal for Monica to refund a half million dollars, finagling the numbers and forging some documents, bills and things that were claimed to have been paid by Monica on the old lady's behalf, to help show Ted Bennett and his long-haired drug abusing client that his numbers were mistaken. In return, Monica would accept a deal for a one-year suspension.

"At first, Bennett went along with it, got sold a bill of goods by Percy, who as you know, can fake it with the best of them. He had Bennett convinced that this was a fair deal, the best he was going to get, one in which everybody won. And Bennett talked his client into going along with it. But then, by dumb luck, Bennett happened to run into Percy and Monica making goo-goo eyes and doing some other things in Percy's Lexus in the parking lot outside some local restaurant whose name I forget. I mean, by now, Percy was off the deep end with this girl, and, I guess, like most cheaters, had long ago thrown caution to wind." Foley had laughed. "Word is Bennett caught her going down on him. Well, Bennett put two and two together, started digging a little harder, and found out that his original numbers were pretty much right on the mark.

"And that's when he went to the CJ, because he wasn't sure if anyone else in the LDO was in on it."

"Fuck," had been Dean's only response to that.

Though Madison had to quit as LDO Director, he kept his law license although he had to certify his "retirement" – that is, that he never ever intended to practice law again not only in New York, but anywhere else. He was set to receive a fairly lucrative state pension anyway after twenty-eight years of employment that included health benefits at a relatively young age. And although Monica Harding had to give back a hefty amount of the money she had siphoned off old lady Weiss, Foley claimed that she still walked away with about half a mil plus the beach home in Antiqua, where she still spends her winters.

So, in the end, according to Foley, both Monica Harding and their former boss got off pretty easy, yet another example that what goes round does not come round.

Dean disagreed with that sentiment to some extent as Madison had to retire in disgrace from a job he loved, quit practicing law, and lost his wife, Beth, after thirty-three years of marriage. As for Monica, she ended up giving back most of the money she had embezzled from the old lady, which went to her rightful heir, Mr. Weiss' nephew, a kid of dubious character, granted. And, she lost her law license in the process.

"She should have gone to jail," Foley had said. "She walked away with a small fortune, a house on a lovely beach in Antiqua, and she still has her looks and wiles and will use both of them to trap another some unsuspecting idiot like Percy." He had laughed. "I mean, I'd jump for that and I know what I'd be getting."

Dean gave him that you-are-a-dirty-old-man look again.

"And last I heard," Foley went on, "Percy and Beth reconciled and bought a nice place near Orlando after he got a job teaching at some community college. Worst of all, the rest of us, especially you, got tainted by the scummy things he did. You heard the whispers, including from some members of the Court, and the CJ as well, how could we have missed what was going on? There was even some talk of firing the lot of us and giving the office a fresh, clean start. And to add insult to injury, we had to clean up the mess. It'll probably cost you the Director's job, or be used as a convenient excuse to justify hiring somebody else, some political hack."

Now, sitting before the new Director, Bradley T. Gunther, thinking of the sordid details of the "Percy Madison affair," as it had come to be called, that he had learned from Foley in The Pub that night now a year and a half ago, Dean realized that Foley had been right all along.

What goes around definitely does not come around.

Chapter Thirteen
The New Director

"You out late last night, Dean?" Gunther leaned back in the black leather swivel chair, formerly occupied by Percy Madison, and regarded Dean with a kind of malicious snarl.

"Excuse me?"

"Late," Gunther said. "As in past Midnight late. Maybe why you were late getting to work this morning?"

Dean thought a moment, and decided to tell Gunther what it appeared he already knew.

"Yes," Dean said. "I was at a bar called The Pub."

"I know," he said and smiled. "You were having a beer with Investigator Foley. The LDO's very own Investigator Foley. At a bar called The Pub."

Dean nodded. He had no idea where this was going, but he could tell by the smirk on Gunther's face that it was going nowhere good.

"Yes," Dean said, trying not to stutter, "Stu and I, Investigator Foley, we sometimes meet for a beer or two at The Pub."

"And do you have any idea what Investigator Foley was doing before you met him at The Pub?" Gunther asked.

Dean shrugged. It was becoming crystal clear that Foley had been bagged following the DA. He shrugged again and tried not to squirm out of his chair.

"Well, let's stop beating around the bush, shall we, Dean," Gunther said. "We both know what Foley was doing before he met you. So you want to tell me why the LDO's very own Investigator Foley was following the county District Attorney around town last night?"

Dean sighed. Busted, he thought. So very busted. There was no use beating around the bush, as Gunther had put it. But before Dean could figure out how and what exactly to tell him, Gunther continued, "I mean, it couldn't be related to an ongoing investigation, could it? Because I had Liza Hartman help me check the computer database first thing this morning, and there doesn't seem to be any files opened on the District Attorney."

"Well," Dean said with a weak smile, "that's because there aren't any."

Gunther frowned as he leaned forward in his chair and clasped his hands before him.

"You want to explain to me then," he asked, "what Investigator Foley was doing following him?"

"Well, we, we had some concerns," Dean said, thinking a moment, then turning and adjusting in his chair, "legitimate concerns, I think, about the District Attorney's handling of the Laurence shooting." He sighed. "Based on the involvement of his first assistant district attorney and all."

"So you knew about this? That an investigator of this

office, its chief investigator, no less, was going to follow an attorney, the District Attorney, regarding an investigation that had not been officially opened?" Gunther asked. "You approved that?"

Dean nodded. "Yes," he said. "I did."

"But you didn't open an official investigative file, did you?" Gunther asked.

"No," Dean said. "I did not."

"So everything Investigator Foley did last night was unofficial," Gunther said.

Dean shrugged with acknowledgment.

"And what would have happened had something happened to Foley while on this unofficial investigation?" Gunter asked. "This fishing expedition or whatever it was?"

Dean sighed. He had never expected that this would come of Foley's suggestion that he follow the DA. His complete emasculation. And quite frankly, he didn't blame the new Director. He would have been angry as well had the shoe been on the other foot.

"Well, I am amazed at your complete lack of judgment in authorizing something like this," Gunther went on. "I am quite beside myself about it, in fact, especially in light of what's been going on around here the last few years."

Now, Dean frowned. "What's been going on around here?" he asked, not liking the implication that he was somehow involved in something untoward or inappropriate "the last few years," as he had put. He had nothing to do with what Percy Madison had tried to pull, and there was nothing to indicate that he had any knowledge of it.

"I'm not sure what you mean," Dean said, but Gunther

would not let him finish.

"And what did Investigator Foley find out last night," Gunther went on, "based upon his unofficial surveillance of the county District Attorney? Where did he follow the District Attorney to?"

"He followed him to The Pub," Dean said, "and he saw him meet with you."

Gunther slowly raised up his hands and clapped.

"What stellar investigative work," he said, "because that's exactly right. Investigator Foley followed the District Attorney, who had come to The Pub for a celebratory drink with his old law school chum – me. And do you know what I was celebrating, Dean?"

"I would think," Dean said, "your appointment as Director."

"Exactly right," Gunther said, "my appointment as Director. Me."

Gunter sighed and leaned back in his chair.

"When did you learn that fact, Dean?" Gunther asked. "That I had been appointed Director. When did you receive the official announcement from the Court?"

"Early afternoon," Dean said. "Around the lunch hour, twelve thirty or so."

"And yet," Gunther went on, now conducting, it seemed to Dean, a sort of cross-examination of him, "knowing that I was officially in charge of this department, you took it on your own to commence a secret, unofficial investigation into the district attorney of this county and authorized the use of LDO manpower for that purpose?"

"I suppose so," Dean said. There was nothing else to

say. It was true. With full knowledge of all that, he had approved Foley going out there and conducting a surveillance.

"But I think our intentions were sound," Dean blurted. "I mean, quite frankly, what the DA did in closing his investigation into the Kent Laurence shooting was quite curious, at best, and, I felt, and still do feel, a conflict of interest that may require adverse comment."

"You couldn't have waited a day, less than a day, and confer with me, your new boss, about it?" Gunther asked.

Dean nodded his acknowledgment. That certainly would have been the wiser thing to do. But he had done what he had done, solely for the purpose of getting down to the DA's motives, to help determine if there was something more to his decision to dismiss a serious criminal investigation into the shooting death of a man by the hand of the man's trophy wife, who happened to be the DA's first assistant district attorney. To get down to the nitty-gritty as to whether his decision not to prosecute was beyond hubris and/or stupidity and might be based on lust, or worse, a combination of lust and greed.

"In hindsight, I suppose I should have," Dean said.

"In hindsight? You suppose?" Gunther leaned forward and slapped a hand on top of the desk. "I think you are letting yourself off too easily."

"But as I said…"

"You want to know how I know about all this," Gunther asked. "That Foley followed the DA last night out to meet me?"

Dean shrugged. He had definitely not made a favorable

first impression on his new boss. Gunther was red-faced, upset. Being late was one thing, but acting *ultra vires*, beyond his powers, confirmed what Dean suspected the Court thought about him, that he was overaggressive in pursuit of lawyers gone bad to the point of being reckless.

"The District Attorney called me around one this morning," he said, "and you know what he asked? Why is one of my investigators following him around? And why is he meeting with the deputy LDO director at The Pub after I had met with him?

"My first question, naturally," Gunther went on, "was how did he know all this – that Investigator Foley had followed him, and then met with you at The Pub after Foley apparently watched me and him have a couple beers in a back booth there? Well, you see, Dean, the DA hired a bodyguard soon as he took office five years ago. You would be amazed how many death threats a District Attorney receives in the course of a month. Anyway, this bodyguard is charged with not only making sure that the DA's house is secure, but that nobody is lurking about, stalking him. Someone who might have it in for the DA. This bodyguard is trained to spot people following him out to bars late at night, where he might meet with his friends or political allies. You get my drift, don't you, Dean?"

"Yes," Dean said, "of course."

"Anyway, it was this bodyguard who spotted our Investigator Foley," Gunther said, "both following the DA in his car, and following him into The Pub. In fact, Investigator Foley's quite fortunate that the bodyguard didn't intervene at any point during the night. I hear the man, a former police officer, is one tough character, a martial arts expert."

Dean didn't offer his opinion that he felt secure Stu Foley could have handled himself quite well had the DA's bodyguard, whomever he was, confronted him last night.

"This bodyguard was also the one who reported," Gunther continued, "that he saw Foley meeting with you and sharing a beer at The Pub around midnight, a bit after the District Attorney and I had left the place."

Gunther sighed and leaned forward.

"What were you hoping Investigator Foley would find from following the District Attorney?" he asked.

"Him meeting with her," Dean said, "his first assistant. Mrs. Hines-Laurence."

"And that would mean what?"

"I thought that might enhance our concern that the DA had engaged in a conflict of interest in making a decision on the criminal investigation into Kent Laurence's shooting," Dean said. "In closing it out. I mean, it was bad enough that his first assistant was a suspect in a potential murder investigation his own office was conducting, but it would be a hundred times worse if he was having an affair with her during it. I mean, his professional judgment would certainly be affected by that. Under Rule 1.7…"

"Don't quote the Rules to me," Gunther said, holding up a hand. "What you did was completely unauthorized and demonstrated a complete lack of good judgment. And perhaps, what you did broke a few professional rules as well. And to add insult to injury, I guess, your unofficial investigation with Mr. Foley demonstrated nothing, only that the District Attorney met an old friend, me, in a bar for a celebratory drink."

Gunther drew in a breath.

"And furthermore," he said, "all your concerns of a Rule 1.7 conflict are going to be resolved sometime this morning if they haven't been already."

"What? Why?"

Gunther swiveled around to a table at the left side of his desk on which his official LDO laptop had been set. He powered it up, typed in his username and password and a moment later, the screen popped to life with three rows of icons against the factory default background depicting a rolling spectrum of icy colors. He clicked on the internet browser icon and after a moment, the official Supreme Court homepage filled the screen. There was a link to the local newspaper digital page. He clicked on that and a moment later, that page filled the screen. "Here it is," Gunther said to himself.

Gunther found the print icon and clicked on it. A few moments later, his printer on a smaller print table to the left of the computer table came to life and started churning out a printed document. Gunther bent down and retrieved two pages, stapled them, swiveled around and placed them at the front of his desk.

"Take a look at this," Gunther told Dean.

Dean reached for the pages and saw that at the top of the page, under the heading, "Breaking News," was the title to a story, "DA Re-Opens Laurence Investigation." Dean read the story's sub-heading: "Has Authorized a Grand Jury Presentation Against his First Assistant DA."

"Looks like the DA came to his senses," Gunther said.

He flashed a mirthless smile. "Nothing for us to open now, wouldn't you agree Dean?"

Dean nodded.

"I guess not," he said.

Now he knew what Gunther and the DA had been meeting about at The Pub last night.

Chapter Fourteen
Foley's Bad News and Worse News

Half an hour later, Stu Foley came knocking at Dean's door. Upon entering, Foley goose-stepped several paces toward Dean's desk, stopped abruptly before it, stood sharply at attention, banged his left fist against the right side of his chest and then stuck his left arm out above his head in a Nazi salute.

"I have just come from the office of our new Fuhrer, Herr Gunther," he said in an obviously fake German accent. Foley sighed and relaxing suddenly, seemed to melt into the back of the chair facing Dean's desk.

"What an asshole," Foley said.

"I had the exact same reaction," Dean said. "So how'd it go? Though I think I know."

"Well, I have bad news and worse news," Foley said. "Or is it worse news and worst news. Which would you like to hear first, Comrade Alessi?"

"The worst news, always," Dean said.

"I'm retiring," Foley said. "End of July."

"Retiring?" Dean scowled. He jerked back and his

expression turned from a frown to one of shock. "Just last month ago, you promised to give me two more years. Until you hit sixty-six. What happened?"

"That was before Herr Gunther took charge of Stalag LDO," Foley said. "I couldn't put up with his bullshit for two years. That Nazi sneer of his, his bully gotcha approach."

"But geez, Stuey," Dean said.

This turn events both surprised and concerned Dean. Foley was his main, and most times only, ally in the office, not to mention that he had become a good friend, like the older brother he never had. A best friend, in fact. And certainly, especially when it came to Laura, a shoulder to cry on.

He sighed and asked, "Really, Stu?"

"Really," Foley said. "I hate to do this to you, boss. But that guy is nothing but heartburn. And at my age, I certainly don't need a case of that. I already have Ginny."

"Well, unfortunately, I have another fifteen years of heartburn," Dean said. "At least another fifteen, if I last that long. And now you chicken out and I have to go it alone?"

"Believe me," Foley said, "I am not chickening out. If I stay in this job, the day would come that I would kill that man." Foley frowned. "He likes to repeat himself, doesn't he? Herr Gunther."

"That he does," Dean said. "He brought up the fact that you were busted following the DA, I take it. And then meeting me at The Pub."

"That he did," Foley said, "several times. So you already know my bad news. That last night was for naught, one big fucking disaster."

Dean lifted the local news article printed from the internet and flipped it.

"And then there's this little surprise," Dean said. "Looks like District Attorney Marcum finally came to his senses. That takes the heat off him, I guess, as far as we're concerned. His out. Even if the grand jury no bills the case…"

"Which is a possibility after the shit-ass investigation the DA and the Manchester PD did," Foley added. "I'd sure like to get to the bottom of that. I had always thought that Eric Baldwin, their chief, was a decent guy."

Foley sighed, and looking distressed, went on, "The whole thing stinks to high heaven. One day the DA's shit-canning the case and protecting his lover …"

"We don't know that yet," Dean said. "That Mrs. Hines-Laurence was, is his lover."

"Well, to protect his first assistant then, if nothing else," Foley said. "And the next day, after a late night meeting with Herr Gunther, he miraculously reverses himself and decides to indict her."

Dean thought a minute.

"Stuey," he said, "so you're saying you think Herr Gunther was involved in that decision? That that's what they talked about last night?"

"That would be a fair surmise," Foley said. "It's classic Sun Tzu." Foley thought a moment, "Attack him where he is unprepared, appear where you are not expected." Then, he smiled, proud of himself or something that he could actually remember it.

"Don't give me your Sun Tzu bullshit," Dean said. Foley was an avid reader of that famous fifth century B.C.

Chinese general's *The Art of War.* Claimed he lived by it.

"Gunther said they were celebrating," Dean said.

"Yes, celebrating the demise of the honor of the legal profession in these parts," Foley said. "At least what little there is left of it."

"You have turned into a bitter old man, my friend," Dean said. After a moment, he remembered Foley's "worse" news.

"Did you tell him?" Dean asked. "That you're retiring?"

"Yeah, I barked it out during his third tirade regarding my insubordination and lack of judgment only surpassed by yours," Foley said. "Just stood up, told him I was outta here. End of the month. Almost said, fuck you, 'Sieg Heil,' with the Nazi salute on my way out of his office."

"But, Stuey..."

"Don't but Stuey, me," Foley said. "What's done is done. He did nothing to stop me, anyway. Didn't try and talk me out of it. Just sat there with his smug, authoritarian bullshit expression that I wanted to knock off his face." Foley sighed and looked at Dean. "I did him a favor, I guess."

"Yeah," Dean said. "One big favor. With you gone, he gets to decide the next Chief Investigator. Dawn Smith, I would think. And you know what an incompetent, kiss-ass douchebag she is."

Foley crossed his arms and his expression turned grave as he looked away and thought over his options. Finally, he shook his head as he looked back at Dean.

"No, I'm not going back in there to un-retire," he said. "I'm done, out of here."

"But Jesus, Stuey, that's only what, five, six weeks

away," Dean said. "You really sure about this?"

"Yeah, I'm sure," Foley said. "Like I said, it's either that or I end up facing a murder charge." After a moment, he sighed. "Look, Dean, I know this seems like a bad deal for you, a coward's way out, me walking out on you. But when you reach my age, you've seen just about all the bullshit in life there is to see. And you are just figuring out around then, as you hit the big six five, with death staring you in the face, that if you don't have to put up with any more bullshit, why do it?"

After a time, Dean sighed, nodded.

"No, I understand, Stuey," he said. "You gotta preserve your health and sanity, especially when you have the opportunity to do so."

Foley sighed and looked Dean straight in the eyes.

"One thing, though," he said. "I want to stay on the case."

"What case?"

"The unofficial DA case," he said and smiled. "It's still open isn't it?"

"And do what?" Dean asked. "You trying to get me fired?"

"I promise not to be a dumbass and get made again by Stan Mazurka," he said. "An even bigger dumbass than me."

"Who's that?"

"That's the DA's bodyguard," Foley said. "The guy who followed me following the DA last night, then watched me meeting you."

"How do you know that?" Dean asked.

"Herr Gunther told me," Foley asked.

Dean nodded, shrugged.

"You know him?"

"Yeah, we crossed paths before," Foley said. "Years and years ago. During my brief stint as a Buffalo cop."

"That's what he was?"

"Well, I suppose you could call him that," Foley said. "Thug and bully is more like it. Like one of those hoodlums in *Clockwork Orange* who ends up on the police force solely for the pleasure of harassing people and beating them up, legally. And then finally, one day they caught onto him. Kicked him out, though they called it retirement.

"What I heard was that it had something to do with groping his partner, some rookie gal cop that had the misfortune of having to train with the dumbass fresh out of the police academy. Her first day on the job, he came onto her. By the end of the month, he cornered her in some dark parking space in a city park. Word is, he almost raped her. Had her pants down to her ankles when she managed to smash the back of his head with her billy club. A month later, they were holding a retirement party for him. And after that, he opened a security business. And to prove again that what goes around does not come around, he's made a fortune at it. He's cornered the market pretty much and gets some fairly important customers."

"Including our illustrious DA," Dean said.

"Yeah, apparently, including him," Foley said. "But like I said, bottom line, he's a drunken, dumbass bully. And dumbass drunken bullies go down eventually."

"I thought what goes around never comes around," Dean said and smiled.

Foley shrugged.

"Yeah, I guess you're right," he said after a time. "I forgot that. He'll probably die a rich old bastard while being sucked off on the beach by some nineteen-year-old, bikini-clad, Swedish blonde. Life sucks, you know that boss?"

Foley stood and grabbed the internet article from Dean's desk and began reading through it. After a time, he looked up.

"So he's not going to present the case himself?"

Dean shook his head.

"No way," he said. "He's assigned that pleasant task to some assistant…"

"Yea, Larry Donnelly," Foley said.

"You know him?" Dean asked.

Foley thought a moment, then said, "Yeah, that's gotta be him."

"What?" Dean asked as Foley continued to chew it over in his mind. Finally, Foley nodded.

"I think his father was the one who ran a bunch of dry-cleaning businesses in the city," Foley said. "Donated a shitload of cash, from what I heard, to the Democratic Party over the years. And to the DA's last campaign especially. See, little Larry Donnelly was attending law school at the time, and what better way to move up the political ladder to a judgeship the old dry cleaner envisioned for his namesake than by starting off your legal career as an Assistant DA. Right?"

"Sure. A lot of our illustrious judges started out that way," Dean said.

Foley lifted up the article and shook it again.

"Well, the fix is definitely in then," he said.

"You think?" Dean asked.

"I know," Foley said. "Just don't know how they're gonna fix it."

"Probably have the grand jury no bill it," Dean said.

"No, that's too easy," Foley said, "and doesn't really take the heat off the DA. A no bill would open him up to criticism that his investigation was shoddy. And why was it shoddy? Because he was investigating his own lover."

"Stuey," Dean said. "I keep telling you, we don't have any proof of that."

Foley shrugged and said, "Well, all I know, the fix is in."

"Perhaps, someone with a cynical heart might think that," Dean said. "So what's the next step in the investigative agenda for the unofficial file opened against the DA? A file, mind you, after this conversation, I really don't ever want to hear about again?"

"Well, I follow him again," Foley said. "This very evening. Except, as I said, I don't allow myself to get bagged by Mazurka. And hopefully, the DA feels safe enough that he goes out and meets his lover, the lovely, now on paid administrative leave, first assistant DA."

Dean's phone buzzed and he picked it up. It was Kathy Barnes, telling him that Peter Antonio had arrived. Dean was going to show Antonio bank records demonstrating that he had stolen over fifty thousand dollars from a real estate client.

Dean gathered the file and Foley stood, knowing he had to run.

As he followed Foley out the door, he said, "Oh, and guess who went into Herr Gunther's office after I left?"

Dean looked back at Foley and shrugged.

"Your best buddy," Foley said. "Liza Hartman."

Chapter Fifteen
Kat Franklin

Dean's meeting with Peter Antonio didn't last long, a mere fifteen minutes. Once the lawyer saw the damning trust account records, and finally accepted in his own mind that his legal career was over, he leaned forward and, much like Frank Martin had done the morning before, covered his face with his hands and started crying. Dean gave him a blank resignation form and advised him to consider submitting it to the court, like Martin had, after reviewing it with an attorney, if he wanted. Moments later, on his way out of the conference room, Antonio walked over to Dean, embraced him and held on for a woeful thirty-second sob.

Not a minute after returning to his office, there was a knock at Dean's door. He called out for whoever to enter; Kat Franklin walked in. His spirit soared momentarily at the sight of her, but seeing her sour look, he frowned.

"Can we talk?" she asked from the doorway.

"Sure," he said and waved her to come sit in the chair before his desk.

"What's up?" Dean asked when she had sat and crossed her legs. She looked awfully good that morning, too good. "You ready for court this afternoon?"

Kat's case involving Leslie McMahon was scheduled for final argument before a five-justice panel of the Supreme Court, after which they'd render a decision, either approving the LDO's two-year license suspension recommendation or sending it back to the LDO for a hearing before a judicial hearing officer.

"The CJ's on the panel, you know," Dean added.

"Yes, Dean," Kat said. "I know, I know. You told me like a hundred times already."

"Well, you know how what a stickler he can be," Dean said, "especially when he takes a special interest in a case like this."

"Stickler? Pain in the rear end is more like it," Kat said. "That man has no ethics. All these *ex parte* communications with us. If the respondents and their attorneys only knew."

Dean shrugged. There was nothing further to say about that. They had had this conversation before. There was no way to justify the CJ's habit of calling them about formal disciplinary charges pending before the Court, even on cases over which he was presiding and would therefore have a primary role in deciding. Like the Leslie McMahon case. Dean knew that in a large sense, the CJ felt he was above the law, better than it, which was the only explanation for his antics. He certainly was not a stupid man and fully understood the concept underlying the prohibition against an *ex parte* communication between a lawyer and judge without the opposing party's lawyer being informed of it.

"How could you come in late on his first morning?" Kat asked.

Dean shrugged.

"Something wrong with Laura?"

"No," he said after a sigh. "I was out late last night. With Stuey. Drank a tad too much. Forgot to set the damn alarm."

That got him thinking about his aching head and tired mind.

"So how'd your meeting go with Gunther?"

Dean told her about how disagreeable it had been, for him and then Foley, and the reason why.

"Stu was following the DA?" she asked and frowned not one hundred per cent getting it.

"Yeah, except he was followed by the DA's bodyguard," he said.

Kat sat there for a while trying to process what Dean was saying.

"And the DA met up with Gunther last night?" Kat asked.

"Yeah," Dean said. "At the Pub. They're old law school friends or something."

"Figures," Kat said.

"I thought he was going to fire me on the spot," said Dean. "You're right, this is not starting out in a good way between us. And it has little to do with me being late this morning. It's way beyond that."

"He's an arrogant, cold-hearted prick," Kat said, and Dean looked up at her. "I could tell that the moment he strode into the conference room."

Kat's face hardened into an intense scowl, which, he had

always thought, made her look all the more desirable. At least, to him. She had a pretty smile that showed off her high, sharp cheekbones, and Dean wished she would stop wearing her hair up in that bun that made her look so severe, stark. He wished instead she'd wear her hair down, loose, let it flow. She looked so much better then, sexy.

"You should have seen how cocky he was during the meeting," Kat said. "He actually boasted about his resume, how he was concerned about taking charge in short order, shape things up around here. That he was a quick study, as if what we do around here is easy as pie."

Dean shrugged.

"Prick or not," Dean said. "He's the boss."

"Yeah, I know. And Liza Hartman seems to like him," Kat said. "On my way over here, I saw her leaving his office. She gave me that snide look as she walked past me. I wanted to bop her one."

"Just what I need," Dean said. "Them becoming close pals."

A German prick and a lady prick with daddy issues, Dean thought. After a time, he shook himself.

"But this is wrong, too," he said. "We shouldn't be doing this. We should give the guy a chance."

"You really believe that?"

"No," he said and laughed. Then after a moment, he sighed and looked down.

"What's wrong," she asked.

"Foley just told me he's retiring," Dean said, looking up, "end of July. July thirty-first will be his last day. Said he can't put up with the place now that Gunther's in charge."

"Crap," Kat said. "Not that I can blame him."

They sat and mulled Foley's departure for a time.

Finally, Kat said, "So what about the DA case? We doing anything with that?"

"No," he said. "First of all, Gunther is his friend. And second of all, take a look at this."

Dean handed Kat the internet article.

"Practically speaking, there's no case, now," he said.

"This doesn't change a thing," Kat said. "His office shouldn't be handling a case against its second in command. That's the conflict."

"She's the former second-in-command," Dean said. "She's been put on paid leave."

"Doesn't matter," Kat said.

As usual, Kat was right, factually and legally. But the DA's reopening of his office's criminal investigation into Kent Laurence's shooting by his wife, Sarah Hines-Laurence, the first assistant district attorney, who was now on paid administrative leave, had practically resolved the problem. Practically, it was done as a disciplinary case. Period.

As Dean told her just that, Kat scowled her pretty (to him, anyway) scowl and said, "No, that's not what I'm talking about. What I'm talking about is what's really going on here. Knowing Sarah Hines-Laurence, I know that this is much more than that kind of simple, basic ethical conflict. What this is, is murder."

Dean frowned, then let out a small laugh.

"What? Murder? I think you've been watching too much CSI."

"I don't watch lawyer shows," she said. "I get enough

bullshit dealing with them in real life."

"You know Sarah Hines-Laurence?" Dean asked.

"I went to law school with her," Kat said. "She's a heartless bitch. Even more heartless than Liza. We participated in a couple study groups together. She slept with a couple guys in those groups just to get their notes. And there were rumors of her sleeping around with professors, men and women. That and some other things she did in law school made me realize she has absolutely no morals. Sarah is the kind of person who's only satisfied by getting everything she wants. I don't even think it's the getting part that drives her. It's the thrill of the hunt."

"Nice armchair psychological analysis," Dean said. "But what's your point, Doctor Franklin?"

"My point is," Kat said, "Sarah Hines-Laurence is quite capable of murder. Especially if it means inheriting lots of money and obtaining control, power. And she's also quite capable of using her body, and her charm, to get someone to help her pull it off. In this case, who better than the DA."

"Well, that's a nice theory," Dean said. "But right now, there's absolutely no proof of it."

"So when do we get it?"

"Huh? When do we get what?"

"The proof against the DA and Sarah Hines-Laurence."

"Never, if I want to keep my job," Dean said. "I already have to get past the problem of Stuey going rogue on me."

"So we're not doing anything?" Kat asked. "Not even something unofficial?"

"No," Dean said. He sighed. "Not with my approval, I mean."

"So we are doing something," she said. After a moment, she cocked her head slightly to one side and smiled.

Perhaps because of the German connection to all of this, Dean thought of the old 60s TV show, "Hogan Heroes," and said, "I know nothing."

"So can I be part of the unofficial DA investigation?" Kat asked.

"I told you," he said, "I know nothing." Dean sighed. "But do whatever you want. Foley's in charge of it, ask him. But, as I said, I disavow any knowledge."

"What, are you into sixties shows or something?" Kat asked. "That's from the old 'Mission Impossible,' 'Good morning, Mr. Phelps.'"

"I loved that show," Dean said.

"So, I should talk to Foley," Kat persisted.

"Yes," Dean said. "Talk to him to your heart's content. I'm not sure how he can use you, though."

She shrugged and gave him a meek look.

"See, I didn't even have to use your lapse of judgment during the Christmas Party as leverage," Kat said. When Dean smirked, then looked away, she added, "I'm sorry, Dean. I – I shouldn't have brought that up. Made light of it."

Dean looked sharply at her.

"We never properly talked about that night, have we?" he said.

"Look," she said. "There's nothing to talk about. You're having problems with Laura. I know that. Everyone knows that. So you needed a shoulder to cry on."

"Well, it ended up being more than that," he said. "And I'm sorry."

"It was a kiss, Dean, that's all," Kat said. "A ten-second kiss. You were drunk, and so was I. And you've already apologized. Case closed."

Dean sighed and looked away, thinking how wonderful that shoulder crying incident had been. And the ten-second kiss that was part of it, though he remembered it being longer. After a time, he looked back at her.

"Alright," he said.

"Alright, what?"

"I don't know," he said. "Just alright. We'll go up to Court at one."

"Yes, one," she said. Kat nodded, smiled curiously at him, and he thought again how cute she'd look with her hair worn down. But then his thoughts turned to Laura and he felt bad, ashamed for thinking about Kat Franklin like that again, and about that stolen kiss during last year's Christmas Party.

Finally, Kat got up and, after a long look in which he thought she was going to say something else but decided against it, she left the office. A moment later, he picked up the phone and called Foley.

"What's up, boss," he said.

"Just thought I'd tell you," Dean said. "We unofficially assigned Kat Franklin to the unofficial DA investigation." Foley let out a small laugh. "What's so funny?' Dean asked.

"You," Foley said. "Like all men, like the DA. Always thinking with your balls instead of your brains."

Chapter Sixteen
The State Supreme Court

In 1976, the New York legislature passed a law authorizing the state's highest court, the Supreme Court, to both grant licenses to lawyers and, for proper cause, to take such licenses away. Prior to the law's enactment, both the admission and discipline of lawyers was handled by the state-wide Bar Association. However, because of the public perception that the bar association was more likely than not to sweep misconduct committed by their brethren members under the proverbial rug, the state legislature, most of whom were also lawyers, decided to create the appearance of impartiality in the disciplining of lawyers via the independent, judicial oversight of the Supreme Court. In either case, however, the fact remained that lawyers – whether they be judges or bar association members – were still policing other lawyers, something that no other profession had the luxury of claiming. And, as if to further protect this luxury, the state legislature added a provision at the end of the new statute making all investigations into complaints filed against attorneys confidential and secret until a charge of professional misconduct, based upon probable cause, was filed with the Supreme Court. Thus, during the investigation of a complaint, except for the complaining party, usually the client, the public could know nothing.

In furtherance of the new law, the Supreme Court promulgated rules guiding the ethical conduct of lawyers practicing law in the state. The Court also drafted fairly simple regulations setting forth procedures for the investigation of complaints of professional and ethical misconduct filed against lawyers, and for disciplining them once such misconduct was either admitted or demonstrated by clear and convincing evidence.

Under these procedural regulations, the "State Supreme Court Lawyer Discipline Office," shortened to LDO, was established. It was to become an auxiliary agency of the Supreme Court under its ultimate supervision and control, which allowed for the employment of a staff of attorneys, that is, disciplinary counsel, or dis-cons, as they came to be called, including a Director, as well as professional investigators, to conduct the ethics investigations. A main office and several auxiliary offices were set up around the state and the work came pouring in.

In Dean's sixteen plus years as Deputy Director of the LDO, over forty thousand complaints of professional misconduct had been filed against attorneys practicing in the state. Most of these complaints were from disgruntled clients, including, not surprisingly, a large number from prison inmates claiming ineffective assistance of their defense counsel. Complaints that lacked any real merit were usually dismissed after a cursory review, but some warranted a closer look or, at least, a response from the lawyer. A minute number of those were serious enough, involving theft of client funds, egregious conflicts of interest, fraud, neglect or other malfeasance, resulting in the filing of formal disciplinary charges with the Supreme Court that ultimately led to the court's issuance of a public order disbarring, suspending or censuring the lawyer found guilty of the charges. Thus, the issuance of disciplinary orders was a rare occurrence.

While the great majority of complaints against lawyers were filed by their clients, sometimes judges and other lawyers would do so, though that, in Dean's experience, rarely happened as the rules for such whistle-blowing were colored in many shades of gray. It had also been Dean's experience that most lawyers and judges (who are basically politically motivated lawyers) loathed to file misconduct complaints against their brethren, and did not look favorably upon lawyers and judges who did. In short, as in any profession or endeavor, snitches were despised even among lawyers.

In addition to commencing disciplinary investigations based upon complaints received from clients, adverse parties, other lawyers and judges, the LDO also sometimes opened complaints *sua sponte*, meaning, "on its own," in Latin parlance, based upon newspaper articles, court judgments or other public documents, such as conviction records, that came to its attention. However, investigations based upon the receipt of telephone calls or anonymous complaints, like the one concerning the DA likely received by some disgruntled former employee of that office, were almost never commenced.

The LDO's investigation into attorneys, John McMahon, and his daughter, Leslie, had come about somewhat differently. It was not opened based upon the receipt of a complaint from a client or clients, another lawyer or a judge, but based upon letters and calls received from over 150 debtors from across the USA. The debtors claimed that the law firm which the McMahon's purportedly ran, McMahon & McMahon, had debt collectors in their employ who had harassed them, and sometimes their children, by threatening criminal prosecution, jail, foreclosure, bankruptcy or public embarrassment, among other nasty and mean things, including threatening to inform their neighbors that they were deadbeats, if they did not immediately pay the debts that the firm had purchased to collect. This improper means of collecting debts, of course, if substantiated, constituted serious violations of the federal Fair Debt Collection Practices Act as well as state consumer protection laws.

Some of these debts, known as zombie debts in the industry, were decades old and long ago closed by the original creditor or could not be found to exist at all. But so vehement and harassing were the debt collectors working for the McMahons' law firm, that some of these unsubstantiated and even bogus debts were paid.

Of course, in the year and a half or so while the McMahon's debt collection law business operated and thrived, the McMahons made a lot of money. However, it soon became apparent, first to Dean, and then to Kat Franklin, to whom the investigation was eventually assigned, that neither of the McMahons had anything even remotely to do with the debt collection business using their law firm name. The rarely showed up at the offices upon which their firm sign had been hung, and most of the debt collectors had not been hired by them or even knew who they were. Kat soon discovered that the collection offices were actually run by a couple of ex-con hucksters who had convinced the McMahons to help them make a pile of money from unwitting debtors by using a law firm name and illegal collection methods to scare people into paying debts that were essentially uncollectible. It was well known in the debt collection industry that debtors were intimated when collectors called using a lawyer's firm name as their employer. A debt collector purportedly working for a lawyer always did better in collecting a debt.

After Kat presented the proof to the McMahons, even their attorney, the ever difficult and irascible, Ted Leary, saw the writing on the wall. A week later, Leary called her with an offer: the elder McMahon, who had just turned seventy-two and was obviously both mentally, physically and morally at the nadir of his career, agreed to resign his law license provided that his daughter, Leslie, be given a two-year suspension. In light of the fact that proving the case at a hearing would be expensive, tedious, and in some respects, difficult because all the debtor victims resided out of state, Dean approved the deal.

All that was required now was for the Court to consent to the LDO's recommendation that Leslie McMahon be suspended from practicing law for two years, the agreement that had been reached with her and Ted Leary. What really troubled Dean about obtaining that consent was the fact that

Chief Judge Krane was heading the panel of five judges deciding the case and had already taken a special and untoward interest in it, expressing to Dean on several occasions his deep revulsion for what the McMahons had done.

"That scumbag," had become the CJ's term of choice for John McMahon. "And his scumbag daughter."

At ten minutes before one, Dean, Kat Franklin, and Gunther assembled in the LDO's reception area to take the elevator down to the lobby and then walk six blocks to the two-year-old, lavish and ornate Richard T. Moran Supreme Court Building. It was the longstanding, unofficial duty of the LDO Director to attend all disciplinary proceedings pending before a five-associate justice panel of the Supreme Court as the highest representative of the office. During the recent hiatus, as Acting Director, Dean had satisfied the requirement.

During the elevator ride up to the Supreme Court's courtrooms that afternoon, Gunther turned to Dean and said, "You know, the CJ expressed some concern to me yesterday about the McMahon case."

Kat glanced at Dean and sighed disagreeably. She had her arms wrapped around two thick files up to her chest while Dean carried a third thick folder under his right arm. Gunther's arms were empty.

"What's his problem with it?" Dean asked.

"Should he even be expressing anything?" asked Kat and let out a derisive laugh. "He's on the panel hearing the case."

Gunther scowled at her as the elevator slowed to a stop and the doors opened.

"He's the CJ," Gunther said to her.

"That doesn't …" Kat started to argue but stopped as Dean glared across at her.

"What's he concerned about?" Dean asked as they walked into the corridor winding to one of four ornate appellate courtrooms where lawyers presented arguments to the Court on behalf of their clients. In each of the courtrooms, state-of-the-art microphone and video systems had been set up to record these oral arguments.

Of course, Dean already knew what the CJ's problem was. He wanted both the father and daughter to lose their respective licenses. For some reason, the case really bugged him. In actuality, John McMahon was a half-way decent guy who hadn't earned very much money over a long career, taking nickel-and-dime criminal cases from clients who often stiffed him, or assigned criminal cases where the pay was low. His wife was dying of cancer or had lupus or something, and his daughter was thin and stringy and seemed to have inherited every ounce of her father's mediocrity. Somewhere along the way, years ago, McMahon had represented one of the hucksters in some minor criminal case and, seeing his profits from his already meager legal fees quickly drying up, and wanting to leave at least a little nest egg for himself, his sickly wife and spinster daughter, he jumped at the chance of earning some easy money for a change, the windfall he had never gotten from the benefit of having a law license.

"What's his concern? The disposition," Gunther said as he walked briskly just ahead of Dean and Kat using a classic power stride. Then, he stopped abruptly, turned and glared at them. "He says it's too light."

"Old man McMahon resigned his license," Dean said, "as is his right, and the daughter, admitted only about a year ago, and who was more or less duped or led astray, whatever, into this by her father, is getting two years. Plus, we save an enormous amount of time and expense of a long-drawn out hearing on all the charges we filed and saved a ton avoiding having to fly witnesses in from all over the country to prove our case." He sighed. "I told all this to the CJ."

"Well, as the CJ expressed it to me," Gunther said, "perhaps this was one case where the benefits of an aggressive and expensive prosecution outweighed saving a few hundred dollars and little bit of time."

Dean wondered about why the benefits of an aggressive prosecution did not apply as well to the DA's handling of the Kent Laurence shooting by his first assistant district attorney, but he held his tongue. That comment would surely earn him nothing but scorn and another of Gunther's long-winded, haughty lectures on insubordination and the need to exercise good judgment. And anyway, by now they had arrived in a small vestibule area outside Appeals Courtroom #4, where all disciplinary arguments were presented.

The CJ's clerk, Margo Anson-Clark, whose duties included monitoring the attorney disciplinary calendar, met them. She welcomed Gunther with a broad grin and brief handshake, then turned to Dean with an unfriendly nod, and totally ignored Kat Franklin. She told them that Leslie McMahon and her counsel, Ted Leary, were waiting in the lawyers' consultation room down a side hall.

"They'll be calling the case in a couple minutes," Margo said. "There's been some heated discussion on it." Margo frowned disagreeably at Dean, then said to Gunther, "Let me go back in and see if they're ready."

As Margo entered the courtroom, Dean glanced at Kat, who frowned uneasily. Dean stepped over and leaned into her.

"Just do your best, Kat," he whispered. "This is a good and fair disposition. Stand behind it."

Margo popped her head back out of the courtroom and gestured for them to enter. That also meant that she had buzzed for Leary and his client, Leslie McMahon, to come to the courtroom. As John McMahon had submitted a resignation affirmation, there was no need for him to appear before the Court.

Dean and Kat followed Gunther into the Appeals Courtroom #4, impressive and spacious with dramatically high ceilings and bright oak wood walls. At the front of the courtroom was a long, raised mahogany counter, or bench, with two large, black leather swivel chairs on each side of a center pulpit several feet above the main counter. Chief Justice Krane sat behind the center pulpit with an austere expression, while the black leather swivel chairs on each side of the counter below him were occupied, respectively, by Supreme Court associates justices, Manuel Sanchez, Sarah Smith to his left, and Albert Clermont and Devlin Kingman to his right. Each justice wore the traditional black judges' robe and equally grim expressions.

A few feet before the judges' bench were long, counsel tables, also mahogany, separated by a high, stout podium. The

LDO's dis-cons traditionally sat at the table to the left of the podium while the responding attorneys, or respondents and their counsel, sat at the table to its right. Behind the counsel tables was a small spectator gallery consisting of about a dozen rows of blue cloth chairs attached to a gray carpet. While Gunther stood in the first row in the gallery behind the LDO table, Dean and Kat set down their thick files on it and stood stone-faced before the somber-faced justices. Moments later, Leslie McMahon and Ted Leary finally entered the courtroom, and after a long, slow amble down the center aisle, took their places at the respondents' table.

"Counsel," said the CJ, "are we ready to proceed?"

"Yes, your Honor," Kat said, "the Lawyer Discipline Office is ready to proceed."

Leary then nodded and said, "Respondent is ready as well, your Honor."

"You may proceed, Miss Franklin," the CJ said.

Kat took a deep breath then started with a brief review of the procedural facts, informing the justices that Leslie McMahon had admitted five of the ten charges in the Petition of Professional Misconduct filed against her four months ago, and is accepting a two-year suspension. Kat started to tell the justices that her father and Co-Respondent had already filed his resignation when the CJ interrupted her.

"Pretty light," he said, "don't you think, Miss Franklin? Sounds like the LDO is falling on its sword on this one."

Kat frowned, taken aback and then angered by the falling on its sword comment. She curtly explained the LDO's reasoning for the two-year disposition, avoiding the expense and time of a trial, especially when it might end up with the same result, and watched in horror in the middle of her spiel as the CJ waved a hand dismissively at her.

"Seems like a cave to me on this one, Miss Franklin," he said.

"Your Honor, if I may be heard," Ted Leary said. "From my standpoint, I believe the two-year limit on punishment is overly harsh for my client. We are seeking a lesser punishment, in the interest of justice, especially in light of Mr. McMahon's admission that he greatly influenced my client, who is his daughter, as the Court is aware, to become involved in this situation. She was guided, or I should say misguided to some degree by the love for her father. She had always looked to him for guidance, for mentoring…"

"Look, Ted," the CJ said, "all that information has been eloquently set forth in your papers in mitigation and we will of course take them into consideration. And I'll give you some time to make an oral presentation, if you desire," the CJ said. "But right now, I am inquiring from the LDO's counsel regarding the sufficiency of the disposition that is being proposed in light of the severity of the charges that have been admitted in your client's stipulated admission to this Petition. In short, Mr. Leary, this is between the Court and the LDO counsel."

"Of course, your Honor," Leary said, seeing where this was going, and knowing full well how bull-headed the CJ could be.

Now Dean stood, trying to restrain his anger, hoping not to say anything belligerent.

"Your Honor," he said. "I approved this disposition based upon the facts of this case, the evidence, and Miss

McMahon's disciplinary history. We believe it is a fair disposition that will serve to advance the goals of attorney discipline – protection of the public from dysfunctional lawyers, general deterrence, and preservation of the integrity of the profession."

"And what does your new boss say?' the CJ asked, looking past Dean to Gunther, who stood. "Mister Gunther?"

"Well, your Honor," Gunther said. "As you know, this is my first day in the position as LDO Director and I naturally deferred to Mister Alessi in regard to this disposition. But perhaps, in light of the Court's concern, we should request an adjournment."

"I object to that, your Honor," Leary said. "This case has been hanging over my client for some time. We feel …"

"Request granted," the CJ said to Gunther. He looked at Margo, who occupied a small table inconspicuously set to the far left of the justices' bench. "Adjourn this for the August disciplinary term. August ninth, I believe it is."

"Yes, your Honor," Margo said. "August ninth."

"Will that give you enough time, Mister Gunther, to sort this out?" the CJ asked.

"Of course, your Honor," Gunther said.

The CJ looked to Leary.

"Is that day is convenient for you, Mr. Leary?"

Dean and Kat were seething on the way out of the courtroom. Gunther strode forward ahead of them, seeming imminently pleased with himself.

Outside in the hallway, still walking behind Gunther to the elevator, Kat leaned into Dean and said, "I want off this case."

"That's not up to me anymore," Dean said and nodded forward. "It's up to that asshole."

Chapter Seventeen
Good News and Better News

Just after nine, the next morning, Foley knocked on Dean's office door. Gunther had come in by eight-thirty but left the LDO offices shortly before nine just as Dean was walking in.

"Nice of you to be on time this morning, Mister Alessi," Gunther said as they passed each other in the waiting room. For some reason, he added, "I have a nine-thirty meeting with the CJ."

Foley was smiling as he approached Dean's desk.

"What you grinning about, you old fool?" Dean asked.

"I got good news," he said, "and better news."

"Well, first the good news," Dean said.

"Well, both pieces of news involve breaks in the DA investigation," he said dropping onto the chair facing Dean's desk. "The unofficial DA investigation, I should say."

"So, what's the good news?"

"Well, I told you I was going to follow the widow Hines-Laurence last night," Foley said. "And so, I did."

"No, you didn't tell me," Dean said. "Nobody saw you

this time, right?"

"Don't worry," Foley said, "I was extra careful. Anyway, you'll be interested to know that the widow went out about nine thirty and met – guess who?"

"You've got to be kidding me? Are they that stupid? So that's the good news. What's the better news?"

"No, wait," Foley said. "Let me tell you more about the good news. Want to know where they met?" He waited a moment for Dean to shrug. "At Randolph Park. Some dark nook, off the road back among some trees. A veritable lovers' lane."

"What did you do?" Dean asked. "You didn't go in there?"

"Sure I did," Foley said.

'Jesus, Stuey." Dean was shaking his head.

"By the time I snuck back there," Foley said, "the windows of his BMW were all steamed up."

"You are incredible," Dean said. "Well, did you get any pictures? Video?"

"A couple," he said. "But like I said, his windows were steamed."

"So they were making out? Screwing?"

"I guess," Foley said. "They didn't even stay out there that long. Only a few minutes or so after I got back there. No more than ten, if that many. Then she got out of his car – and yes, I videoed her walking away." He thought back to that moment and sighed. "And you know, she looks better in person, a real looker, with quite the bod, especially in those skin tight jeans or whatever she was wearing. She went back to her car, they drove out of the bushes, and that was it."

"That was a lot," said Dean. "The DA meeting with the target of a criminal investigation whose case his office is putting before a grand jury." Dean smiled. "And, yes, you are a dirty old man."

"It's certainly unusual," Foley said. "And I plead guilty to both of your allegation, and am proud of it."

"Should we tell Gunther?" Dean asked.

Foley frowned, and after a moment shook his head.

"I don't think that's a good option," he said. "First of all, he'd go ballistic for me, us, because he'd figure you were part of it, disregarding his order. Second, he's friends with the DA, remember? And, third, what does it really mean, them going out there? I didn't see any romance – although steamed up windows should at least make one speculate. All I got is them meeting out in the dark in some hidden nook.

"She's a target of a criminal investigation sure, but she's not just any target. They're friends, right? She's his first assistant DA, one of his closest advisers in the office. They could say they were meeting, as friends, colleagues, about some pending cases. I don't know. That it was completely innocent." He shrugged. "It certainly looks inappropriate, but what I did in following her and finding them out there may be deemed even more so, especially after last night's fiasco.

"No, boss, telling Gunther is not an option," he said, shaking his head. "Not at this point anyway."

Dean thought a moment. Finally, he looked at Foley.

"Yeah, you're right, Stuey," he said. "We need to keep this to ourselves." He sighed and wondered again whether Foley was right. It never came around. "So what's your better news?"

"I took a call yesterday afternoon," Foley said. "From the source of that anonymous letter about the DA."

"Really," Dean said.

"Yeah, really," Foley said. "He wants to tell us the rest of the story, as Paul Harvey used to say – or is that before your time?"

"No, I remember him. The guy with the deep voice on the radio," Dean said and Foley nodded. "So how did the call come about? He call asking for you?"

"Late yesterday afternoon," Foley said, "I was going over the Danny Willis case with Pete." He frowned. "Where the hell were you yesterday afternoon anyway? You weren't around when I came looking for you after court."

"I'll get to that," Dean said. "Tell me about the call first."

"Well, I was sitting there with Pete when the call came in," Foley said. "He took it. He's on intake, I guess."

"Yes, right," Dean said. "Intake."

"Anyway, I figured out what the guy was talking about," Foley said, "when the kid mentioned the DA, telling the guy we don't do anything based on anonymous information."

"Well, that's true," Dean said with a shrug.

"I gestured for the kid to give me the phone," Foley went on. "I told the guy who I was and he told me he wanted to meet with someone from the office. Confidentially, he said, and I told everything we do is confidential. But he said, no, what he meant was unofficially, off-the-record. So, since I figured we had an unofficial investigation going anyway, I said okay."

"You what?" Dean sighed. "And Pete was there. He heard the call. He knows you're going out to meet this guy, whoever he is?"

"The kid's clueless," Foley said with a shrug. "While I was on the phone with whomever, he was staring at the spreadsheet on Willis' trust account I'd prepared for him, trying to figure things out. He wasn't paying attention to what I was saying."

"Well, that's good," Dean said.

He sighed and gave Foley a long hard look.

"So when we meeting this guy?" Dean asked. "And where?"

"We?"

"Yeah, we," Dean said.

"Tonight, around nine," Foley said, smiling. "And funny thing. Guess where he wants to meet us?"

"Where?" Dean asked.

"Randolph Park," Foley said. "In that same lovers' lane area off the main road where I spotted the DA and his first assistant last night."

"That's spooky," Dean said. "Or creepy, I'm not sure which. Just hope that the DA and Hines-Laurence don't decide to go out there again tonight."

"Yeah," Foley said and laughed. "So what were you caught up with yesterday afternoon after court? Like I said, I came looking for you after the call. You with Herr Gunther?"

"Unfortunately, yes," Dean said. "He was berating me again over the other night, you following the DA and my lack of judgment for allowing it to happen. And he was also upset about how we handled that McMahon case."

"McMahon? What's wrong with it?" Foley asked. "I thought it turned out pretty well."

"Well, the CJ, with the support of the Herr Gunther, as you call him – because I would prefer not getting into the habit of calling him that in order to keep my damn job – they pretty much nixed it and now we're back to square one, even with old man McMahon. It turned out to be a big clusterfuck which by his standards was pretty much all my fault, another demonstration of poor judgment."

"Screw that Nazi," Foley said and squirmed disagreeably in his chair.

"Anyway," Dean continued, "he had me in his office until five-thirty berating me for this and that, going over damned files that had been closed two years ago, wondering why we did this and didn't do that or vice versa. Then, I went home and found Laura passed out drunk on the living room couch again and nothing to eat except stale bread and an old microwave dinner."

"You need to get her back in rehab, boss," Foley said.

Dean waved a hand at him.

"I need to do a lot of things, Stuey," he said and sighed.

Finally, he looked back at Foley and asked, "So what time you picking me up tonight?"

Chapter Eighteen
Randolph Park

The road around Lake Randolph was in desperate need of re-paving. Its three mile roughly elliptical route was marred by variously sized pot holes after several winters had come and gone since its last re-paving. Fortunately, the speed limit along the route was only fifteen miles per hour, limiting whatever damage might be done to a car's suspension or undercarriage by striking, or falling into, one of them.

As requested, Foley had come for Dean at eight-forty-five for the fifteen-minute ride to the park. The meeting with whomever had sent the anonymous DA letter was set for nine in a nook back from the road among some old maple trees and brush. The spot was often used for teenagers and sometimes older folks, like the DA and Susan Hines-Laurence yesterday evening, looking for a little privacy for some serious necking, petting, or perhaps even more than that. It was one of several such nooks along the pock-marked road that provided an intimate escape. Sometimes, if they had nothing better to do, cops assigned to the south Buffalo precinct in which the park was located would sneak back into one of these nooks and, on a better night, surprise a couple, man and woman, or better yet, according to the cops, woman and woman, doing something privately embarrassing, by shining a light in the dark car windows.

On the way over, Foley brought up a phone conversation he had late that afternoon with Myra Styles, the secretary for longtime Supreme Court Associate Justice Alan Myers.

"Myra and me go way, way back," Foley said. "Certainly long before your time. I dated her a few times."

"Last century or the one before that?"

"Don't be a wise-ass."

"What'd she want?" Dean asked.

"She called in a panic," Foley said. "It seems that old Myers is not long for this world, and she's worried about finding a new job."

"Really? I hadn't heard anything. What's wrong with him?"

Myers was an old-timer, seventy-four years old. He'd be placed into what was known as "senior status" upon his seventieth birthday and then after six years in a semi-retired capacity, by state law, he'd be forced off the bench and formally and finally have to retire. Dean always marveled how some judges clung to their jobs well past their prime and need for money. Why work at that age when you could be on the golf course or on the beach in sunny Florida? Dean figured it must simply be the ego boost some of them got wearing judicial robes.

"Bone cancer," Foley said. "Stage Four. Three, four

months to live or something like that. Maybe not even that long. My point is, there is going to be a vacancy on the Supreme Court. Probably before Christmas, and Myra will need a new job."

Dean shrugged.

"So?" he asked. "Can you find her one?"

"That's not what I'm talking about," Foley said. They were waiting at another of the many red lights along Ridge Road leading to Randolph Park. "Jesus is this light ever going to change?"

"So what are you talking about?" Dean asked.

"The names that come up for Myers' spot on the Court," Foley said. "That's what I'm talking about."

"Who?"

"Who do you think?" Foley said. "The DA. Our very own, Sam Marcum." He sighed. "That's what Myra told me. Now wouldn't that be a kick in the ass."

Finally, the light changed and off Foley drove the remaining half mile along Ridge Road to the entrance to Randolph Park. As Foley turned left into the park, he said, "It's just like I always tell you, there's no comes around after the what goes around," he said. "For most assholes, it just goes around, in their favor. In this life, anyway, and probably there's not even an afterlife for proper justice to be served no matter what they taught you in Catholic school. And the other thing I tell you..."

"Everything is politics," Dean said.

They merged onto the bumpy, elliptical main road that wound around Randolph Lake.

"Yes," Foley said. "Everything is politics. Getting ahead

in life, for the most part, has nothing to do with talent. It's who you know, how well you're connected, then a little bit of luck. Talent helps, of course, but it's getting the opportunity to apply that talent in some way, and the only way to get that opportunity, most times, is by being born into it or having someone push you ahead of the line."

"Do you know where we're going, Stuey?' Dean asked. He'd heard this spiel a hundred times before, maybe more.

"Yeah," he said. He was doing the speed limit, barely fifteen miles an hour, and the car was having a hard time going that slow. "It's on the other side of the lake.

"And that goes for everything," Foley continued the spiel, barely missing a beat, "even in pro sports. For each and every ball player who makes it, there are ten lined up equal to them who'll never get the opportunity to shine. And why?"

"Politics," Dean answered.

"Damn straight," Foley said. "Pol-oh-ticks."

He drove on in silence for a few moments looking for the turn-off, then slowed to a crawl, saw the entrance into the lover's lane he was looking for and made a hard right-hand turn.

"How'd you know this is the one?" Dean asked.

"There's a speed limit sign a few feet before the entrance," he said. "Has a graffiti drawing of Mickey Mouse on it."

Foley negotiated a narrow path with the tires crunching the dirt and gravel that opened to a cramped clearing surrounded by some tall maple trees and pines. He pulled alongside a dark car parked at the far end. Foley turned off the car and they waited in the darkness.

"Now what?" Dean asked.

"We wait," Foley said with a shrug.

After a minute or so, the driver's side door of the other car opened to a glare of interior lighting and the *ping-ping-ping* of the car's warning chime. The driver cursed, pulled the keys out of the ignition, stopping the alarm, and gently shut the door. Then, the dark, hunched-over figure walked toward the back of their car along Dean's side. He stopped for a moment, as if calling up his resolve, then proceed along the side of the car, stopped at Dean's window, and knocked at it. Foley pressed the button lowering it and Dean looked into the face of Salvatore Parlatto, the former first assistant district attorney of the county DA's Office.

Chapter Nineteen
Salvatore Parlatto

Dean had never met Sal Parlatto but he knew him from photographs in the local newspaper and from his television interviews over the years regarding several high profile cases he had prosecuted. Indeed, Parlatto had handled some of the most notorious and toughest homicide cases in the county brought by the DA's office over the past fifteen years. He was a well-respected litigator who always earned extra praise for his decency and fairness. But like all occupations, he had lost some of his edge as he got older and fell more into the administrative game.

But his biggest and perhaps dumbest sin was not actively supporting Sam Marcum in the last election. Instead, he had remained on the sidelines, mostly because a good friend, Janet Hayes, was running against Marcum. That decision had cost him a shot at first assistant district attorney when, right after Marcum's re-election, Ken Bishop, who had held the job during the DA's first term, left the office. Bishop joined a rising personal injury firm to try his hand at making some real money. This lack of support also had the eventual side effect of forcing Parlatto out the door.

But now that Dean thought about it, whom he had supported in the last election had nothing to do with why he had not been selected for the job of first assistant district attorney. Perhaps, it was related to human emotions and urges more basic than political intrigue. Perhaps, it had been simply a function of the fact that Sal Parlatto was not as pretty and sexy in Marcum's eyes as Susie Hines-Laurence.

"I'm Sal Parlatto," he said and stuck a hand into the car. Dean shook it. Parlatto was a short man, no more than five feet six, with a thick build, stone-like, chiseled features and a swarthy complexion. He looked like he'd have been just as comfortable being a bricklayer as a lawyer. (Indeed, his grandfather had been exactly that in the old country).

His voice belied his gruff appearance and was surprisingly smooth, sonorous, such that during his questioning of witnesses, even during cross-examination, and especially during summation, it drew one into the subject. Parlatto's voice compelled listening to it. Someone had once put it that Sal did everything smooth and slow, deliberate, purposeful, and by doing so, he slowed down a trial syllable by syllable to make it understandable for the jury and spectator.

There were some who wondered, given his litigation skills and success in the courtroom, why he had remained a prosecutor, and not taken the many purported offers and jumped to one of the high-priced criminal defense firms. The popular thought was that he saw the DA's office as the safe vehicle to some higher office, like United States Attorney, or, better yet, a judgeship. But that never happened for him, probably because as he busied himself with his craft, honing his trial skills, doing his job, he never found time to sufficiently nurture the political connections needed to get beyond the District Attorney's office. Confirming, Dean thought, once again, Foley's cynical view of justice, or the lack of it, in the world.

Now, Parlatto was out of a job, forced into early retirement, and even disgraced to some degree by spurious rumors that his sudden and unceremonious departure had been forced because of an alleged affair with a married secretary compounded by his botching of several recent cases indicating that he was losing, or had lost, his litigator's curve ball at the relatively young age of sixty.

"I'm Stu Foley," Foley called over to him.

Parlatto nodded.

"Can I get in?"

"Sure," Foley said and a moment later, Parlatto was sitting in the back seat. He had brought with him a file folder that now rested on his lap.

"So you wrote that letter?" Foley said. "About Marcum."

"Yes," Parlatto said and looked out the window. He did not look happy to be here. Though the reward might be great, Foley appreciated that taking revenge was usually a lonely and unappetizing business. Even for a prosecutor, being a snitch was not a good thing.

"So what else you got?" Foley asked. "What's the more to come part? Like the letter promised."

Parlatto stared out the back window for a time at the

thick darkness of the nook, lamenting something, the state of his life perhaps. Finally, he turned to Foley and in his smooth, silky, unhurried voice, said, "Know why I'm here? Because assholes like Marcum always get ahead in the world and guys like me get screwed. Marcum fell in love or lust or whatever with Susie Hines the moment she waltzed into the office what, six, seven years ago. He was a bureau chief back then, headed special investigations, bunch of bullshit white collar crime cases, no heavy lifting. Guys got transferred to special investigations at the end of their career, somewhere to put them where they could do no real harm. But the former DA, Hargrave, he liked Sam. Plus, Sam's Uncle was that congressman downstate with ties up here who could help him get votes. Same old story."

Parlatto sighed.

"Anyway, at the Christmas party a couple years after they hired Susie Hines, Marcum was all over her. His wife is this fat lady, Joan, a truly nice gal with a big laugh. But heavy, you know, grotesque. Years ago, she was pretty. At least, I thought so. But she had ballooned over time, ate too much. You know the story for some women who were once pretty but don't age very well. I don't know." He laughed. "I got a woman like that. Maybe most of us do. Anyway, the fatter Mrs. Marcum got, the more unhappy she got. The classic fucking vicious circle."

Parlatto shrugged trying to pick up from where he had digressed by making Mrs. Marcum part of his story.

"Anyway, that night," he went on, "Joan Marcum was balled up at her table with a puss on her face making small talk with whomever, aware but acting oblivious to the fact that her husband was all over a girl almost half his age. Susie, of course, was eating it up, making him beg for it. She saw possibilities in Sam that he was going far, well beyond his current position and status in life. Maybe, there was more to it than that, that she was attracted to that older man who is ripening in his attractiveness while his wife is growing old and fat.

"Whatever it was, I suspect their affair began sometime shortly after that."

"You *suspect* their affair began?" Dean interrupted. He had turned in his seat and put an arm over the back of it so he could look at Parlatto. "You don't know for sure. I mean, no one else in the office has come forward claiming anything like that. Not that we've looked all that hard."

"I know because I know," Parlatto said harshly. "I mean, I don't have any photographs of them or anything like that. But I used to watch them together, and you'd see it."

"But she married Kent Laurence sometime after that Christmas party," Foley interrupted, himself turning sideways with his right arm over the back of his seat, looking back at Parlatto. "Right? So she was having an affair with Marcum and ended up marrying Laurence. Doesn't quite make sense."

"I'm telling you she was having an affair with Sam," Parlatto said. "I was there. I know it. But rumors started flying that Hargrave wasn't going to run for reelection, and Sam was naturally interested in the job. And should that happen, the last thing he needed was a divorce proceeding hanging over his head, a black cloud. Susie Hines saw this as well, or just got tired of being secretly attached to a married man, no matter how powerful he might end up becoming.

"From what I understand, Susie had been flirting with Kent Laurence around that time, cultivating him, sort of speak, letting him spend some of his money on her and all that. He was going through a late, mid-life crisis thing, and she was, and still is, hard to resist. Best of all, he was single. Wife number three was out of the way a couple years before he had met Susie. So she must have felt it was time to hitch her wagon to him, start earning, and spending, more of the rich old bastard's fortune. So that's how she ended up with Kent Laurence.

"But, soon enough after marrying him, Susie was back at it with Marcum. They were up to their old tricks, giving each other goggle eyes, touching, whispering. Meeting behind closed doors, that sort of thing. It was nothing overt, and they were noticeably discreet. Unless you were looking for it, unless you knew, you wouldn't have known anything was going on, if that makes any sense. But I knew, and I saw right through how they operated.

"Then, it happened. Hargrave announced he wasn't running, and Marcum got the endorsement and easily won the election that November. He had it made, except he was still married to fat old Joan and Susie had married Kent Laurence. Life was complete, but not. So he tried to make it more complete by naming Susie first assistant instead of me after Kenny Bishop left. And then at some point after that, I guess, they starting hatching the plot to get rid of Laurence, who was pretty much a complete asshole in his own right, from what I've heard."

"You guess?" Dean asked.

Parlatto frowned.

"You said, you guess they were hatching a plot," Dean said.

"Yeah, guess," Parlatto said. "What do you think, I have a tape of them plotting to murder the guy?"

"So let me get this straight," Dean said, growing a bit perturbed by the massive amount of speculation and little in the way of proof that Parlatto's somewhat convoluted story relied upon. "Shortly after a DA's office Christmas Party about six years ago," he said, "Marcum and Susie Hines start having an affair. Maybe they even talk about him divorcing his fat old wife, but then, a short time later, he finds out that Pat Hargrave isn't running for reelection and decides he wants to be DA. So now he can't divorce the fat, old wife because that might cause a major problem getting the Democratic endorsement. Susie is being pursued big time by Kent Laurence about the same time, and she decides that something is better than nothing, especially a rich something, and she marries him instead."

Dean took a breath. "Is that about right so far?"

Parlatto nodded. "You seem to be getting it," he said.

"And somewhere along the way," Foley now jumped in, "Susan Hines-Laurence becomes first assistant district attorney, a job that should have been yours."

"It should have been," Parlatto said. "Susie Hines is a lightweight. At least, as a lawyer. As a whore, she's major league."

"So, anyway," Dean continued, ignoring the comment, "Marcum and Susie Hines, now Laurence, continue their love affair that was interrupted by his run for DA. They decide that they can't live apart anymore. But divorcing Kent Laurence might be messy for both her and Marcum, not to mention the pile of money she'd be walking away from." Dean sighed. "So they, what, hatch a plot wherein she shoots him with his own gun and says it was all an accident, banking on the DA's promise to concoct a criminal investigation finding that she was telling the truth – that, as she said, Kent Laurence's death was nothing more than a horrible, ridiculous, tragic accident, when, in fact, it was murder."

Parlatto nodded, brought up his hands and started clapping.

"Very good, counselor," he said, lowering his hands. "Except you can add as their motive for killing Kent Laurence, it appears that he may have been onto their affair, towards the end, I mean." He sighed as Dean and Foley appeared to be digesting what he just said. "And I know, it sounds far-fetched."

"Far-fetched?" It was Foley's turn to chime in. "It sounds like a bad crime novel. You have any proof of any of this?"

"Hey, bad crime novel or not," Parlatto said, "people in real life do some pretty stupid things for love and money, and when both are involved, they get even stupider. Just read the papers on a daily basis. And as for proof, except for my intuition, and observations of them around the office the last six years, I have these."

Parlatto tapped the folder on his lap, then pulled the flap off the Velcro and reached into it. He took out several sheets of paper and handed them up to Dean. Foley turned on the overhead light and Dean started to read.

"Emails?" he said.

"Yep, emails," Parlatto said. "Incriminating emails."

But as Dean leafed through them, seven in all, he soon decided that they weren't as incriminating as Parlatto would have them believe. There was certainly a measure of flirtation that seeped through the exchanges between the DA and his first assistant, but nothing showing that they were having an affair. And certainly nothing proving that they had planned the murder of Kent Laurence and pulled it off. For the most part, they were routine emails involving the day-to-day operations of the office. Spiced in between the business were quips and comments that could leave one to wonder about the exact nature of the relationship that existed between DA Marcum and Susan Hines-Laurence.

After reading each of the seven emails, Dean handed them over to Foley while Parlatto waited without comment in the backseat.

"These are copies, I take it," Foley said as he read through the third one Dean had passed over.

"Sure," Parlatto said. "I got the originals."

"How'd you get them?" Foley asked.

"Well," Parlatto said, "let's just say I have a good friend in the office that the DA doesn't know about, well, at least, he didn't when I got them. A friend I think who will come forward and say some things if the timing was right."

"A married secretary?" Foley asked, remembering the rumors why Parlatto was forced out, deciding perhaps it hadn't seen so spurious after all.

Parlatto grunted. "That rumor's bullshit," he said.

"You can't be more specific than that?" Dean asked.

"No, I can't," Parlatto said. "I'm talking about someone

could lose their job if this came out. Maybe even worse than that."

Foley's frown deepened and he seemed even more troubled than a moment ago.

"So that's it? All you have?" Foley asked. "These seven emails? And someone on the inside who might be able to add something, when the time is right. That's the extent of the more to come part of your anonymous letter?"

Parlatto turned and glared at Foley.

"Take a look at them," he said. "I know some of it sounds innocent, but in context, I think they speak volumes."

"Maybe because you want them to," Dean said.

"What about that one she sent to him that simply said," Parlatto said, "'I think he knows.' That was about two months before Laurence was shot, murdered. And that shows the motive for killing him I was just talking about. They were worried all of sudden that he was on to them."

Dean shrugged, then leafed through the emails and found the one Parlatto was talking about. Squinting in the bad light, he read it. It was from susan.hines@erieda.gov.state.us addressed to DA.Marcum@erieda.gov.state.us, and stated, "I think he knows. Talk later." There was no message in response.

"So this means he was on to them," Dean said. "Their affair."

"What else could it mean?" Parlatto said and from Foley came a short laugh. Parlatto turned and glared forward at him. "What else?"

"Just seems there's a lot of blanks to fill in to get to that conclusion," Foley said.

Dean sighed.

"So that's it?" he asked. "Your more is coming proof? Of what, murder?"

"Yeah, murder," Parlatto said. "That's it. These emails. Take it or leave it." Parlatto added, "That and the fact that Kent Laurence was shot to death and the DA tried to cover up what really happened."

"You read the papers, right?" Foley asked. "The DA's changed his mind and is going to present a case against Susie Hines-Laurence to the grand jury. She may end up being indicted. So what does that do to your case?" He hesitated a moment. "Same as ours."

"But all that has got to be a setup," Parlatto said. "There's something fake about it."

"We think so, too," Dean said.

"You never followed him, or her," Foley said. "Or had them followed. To confirm their affair?"

Parlatto looked down. He seemed to be losing confidence in his attempt at revenge, seeing maybe that it was going down the tubes.

"No," he said. "I never thought it would lead to anything. To murder. To my ..."

He looked up.

"So that's it?" he asked. "They get away with ...murder?"

Foley sighed and looked forward.

"You want them?" Parlatto asked. "The emails?"

Foley looked down at them in his hand.

"Can't hurt to have them," he said. "Who knows?"

Parlatto nodded and without another word, he opened

the back door.

"Like I said," Dean said, "we think the whole thing smells funny, too. Only thing is the lack of proof."

"You don't need to tell me about proof, counselor," Parlatto said. "I always managed to find enough in twenty years as a prosecutor to put plenty scumbags behind bars. I know full well that's the trick. Proof."

Then, a moment later, he stepped out into the chilly night and slammed the door behind him. He walked solemnly back to his car, got in, started it, and slowly maneuvered out of the clearing.

"Well, that was a complete waste of time," Dean said.

"No," Foley said. "It wasn't."

"How wasn't it?" Dean asked.

"Because while Sal might not have had all the proof," Foley said, "his analysis was spot on."

"So you think the DA and Susie Hines murdered Kent Laurence?" Dean asked. "Is that what you're telling me? This makes our Rule 1.7 conflict of interest a joke compared to that – a case of murder."

Foley shrugged and switched off the overhead light. He started the car, put it into reverse and started backing up.

"Stuey, tell me what you're thinking." Dean waited a time as Foley put it into drive and drove them back to Franklin Park's main road.

"Stuey?"

Chapter Twenty
The Retirement Party

Six weeks later, at seven on a Thursday evening on the thirty-first day of July, coinciding with his last official day as Chief Investigator for the Lawyer Discipline Office and as am employee for the State of New York, Foley's retirement party was held at Scianno's Restaurant. Scianno's, an Italian eatery out in the suburbs, had become Foley's favorite restaurant in the area. About a half hour before the party was set to start, Scianno's long-time owner, Enrico Scianno, who had emigrated to the United States in the late 1940s from the Abruzzi Province while still a young boy, came out to greet Foley and Ginny upon their arrival with Foley's brother, Mike and his wife, Gloria. Enrico led them into the bar off the main dining room and bought them a round of drinks.

"Glad you a come, *paisano*," Enrico said.

He still spoke with a heavy Italian accent that some said was only for show. He was a large man with an expansive, welcoming style who always seemed happy and full of life. Of course, Ginny Foley dourly attributed his happy-go-lucky attitude to the many years of his restaurant's success and the riches he had accumulated because of it. But for once, Foley wasn't so cynical, feeling that the man simply knew he was blessed with a good family and riches and appreciated it. In short, there was nothing for him to be unhappy about.

Upon ushering Foley and Ginny and Mike and Gloria to the bar for their drinks, Enrico ordered a glass of Sambuca for himself with a few coffee beans settling on the bottom and held it up for a toast.

"To a my friend, Stu Foley," Enrico said, "Have a fun on this a special night. *Cento di questi giorni.* May you a live a hundred years. Ah, Salute!"

Dean arrived just as they were downing their glasses. He was a regular at Scianno's as well and when Enrico saw him, he put his thick arms around his shoulders, brought him over to the bar and told him to order a drink.

"On-ah me," he said and slapped Dean on the back.

"I'll have a Black Russian," Dean told Mike, the long-time bartender.

Enrico said his goodbyes and went off to greet other patrons and to generally oversee the operation of the restaurant, which was already almost to capacity even on a Thursday.

"Where's Laura?" Ginny Foley asked Dean as he took a sip of his drink. The question earned a sideways frown from Stu. Ginny was a fan of juicy gossip, other people's troubles.

"Home," Dean said with a shrug. "Not feeling good."

"One thing I have never understood," Mike Foley boomed as he patted his younger, and smaller, brother on the back, "is how a total Mick like you likes Italian food. You should be eating bangers and mash instead of spaghetti and meatballs."

"Well," Stu Foley said, turning to his brother, "if you studied your history, you'd know that the Romans conquered the little isle of Eire back in the second century AD. So we all carry around in us Italian blood and a taste for red gravy and meatballs."

They laughed at that but soon Foley edged his way down the bar to Dean.

"She drunk again?" he asked.

"What else is new?"

"You okay?"

"Well, I'll enjoy myself tonight a hundred times more without having to worry what a fool she's making of herself."

Foley nodded. He looked up to the TV on a shelf over the bar. Highlights of some afternoon baseball games were playing on ESPN Sports Center.

"You watch the news?" Foley asked.

Dean nodded and took another sip of his Black Russian.

"Looks like our theory about the DA is down the drain," Dean said. "What were we dreaming, or smoking, I should say." He shook his head and laughed. "Murder."

"Yeah," Foley said and shrugged. "I guess you can close that unofficial file. Fitting isn't it. I lost my last case."

"Don't consider it a loss," Dean said. "Maybe for once, it came around."

Foley laughed, but after a time settled into a cold frown.

"What?" Dean asked. "You got that look, the look I never like but will miss horribly, asshole."

"I don't know," Foley said. "Something still bothers me

about it. So he indicted her on a voluntary manslaughter charge. Why not murder second?"

Dean shrugged.

"Well, isn't such a great case, for one thing," Dean said. "I mean, there was just him, a dead guy, and her, for witnesses, and she claims it was an accident. So all the DA has if forensics, which I guess puts that claim into question. Plus, she can get fifteen years for manslaughter, right? And it's easier to prove. Sometimes it's better not to over-charge."

"I know, I know, but…"

Just then, Pete Lassiter, one of Foley's former partners from his private investigator days nudged between Foley and Dean at the bar. Some other invitees had arrived and were assembling in the banquet room at the back of the restaurant where the party was to be held.

"Hey, no talking shop,' Pete said. "It's a party and you're no longer on the clock."

Foley stepped forward and hugged his old partner and, stepping back, told Pete he looked great. They had formed Foley, Lassiter and Bain more than thirty-five years ago shortly after Stu had quit the Buffalo PD only a year after his discharge from a six-year stint in the Marines. After ten years chasing cheating husbands and wives, following and photographing malingering workers and workers' comp cheats, and interviewing accident witnesses, Foley got hired as a tax investigator for the state finance department and, then, seventeen years ago, transferred over to the Legal Discipline Office.

"So what you gonna do now?" Lassiter asked him. "Retire down to Florida? Die in an old folk's home?"

"Screw you, Pete," he said.

"Hey, I'm still looking for a partner," he said. "Seriously, you interested in some part-time work?"

"Let me think about it," Foley said. "Get back to you."

By now, it was time to get over to the banquet room where eighty or so guests were gathering and finding their assigned tables. Dean followed Foley and Ginny, Pete Lassiter, and Mike Foley and his wife through the large, noisy dining room to the banquet hall. There was a long main table along the far wall and Dean found his place setting and sat down. A few moments later, Brad Gunther strode pompously in and sat in his assigned chair next to him.

"Hello, Dean," he said with a cold nod.

"Hello, Brad." Dean looked out at all the people settling around their tables.

"Nice gathering," Gunther remarked curtly and Dean merely nodded. It seemed offensive that Gunther was there, celebrating Foley's many years of dedicated service to the State of New York considering it was Gunther who drove him to an early retirement.

Without further comment, Gunther scanned the room at the ten or so round tables filling up with guests. Kat Franklin was already sitting at one of the tables directly in front of the head table. She nodded to Dean and to the empty chair to his right that had been reserved for Laura, and he shrugged. Kat gave him a sympathetic pout. His heart lost a beat, it seemed, with that gesture.

Gunther waved at Kat and she gave him a weak smile. Ever since the McMahon episode six weeks earlier, she had become leery of him.

The table where Kat was sitting, a second and third, were reserved for LDO employees. They were divided by disciplinary counsel at one, and the investigators and clerical staff at the other, together with their significant others. Kat, of course, had come alone. Sitting next to Kat was Ed Chase's wife, the heavy-set and blustery Olive Chase. Liza Hartman and her husband, Ken, a mild-mannered guy who was himself a lawyer and seemed to be well under Liza's control, were next around the table looking stiff and bored. Pete O'Brien had also come alone, and traveling from one of the satellite offices was dis-con, Don Asperante and his wife, Nancy.

Around the adjacent table were the investigators, Dawn Smith, also dateless, and the mostly silent, nondescript, Larry Stevens and his wife, Moira. Joe Canistrari from Asperante's office and his wife occupied two more chairs and next to him was the dour Paul Koslowski from another of the satellite offices.

Occupying the next table over were the LDO legal assistants, Kathy Barnes, Carol Pelowski, Gina Cammeroni, and the brand new lady, Anna Golson. Each of them had their husbands in tow.

Ed Chase had been designated early on as the party's official Master-of-Ceremonies. He was relaxed and funny in front of a crowd, especially after a few drinks. It was already a few minutes past seven by the time he stood and stepped behind the podium that split the head table in half. Foley was to his immediate right, next to Ginny, with Gunther next to her.

"Alright, ladies and germs," Chase said and tapped into the microphone several times causing an annoying, *boom*,

boom, boom effect.

"Ladies and germs, please take your seats," he called out again and waited a moment as the guests started paying attention and finally proceeded to their seats.

"Some of us are starving, especially Stu." Chase laughed. "You know how Stuey hates it when you're late for dinner. Late for anything. Your own funeral even."

Stu Foley was, in fact, notoriously early for everything and it was well known that his pet peeve was even the slightest tardiness.

"Old Stuey will show up early for his own funeral," Chase added as a crass afterthought, causing Gunther to turn and glare at him.

When everyone appeared to have found their seats and were paying attention, getting ready to eat, Chase looked to his right and, finding him, said, "Father Murphy?"

A thin, frail-looking old priest with a chalky complexion and stark white hair stood and hobbled over to the podium. But his sickly appearance belied a strong heart and mischievous attitude. He looked about the assembled guests and grinned.

"They asked an Irish priest to do the benediction," he said. "And they expected him to be sober?"

There was a titter of laughter from the audience.

"When they called me about Stu," Father Murphy went on, undeterred, "I thought they were asking me to his funeral mass."

More tittering rose up.

"Alright, alright," he said and brought up his hands to playfully calm down the audience. "So Henna Youngman, I'm not. Here's the damned benediction. I know you're hungry."

After another round of suppressed laughter, Father Murphy bowed his head slightly and closed his eyes. Everyone else, it seemed, including Dean, did likewise.

"Let us pray," Father Murphy began. "Heavenly Father, thank you for allowing us to gather here today for this joyous celebration and we pray that you impart your favor upon each of us. And I implore that you bestow a special blessing on your son, Stuart Foley, as he enters his new life in retirement. We also give thanks for granting us this celebration and the food and drink that comes with it. Through Jesus Christ our Lord, amen."

Foley's family and friends offered a half-hearted, "Amen."

"Let's eat," Father Murphy said and off he went back to his chair at the main table.

"He's too much," Dean heard Ginny whisper to no one in particular.

Scianno's waiters and waitresses worked fast to deliver the family style dinner for each table, plates of pasta, meatballs, chicken cacciatore, roasted potatoes, and fried vegetables.

"What a feast," Foley said as the servings kept on coming and he piled all of it onto his dinner plate.

Dessert was cherry cheesecake and cannolis.

Just as fast as the food came, Scianno's busboys cleaned up the tables and Ed Chase was back at the podium. With coffee and tea steaming in front of the guests and the honoree, Chase launched into his standard routine.

"May I have your attention, please," he began. "Well,

now we're at the point in the night after a great dinner when, if we are still awake, we have to honor the honored guest, in this case, Stu Foley, who is leaving state service after how many years, Stu?"

"Twenty-eight," Foley said and coughed.

"Twenty-eight long years," Chase said. He yawned. "Twenty-eight wasted years."

More unenthusiastic tittering rose from the audience.

Chase got better telling a series of almost obligatory retirement jokes, and three or four even drew some genuine guffaws and applause. He ended with this one, "And remember, Ginny, a retired husband is a full-time job. And with that, I'd like to call up to the podium to relieve me of these unpleasant duties, the Director of the LDO, Brad Gunther."

As Gunther pushed back his chair, stood and headed toward the podium, Chase started down the other way. On his way past Foley's chair, he bent down, slapped him on the back, and said, "Gonna miss you, old pal," before making his way past Dean to his chair at the very end of that side of the main table. But as he walked past, Dean reached around and grabbed Chase by the left sleeve of his sports jacket and pulled him down to him.

"What the hell, Ed," Dean whispered, "I thought I was supposed to go up next."

Dean had written a short speech, a tribute, with some funny and touching things to say about what a wonderful friend and mentor Foley had become to him, after all their years fighting lawyers who'd gone bad.

Chase jerked back toward the podium, where Gunther

was now standing getting ready to speak.

"He told me no," Chase said. "Tonight, just before I went up there. He asked what the agenda was, so I told him. He said, and I quote, scratch Alessi off the list. Unquote."

Dean let go of Chase's sleeve and swiveled around toward the front. He turned and looked up at the podium, just in time to hear a punch line of Gunther's obligatory retirement joke that drew a decent round of laughter and applause.

Chapter Twenty-One
After-Party Blues

Foley's retirement party was officially over at ten and the guests started shuffling out of the banquet hall for home, Gunther among them. But Foley and Ginny and Foley's brother, Mike, and his wife, Gloria, Pete Lassiter and a couple other old friends, Dean among them, stuck around and took over Scianno's bar. Enrico Scianno joined them for drinks, including a couple shots of bourbon, toasting to Foley's long and healthy retirement.

"You a go to Florida," Scianno told him, laughing, "have a fun in the sun a watching Ginny in her bikini."

At some point, Dean found himself in the corner of the bar sipping another Black Russian he didn't need or want, courtesy of Mike Foley. After a time, Stu Foley made his way over to him with a wide grin and wide eyes.

"Happy that shit's over," he said.

"Ginny's driving, right?" Dean asked. "You're sloshed. Nice speech, though. Thanks for all the kind words."

"You deserved it, pal," Foley said. "If it wasn't for you,

there'd be no LDO. And what the hell happened in there? I heard that fucking Gunther wouldn't let you say a few last words in tribute for your old friend."

"That's pretty much what Ed Chase told me," Dean said and took a sip of his drink. "Something's fishy going on."

"Well, the hell with him," Foley said and slapped Dean on the back. "Forget that bullshit tonight. In no time, he'll figure out what you mean to that office like Madison did, and leave you about your business."

Dean shrugged. Looking away from Foley, who was feeling no pain slurring his words and not making much sense at this point in the night, he saw Kat Franklin lurking in the entrance to the bar off the foyer of the restaurant. She saw him and Foley and walked over.

"I didn't get the chance to personally congratulate you, Stu," Kat said and she gave him a hug.

"Thanks, Kat," Foley said.

"Hey, I thought you left," Dean said.

"I did," she said. "But I figured you guys would stick around for a while."

Someone was calling Foley back to the bar for another round of shots.

"I've got to get back, my admirers call," he said, and then he turned to Kat. "You guys want to join us?"

"No, over here is just fine," Dean said.

"Some of us have to work tomorrow," Kat said, begging off as well.

"You take care of this guy," Foley told her, slurring a bit, his eyes heavy. "He's a good egg."

"Sure thing, Stu," Kat said.

Foley leaned forward, hugged Dean, slapped him on the back and then he was off for another round.

"Why aren't you there in the middle of that instead of sulking over here?" Kat asked.

"Why? Because I got a lot to sulk about."

"Like what?"

"Like my life is crumbling around me," Dean said. "First of all, there's this. Foley's actually leaving. He's been well, you know, like the older brother I never had. You know, a mentor. I don't know. Anyway, I'm going to miss him."

"Yeah, we're all gonna miss him," Kat said. "Except assholes like Liza Hartman and Dawn Smith and Brad Gunther."

"You hear about the Hines-Laurence indictment?" Dean asked.

"Yeah, it was all over the news."

"Well, now I really look like a damned fool to Gunther," he said. "Took the damned wind completely out of my sails." He took a long, tired sigh. "And then there's that other bullshit tonight, not letting me say anything during Foley's ceremonies. What the hell was that all about?"

"I'm not sure," Kat said. "But, I agree he's up to something, something that doesn't appear to bode well for you. Do you know who spent an hour and a half in his office again this afternoon, behind closed doors?"

"Yeah, I know," Dean said. "Our lovely Liza Hartless-man."

"And that Dawn Smith's another one," he said. "She's bucking to get Foley's job for sure. And because Foley hated her, and Liza Hartman likes her, she's likely to get it even though, as we both know, she's incompetent as the day is long."

"More proof of Foley's view of life," he said.

"What?"

"Nothing."

A roar of laughter went up from the contingent of friends celebrating with Foley by the bar.

"Anyway," Kat said. "I heard Dawn saying something derogatory about you to that new secretary, Anna. Something about keeping her advised of what you are saying about things."

"Really, you heard that?"

There was another rise of laughter from Foley's group at the bar. The bad dirty jokes were flying.

"Look, I can't hear myself think in here," Kat said. "Let's go outside. I have to get home anyway."

Their leaving the bar went unnoticed. As Dean walked with Kat through the restaurant parking lot to her car, he started talking about Laura, how she was getting worse, that he needed to do something, but wasn't sure what. They were standing at the driver's side door of Kat's Honda Civic, within a couple feet of each other, when he shook his head and told her his life was a frigging mess.

"It sounds like you have to get her into rehab again," Kat said. "Do another intervention."

Dean leaned into Kat and brought her into his arms. Then, he moved back, looked into her eyes momentarily and lowered his lips to hers. They kissed. It was a gentle, short kiss.

"No, Dean," she said after a moment, then jerked back.

But he leaned forward and this time kissed her passionately, and she returned it.

Finally, she pushed him away again.

"No." Her whisper was harsh, urgent. "No."

He stepped forward into her but this time she pushed at his chest with some violence.

"I said, no," Kat said in a dry, no-nonsense tone.

"I'm sorry," he told her, then after a time, reached around her and opened the car door. What else was there to do? He was married to a drunk that had lost a baby fifteen years ago but who still grieved over it, and probably forever would, and Kat was denying him anything, Kat being Kat. Perfect way to cap off a bad night.

"Look, Dean," she said, "we've talked about this. What happened Christmas can't happen again."

"Nothing happened," he told.

"No," she said. "A lot happened. Too much."

"Alright," he said. He turned away from her and looked up into a clear, warm sky. After a sigh, he looked back at her.

"You're right," he told her. "You better go."

"You okay to drive?" she asked.

"I'm fine."

She looked up at him for a time, and in the next moment, ever so slightly moved toward him, seemingly to have given in, but then, abruptly moved right and slid into the driver's seat. She sat there waiting and then Dean shut the door. Kat started the car and he backed away as she pulled out of her parking spot and slowly drove off leaving him standing alone looking after her.

Chapter Twenty-Two
Ambush

When Dean woke up the following morning, Laura was not on her side of the bed. He had not gotten home until well after midnight and he was a bit hungover. The red digits of the alarm on the night table next to his side of the bed blared 8:05. He groaned, pushed himself out of bed. He stumbled out of the bedroom, down the hall and breathed a sigh of relief when he found Laura sitting at the kitchen table sipping a cup of coffee.

"You went without me last night?" She stared into her coffee, then looked up at him.

"You were asleep on the couch when I came home from work," Dean said. He walked over to the counter and poured himself a cup of coffee.

Laura nodded, took a sip of her coffee.

"You hung over?" she asked.

He shrugged as he came over and sat next to Laura.

"Not too bad," he said and laughed. "But I bet Stuey is."

179

Laura brought the cup to her mouth but didn't drink. She put it down and looked over at Dean.

"So was she there?"

"Who?"

"You know. Kat." Laura lowered her cup to the table and glared at Dean. "What the hell kind of name is that anyway. Kat."

"Why do you have to always bring her up?" Dean asked. "There is nothing going on between us. I keep telling you that. Nothing."

"You're lying," she said and looked away from him. "I'm a drunk, not an idiot."

She sighed and, after a time, turned back to him. "You want breakfast?"

"We need to talk about that," Dean said. He took a sip of coffee, put it down. "Your drinking."

"No we don't," she said. "I'm not going back to rehab."

"Laura…"

"I asked you, do you want breakfast?"

"No," he said and stood.

He was thinking about Kat. That kiss he gave her last night, and her momentarily lapse as she kissed him back.

"I'll get something on the way to the office," he said. "I'm late. I'll stop at Tim Horton's."

"Why go in?" she said. "Stay here. Fuck me."

He looked over at her and she smiled. Something was pulling at him to do just that. Call in sick, spend the day in bed with her. Fuck her.

But then the thought of Gunther thinking he was simply hung-over. Another demerit, and a step closer to unemployment.

"I've got to go in," he said. "I told you what an ass Gunther is."

Laura looked away and he was torn again, but then she said, "And she's there. Maybe you can fuck her in your office."

"Kat – I mean, Laura…"

But now it was too late. He had called her, Kat. She shot him a look, a knowing smile.

"Laura, please," he said. "I don't have time…"

"Do whatever you want, Dean," she said.

Laura gave him a suit-yourself kind of shrug and looked away. She looked so worn out now, her skin pale, slack, and her hair unkempt lacking any sheen from not being colored in so long. She's really sinking lately, he thought. But in her heyday, when things had not been going so bad in her mind, when she had not been drinking so much, Laura had been attractive, hot. At least to him, and no matter what his mother thought.

Hotter than Kat.

On his ride in, Dean regretted not taking Laura up on her proposition. He thought of going in, then checking out by mid-morning. He was behind his desk by five after nine. It was sad to walk past Foley's empty office on his way back to his own decent-sized space that he'd occupied for over sixteen years already. He still had another fourteen or fifteen years to go before he could realistically retire. But then, what would there be to look forward to?

He hit the power button on his laptop and got annoyed

waiting for it to boot. Time for new machines, he thought, something he'd been futilely clamoring for from the Supreme Court tech guy the last two years. All the justices had gotten new computers while the auxiliaries like lawyer discipline and mental hygiene languished. Finally, he was up and he immediately clicked on his email link. There were several messages highlighted in bold black lettering. The top one was from Gunther. It had been sent at 8:55 AM.

"Shit," Dean said and sat straight up. He clicked on the message and read:

Come over to Chief Clerk Anson-Clark's office at 9:45 AM for an important meeting.

Dean frowned and wondered what the hell this meeting could be about. If Foley was still here, he would go down and talk to him about it. Once, a few months back, the CJ had sent him a similar, cryptic note directing him to come down to the CJ's official chambers. That had been about the McMahon case, and the CJ railed on for about an hour how worried he was that "that scumbag" and his daughter were going to get away with "it." Dean had listened and tried to downplay the impropriety of the *ex parte* communication about a case pending before the Court, a case in which the CJ would later assign himself to decide. For weeks after that, he had been conflicted about reporting this to someone. It was Foley who had talked him out of it.

But Foley had officially retired yesterday and was probably sleeping off a long, hard drunk from the night before.

Dean checked his watch. It was only nine fifteen. Still,

another half hour before he had to head up to the so-called "important meeting," with the dour Chief Clerk Anson-Clarke and arrogant Brad Gunther. He had work to do, a respondent coming in with his counsel at eleven to review a trust account that Dawn Smith had compiled, indicating that the lawyer was out of trust over twenty grand for a whole month, In short, he had dipped into his clients' funds to pay for things unrelated to their cases. What those other things were, Dean didn't know. But he intended to find out. No matter what, the lawyer was in deep trouble.

Dean walked down the long hall from his office to the kitchenette and poured himself a stale cup of coffee. It was dark and bitter, but he drank it anyway. Kat walked in and saw him sitting forward on a chair at the small kitchen table.

"You alright?"

He shrugged. He decided against telling her what he was facing within the hour. And he truly didn't know. Could be nothing.

"What are you up to dressed so nice and all?" he asked.

"I've got Nelson Kelly coming in with his client, that scumbag Joe Cardoni," she said as she fixed herself a cup of tea.

"Under oath?"

"Yes," she said. "You approved it a couple weeks ago. What's the matter, Dean? You seem nervous."

"Nothing," he said. He got up with his coffee and left Kat alone in the kitchen. "Pooped and a little hung-over from last night. That's all. One too many Black Russians."

She looked like she wanted to add something to that, and glanced behind her. Something about the second kiss that

183

had passed between them. But then, she thought better of it and simply shrugged and went to fridge, got a yogurt and went back to her office.

Finally, it was 9:35 and Dean got up. As he walked through the reception room, he told Kathy Barnes he was off to the court for a meeting with the Chief Clerk.

"You, too," she said. "Mister Gunther went up there just after nine. What's going on?"

"You know as much as me," Dean said with a shrug.

By 9:45, Dean was sitting in the small, boxy waiting room off the Chief Clerk's office. Her chirpy secretary, Kim Barber, was typing something on her laptop keyboard and answering calls from time to time within her small kiosk along the wall next to the door leading into the main office. Finally, Kim called happily out to Dean.

"They'll see you now," she said.

As Dean got up and walked to the office door, he wondered if he might be dusting off his resume later that morning at home.

There were four people sitting around a conference table in the middle of the spacious Chief Clerk's office – the Chief Clerk, Margo Anton-Clarke, of course, sat on one side closest to Dean, to the left of her, Deputy Pam Wilson. On the other side across from Pam sat Jenny Ziniski, the Supreme Court's HR director, and across from the Chief Clerk sat a stone-faced Brad Gunther with his arms crossed on his chest. There was an empty chair at the head of the table, apparently reserved for Dean.

"Take a seat, Dean," Margo Anson-Clarke said.

Dean walked over, sat, for some reason smoothed his

gut and thighs and looked at the four of them staring at him. He had a hard time breathing for a few moments but, after a time, he looked down and saw a memo on the table.

"We've drafted out some things, Dean, in the memo before you," Margo said. "Could you please take a moment to look it over?"

Dean picked up the memo and started reading but his brain would not register anything.

"What – what is this about?" he asked and emitted a nervous laugh. For some reason, he looked across at Jenny Ziniski.

"It's a counseling memo, Dean, if you will," Margo told him. She looked at Gunther and said, "Brad?"

"The memo lists some of my concerns regarding your conduct as an employee for the Lawyer Discipline Office that I have observed over the last few weeks," he said methodically, like a recording. "And that some others have observed over the last year or so."

"The last year?"

Gunther looked at Jenny Ziniski and nodded, then back at Dean.

"At least," he said.

"Like, like what?" he asked.

"Well, first of all," Gunther started, "your meeting with Sal Parlatto in Franklin Park about three weeks ago. With Stu Foley." Gunther glared at him. "Did that happen?"

Dean thought a minute, wondering if he should call this ambush off and walk out. Hire an employment lawyer. However, he knew that as a management-confidential employee for the Supreme Court, no union protected him and he could be fired at will. And, worst of all, it was true. He had met with Sal Parlatto about the "unofficial" LDO case involving the alleged professional misconduct of the DA.

"Yes," Dean said with a shrug. "We met with him."

"About what?" Gunther asked.

"Parlatto provided us with information about a case," he said. "I can't discuss it here. I feel confidentiality rules would prohibit it." He looked at Jenny Zinski and Pam Wilson. "Because of them."

"No, there was no case," Gunther said, his voice strident now, demanding. "And it involved your surreptitious gathering of information with Stu Foley about a case that I had directly told you we were not going to pursue."

"But there was nothing wrong with listening to the guy," Dean said. "I had no idea what he was going to tell me. Maybe it would have resulted in something."

"It resulted in harassment of an esteemed government official," Gunther said, "and might have brought further shame and discredit on the LDO. And it was in direct contradiction of my express order."

"Can I ask," Dean said, "how you know about that meeting?"

"That's irrelevant to this inquiry," Gunther said. "The fact is that I know about it."

Dean sighed.

"And it's a further demonstration of the lack of judgment you previously demonstrated by authorizing Investigator Foley to follow the District Attorney of this county the night before my first day on the job but when you already knew I was in charge," Gunther went without taking a breath. Then, he stopped, swallowed, and added, "There is no question that you and Mister Foley have engaged in some kind of obsessive fishing expedition in search of proof of professional misconduct that did not and does not exist."

Dean was about to respond, "But it does exist." That he and Foley had indeed subsequently discovered that Sam Marcum and his first assistant district attorney were having an affair. And that the affair had likely started and was continuing right up to the time when she had purportedly "accidentally" mortally wounded the dear husband she happened to be cuckolding.

Instead, Dean looked down at the memo, but his mind was still so clouded that he could not read it.

"I have also identified at least ten cases," Gunther went on, "that were inappropriately, incompletely or incompetently investigated, or demonstrated a certain level of judgment lapses on your part."

"Which cases?" Dean demanded.

"They are listed in the report," Margo Anson-Clarke said, nodding to the memo. "You will have an opportunity to respond to them if you like, in a rebuttal memo that will be placed in your personnel file."

Dean shook the memo and looked at Jenny Ziniski. Across from her, the deputy clerk, Pam Wilson sat stone-faced.

"This is going in my file?"

"As Margo said," Jenny said, in her chirpy voice, smiling, trying to put a happy face, as she always did, on something unpleasant, "you'll have an opportunity to file a written rebuttal, or as called in court regulations, a formal explanation."

"There's more," Gunther said.

Dean looked at him. He felt totally defeated, or at least that this was the beginning of the end. He was in the process of being terminated from the job he loved and had done so well performing the last sixteen years by this cruel and mean-spirited ambush.

"And it involves probably the worst problem of all," Gunther said. "A claim of sexual harassment."

Dean looked down at the memo in his now shaking hand trying to find the details of that allegation. But after a moment, he looked up and asked, "What sexual harassment?"

"Do you deny," Gunther went on, "that at the Christmas Party last year, you got intimate with a subordinate LDO attorney."

Of course, Gunther was talking about the necking between Dean and Kat Franklin in the small dark hallway separating the men's and women's bathroom outside the ballroom where the Supreme Court held its annual Christmas Party. He remembered seeing Dawn Smith lurking near the entrance to the hallway as he and Kat had walked out from the shadows back there shortly after Kat had told him for the first time that what they were doing was wrong. That he was in love and had an obligation, a vow, to Laura. As she had done again last night.

"Got intimate," Dean said. "No, I don't deny it. We kissed each other."

"A Christmas kiss?" Margo asked.

He turned to her.

"No, Margo, not a Christmas kiss," Dean said. "A kiss.

We were both a little tipsy, and it just happened."

"Well," whispered Margo Anson-Clarke.

After a momentarily lull, Gunther mumbled several times that this was serious, very serious, seeming surprised that Dean had so easily admitted kissing Kat Franklin. He then went on for some minutes to repeat his previous allegations of wrong-doing that were apparently set forth in the memo they had given Dean.

Finally, Margo Anson-Clarke said, "I think we've belabored this enough, Brad."

Everyone fell silent for a time. Dean let the memo fall limply to his lap as he looked forlornly down at the crisp new tan carpet in Margo's office.

Finally, he looked up.

"I know I may have been distracted the last few weeks," he said. "But I have a lot of things going on in my life." He looked at Margo. She knew fully well what he was talking about.

But why was there even a need to explain himself. He had been an exemplary employee the past sixteen years, had honestly and fairly and consistently upheld the principles of the Lawyer Discipline Office to protect the public from dishonest and dysfunctional attorneys and thus uphold the integrity and public opinion of the legal community. Why was he being treated so shabbily?

"Look," Margo said. "We just thought you needed this session to let you know about the Court's concerns and Brad's concerns. Brad wants you to think things over and meet with him on Monday. Just you and him. See if this can be resolved, straightened out. If you can come to an understanding, a better professional relationship. Alright?"

Dean looked up and nodded. So he was going to have to suffer through the weekend not knowing whether he'd have a job on Monday?

"Sure," he said.

"We'll meet Monday morning," Gunther said. "See if we can put all this behind us."

Dean nodded.

"Take the rest of the day off," Margo said. "Consider it paid administrative leave."

"I have a respondent meeting this morning," Dean said.

"I already canceled it," Gunther said. "We think it's better for you, for all of us, for the office, if you take some time off."

"And then what?" Dean asked. "What happens Monday?"

"Then, Monday, we talk," Gunther said. "There are some other issues, more minor issues, we need to discuss."

Gunther stood, as did Margo, Pam, and Jenny. After a moment, Dean did as well. Gunther stepped forward and reached out his right hand and Dean shook it.

"We'll talk Monday morning," Gunther said. "See if we can work things out."

Dean nodded emptily, then turned and walked out of the office.

Dean came home to find Laura already passed out on the couch. After a quick change into shorts and a polo shirt that warm day, he drove to Foley's small, neat Cape Cod house in a northern suburb, arriving a few minutes short of

Noon. Ginny Foley greeted Dean at the side door with a curious frown. A cloth bathrobe was wrapped tightly around her considerable, sexless frame.

"He's still sleeping, Dean," Ginny said, but then in the next moment, from beyond the entrance foyer, Foley's gruff voice told them, "I'm up."

Ginny let Dean in and he and Foley, himself draped in an old bathrobe, went into the living room that was dark from the shades still drawn. Foley dropped onto the couch and rubbed his temples.

"Bastards fire you?" he asked.

Dean sat on an old, green loveseat and sighed.

"No," he said and sighed. "Almost, I guess or are about to. This morning, they were content with emasculation."

"I knew something was up when Herr Gunther wouldn't let you speak yesterday," he said. "What happened?"

Dean explained about the ambush while Foley laid back, closed his eyes and listened.

"Bastards," he said when Dean finished.

"See, you're right again, Stuey," Dean said. "There is no fucking justice in the world, just pricks making the rules and guys like me, puppets dancing on the strings of the fucking bastard puppet masters of the world."

Dean turned to Foley with a bleak look.

"And what goes around never ever comes around," he said.

Foley shrugged.

"You got that right, kid," he said.

"Just one thing," Dean said. "How do you think they knew about the Parlatto meeting?"

"I guess I underestimated that Polack, Mazurka," Foley said. "Ah, my aching head."

Chapter Twenty-Three
A Grand Mistake

A month after the ambush in the Chief Clerk's office, as Dean referred to it, now early September, he was still on the job. Eviscerated, effectively powerless, based on Gunther's various new office policy moves, but on the job nevertheless. For how long, he had no idea.

The power vacuum in the office had been promptly filled by Liza Hartman, Gunther's obvious pet despite her inexperience and, some would say, including Dean, Kat Franklin, and Foley, her general incompetence.

"Well, she's got better legs than you," Foley remarked during one of their twice weekly meetings at The Pub following his retirement. The week after Foley's retirement, Gunther had appointed Dawn Smith as the new LDO Chief Investigator and hired a young gal with an unremarkable resume as the third investigator. Then, in an obvious reduction of Dean's powers, he appointed Hartman as head of the investigators. They were to report directly to her on all job-related matters. Dean was out of the loop.

Another change came in the manner in which complaints were assessed and assigned. In the past, Dean had read every new complaint filed in the office, somewhere around twenty a day, and determined whether, on its face, giving every benefit of the doubt to the client, lawyer, judge or other third party making the complaint, to commence an investigation. Gunther ordered that a review of new complaints, and a decision as to what to do with them, was to be by consensus of the attorneys and investigators at weekly review meetings.

"So what's my fucking job?" Dean asked Foley at the corner of the bar in The Pub a few days after that policy changes had been implemented and communicated by Gunther via a tense staff meeting. It was around six o'clock and Foley had agreed to meet Dean after Dean had called around four telling Foley he'd had another long, bad day and needed a shoulder to cry on.

That morning, after meeting with Liza Hartman behind closed doors from nine to ten or so, Gunther had called Dean into his office and accused him of belittling the new secretary, Anna.

"It was a total bullshit lie," Dean told Foley. "But how am I supposed to defend against something like that. Lies against my character?"

"I don't know, bud," Foley said. "I think all you should do is listen. Keep a low profile and keep your head down and especially, keep your mouth shut. Bide your time. Certainly, don't trust anyone in that office, except, of course, Kat. And remember, you make the same money now as when you had more responsibility. But I know you. It's tough to live like that. With your head down all the time.

"And I know you want investigations handled right," Foley added after a moment while Dean looked away and contemplated his advice. "Thoroughly. Fairly."

Dean turned to him

"Fucking right," he said. "But that asshole, Herr Gunther, and his Frau, Liza, are on a mission to screw it all up and screw me in the process. They don't want us to go after attorneys. They want us to sweep things under the rug. Gunther's attitude is unless you murder your client, your ethics are just fine. He's just like the CJ in that respect. Do nothing to upset the apple cart, don't rock the boat. And Hartman is one hundred percent on their bandwagon."

"She's got aspirations," Foley said. "And she believes going aggressively after lawyers isn't going to get her them."

"What aspirations?"

"City Court," Foley said. "That's what I'm hearing on the street. And being on Gunther's side is being on the CJ's side, and that's a hell of a lot of ammunition in helping her get where she wants to go."

"Always fucking politics, eh, Stuey?"

"You got that right, boss," Foley said. "And another thing. Remember when I told you she has daddy issues? Well, Herr Gunther happens to fit her idea of what a man should be. Authoritative and cruel, but compliant and pandering when it comes to woman's rights. A true unmanly Hillary Democrat." He laughed and took a long sip of beer. "Liza's daddy left her mommy when she was like nine or ten or something. The short of it is, she hates a certain kind of man, and unfortunately for you, you happen to be among the kind of men she hates. And Herr Gunther isn't."

"There seem to be a lot of woman out there like that," Dean said.

He took a sip of his beer while Foley nodded, thought a minute, then looked at Dean

"Like I said, the one person you can trust in the office is Kat," he said and smiled. "I think she'd even take a bullet for you. Or take a bullet from you."

"Would you please quit it with that shit," Dean said. "For the hundredth time, no matter what, no matter how bad it gets, I'm still in love with Laura."

"Alright, alright," Foley said and patted Dean on the back, "I know you are. And I respect you for staying with her, living up to your marital vows. But sooner or later, doing that is going to wear you out." He sighed. "And I can tell however you feel about Laura, you feel something for Kat."

"Alright, Stuey," Dean said, "I hear you."

"My point is," Foley said, "you can trust Kat. You have at least one ally in the office. The rest of them will be looking out for themselves, and if that means screwing you, or even going so far as making up lies to fuel what they know Herr Gunther and Frau Hartman want to hear and are trying to do, they'll do it."

"Even Kathy Barnes?" Dean asked.

"Especially her," Foley said.

Dean had looked up to what was playing on the small TV on the shelf above the bar. It was on Channel 7, the local "eyewitness news" station, and there was a "breaking news" event being reported, with a young lady reporter standing in front of the Erie County Courthouse on Franklin Street speaking eagerly into a microphone.

"What's this?" Foley asked as he was now looking up at the TV as well.

"Hey, could you turn up the sound, Ed?" Dean asked the bartender. With a nod, the bored, big-nosed bartender, Ed, picked up the remote and scrolled up the volume until they could hear what the reporter was saying.

"So that's it from county court," she said. "To repeat, a decision has just been issued by Judge Corcoran dismissing the indictment against former first assistant district attorney, Susan Hines-Laurence. And apparently, that will end all proceedings against her in this controversial case involving a charge of voluntary manslaughter against this county's former number two law enforcement official. Sheila Douglas reporting, Dennis, live from the Erie County Courthouse."

"What?" Foley asked and took a sip of beer.

The news flipped back to Dennis Masterson, lead anchor for the six o'clock news, and he said, "Interesting development there, Sheila. I'm sure we'll be following this story in days to come." And that was it, he was on to the next story.

Dean took out his cell phone and started punching in a number.

"Who you calling?" Foley asked.

"Kat," Dean said. "She usually watches the news. Maybe she can tell us what the hell is going on."

Kat answered after the fourth ring.

"Dean? What's up?"

He told her where he was, and that he and Foley had just seen the end of a news story about the dismissal of the indictment against Hines-Laurence.

"What the hell happened?" he asked.

"Oh, you heard about it," Kat said. "Sounds like Larry Donnelly really screwed up. By some grand mistake in the grand jury, he immunized her. Her waiver of immunity was screwed up."

Dean thought about that for a time. He knew, of course, that under state criminal procedure law, someone who was the target of a grand jury proceeding that could lead to a criminal charge had the right to request an opportunity to testify before it. However, to avoid another part of state law immunizing witnesses testifying before a grand jury from prosecution for any crime about which they gave testimony, the target was required to sign a "waiver of immunity" form and, then before giving testimony, swear before the grand jury that he or she had done so. Therefore, signing the form was not enough. The target had to confirm that he or she had signed the form in the presence of the grand jurors.

Most importantly, if the waiver procedure was screwed up, which it was, according to cases, from time to time, the target would be immunized based upon his or her testimony on the crime or crimes under investigation. And if that happened, that target could never be prosecuted for the crime, or any related lesser crime, being considered for indictment by the grand jury in which he or she had testified.

"What did Donnelly do?" Dean asked. "Or forget to do?"

"He had her sign the waiver of immunity form outside the grand jury," Kat said, "you know, back in his office. But then, Donnelly forgot to have her swear before the grand jury that she had signed it. All he had was the damned form. And thus, he inadvertently conferred transactional immunity upon her."

Which meant, of course, Susie Hines couldn't be prosecuted for murdering her husband. She had been forever immunized.

A grand mistake indeed.

"How the hell could he do something as stupid as that?" Dean asked. "It's not like Donnelly's a rookie and never had a defendant testify before the grand jury."

"No," Kat said. "He's one of the DA's favorite sons, from what I hear. Because of who Donnelly's father is."

"Maybe it was accidentally on purpose then," Dean said.

"What?" Foley wanted to know what they were talking about and Dean took a minute to tell Foley what Kat had told him and what it meant.

"What do you mean, accidentally on purpose?" Kat asked.

"Think about it," Dean said.

Kat did just that, kept quiet and thought about it. What a perfect way for the DA to protect his lover from going to jail for a long time than by fixing it so that she was granted complete immunity from prosecution. This would literally help her to get away with murder.

"You really think that happened?" Kat asked. "If so, looks like you maybe should re-open you unofficial investigation against the DA. Assign Foley to it."

"Just what I need," Dean said.

"Ironically enough," Kat said, "know what an earlier story was before that news broke? The DA is being appointed to the Supreme Court taking over the Myers' vacancy."

"Are you kidding me?" Dean said. "Even after this?"

"Well, it wasn't his screw up," Kat said. "It was Donnelly's fault by messing up something so basic. How was the DA supposed to supervise that, see that coming? And how can someone read more into it than that?" Kat sighed. "Looks like it's another example of what Foley always says..."

Dean looked at Foley and finished for her by saying, "What goes around never comes around."

"You got that right," Foley said as he took one last swallow of beer.

Part Two
Comes Around

Vincent Scarsella

Chapter Twenty-Four
A Celebration

The loud popping of a cork off a champagne bottle late on that dark, cold afternoon in early December, and the laughter which suddenly bellowed from the CJ's chambers told the Chief Clerk of the Supreme Court, Margo Anson-Clarke, that the celebration had begun. Among the celebrants were the CJ, Sam Marcum, and Brad Gunther. What they were celebrating was Marcum's appointment by the Governor that very afternoon as Associate Justice of the Supreme Court. He was taking the seat vacated by the death of Associate Justice Myers, who had finally succumbed to bone cancer and been buried a week before Thanksgiving.

The CJ yelled out for Margo to join them back in his chambers for a champagne toast. After all, she had gone to Nason's Classic Liquor Store on Broadway Street to buy the seventy-five dollar bottle, generously paid for by the CJ. Perhaps, she thought, generosity had nothing to do with the gesture. Margo knew that Marcum's appointment, after the mess of last summer involving the dismissal of the murder indictment against Susan Hines-Laurence, was a personal triumph of the CJ's political skills that had gained him yet another ally in his relentless quest for the highest judicial office.

Margo hurried inside the CJ's chambers as he was pouring champagne into a long-stem crystal glass. She took it from him as he ushered her within the circle of celebrants. With her now standing among them, they raised their glasses for a toast.

"I give you the newest Associate Justice of the state Supreme Court," the CJ said, "the Honorable Samuel Daniel Marcum!"

"Here, here," they all said and took sips from their glasses.

It was just short of four months since the so-called, "Grand Mistake," in which ADA Larry Donnelly had now famously botched the waiver of indictment procedure resulting in the dismissal of the voluntary manslaughter indictment against Susan Hines-Laurence, now simply, Susie Hines, and barred forever her prosecution for the shooting death of her late husband. Ever since there had been whispers behind Sam Marcum's back among members of the Bar. Talk in the local courthouses, dark corners of bars where lawyers often gathered for beers and cocktails and gossip after work, in front of law firm water coolers, and other places where lawyers and followers tended to congregate, speculated if Donnelly's blunder – "The Grand Mistake" – had been intentional and at Marcum's direction. Most of the opinion fell on the side of intentional. Of course, the whispering only intensified when it was rumored that Donnelly was to be named as Associate Justice Marcum's confidential law clerk after his nomination for the appointment by the Governor was made known, which, with the CJ's backing, seemed like a sure thing.

"And here's to the end," Gunther said, raising his glass to offer his own toast, "of all that vicious gossip about you, Justice Marcum."

The CJ winced and Justice Marcum gave a weak smile. It had been a stupid thing to bring up during this celebration. A *faux pas* on Gunther's part to say the least.

Each of the celebrants took brief sips from their glasses.

"Once Sam is sworn in Monday morning, all that talk will cease to matter," the CJ said. He turned to Marcum, grinned and slapped his back. "It's a goddamn lifetime appointment."

Not, of course, the CJ thought to himself, and perhaps the others as well, including Marcum, if somebody was to prove that he had concocted the botched waiver of indictment plan, and bribed Donnelly with the confidential law clerk position for him to go through with it, in order to help his lover get out of a terrible jam. Or worse, that Marcum was somehow involved with Susan Hines-Laurence in the plot to murder her rich, much older husband. Not even a murderer can remain a Supreme Court associate justice.

Of course, the CJ was ever mindful of the damage that would be done to his reputation should Marcum be implicated in something as sinister and scandalous as that, in light of the fact that he had pushed so hard to get Marcum on the Supreme Court. His lack of judgment in supporting such an obviously disreputable and terrible man would surely be mentioned, highlighted in fact, and probably scuttle his rise to higher judicial office. It might even require lead to calls for his resignation from his current, much-coveted office.

But on that afternoon, the CJ joined with Gunther and Marcum and the Chief Clerk in hailing, "Here, here," and drank up whatever champagne was left in his glass.

After Margo poured them each another half glass, the CJ grabbed Marcum by the elbow and gently tugged toward the back of his chambers. Gunther remained speaking with Margo, asking about her recent vacation to Ireland.

"You sent in your recommendation for Brad for DA with the Governor's office, haven't you?" the CJ asked.

"Of course," Marcum said. "A week ago. Once we got by that last hurdle after I thought he was gonna back out of our agreement."

"Yeah, the Governor," CJ said. "He can be a bit too careful sometimes."

"Should be a cake-walk for him next November," the CJ said. "Brad makes a pretty good impression, speaks well in front of a crowd, even though, deep down, he's a complete asshole."

The CJ laughed to himself as he looked over at Gunther chatting with Margo while Marcum raised his glass in salute, signifying his complete agreement.

"But I have to say," Marcum said, "that suggestion he gave me last summer to take the heat off was a master-stroke."

"Don't know anything about it," the CJ said.

"Sure," Marcum said with a laugh, "even though it was a case you decided, what six years ago, that Brad cited to me.

People versus Oliver." Marcum sipped from his glass of champagne. "You made the law that got Susan off."

"Well, she's innocent, isn't she?" the CJ asked. He quickly looked away, as if not interested in seeing Marcum's expression in response. After a sigh, the CJ looked back at Marcum.

"Isn't she?"

Marcum frowned, nodded. The CJ edged closer to Marcum and looked squarely up at him.

"You're not still seeing her, are you, Sam?" he asked.

"Not officially," Marcum said. "But…"

"Not officially? Don't be a damn fool," the CJ said. "I told you that thinking with your small dick instead of your small brain will only get you into big trouble."

Marcum swallowed, thought about that, nodded. It was true, the CJ certainly had a way with words.

"Just be careful whatever you do," the CJ said. "Go slow. Now is not the time for anyone to find out that you're currently dorking little miss Hines, no matter how good she looks in tight pants." He sighed, turned sideways, staring again at Gunther and Margo talking away. "Did she get her money from his estate?"

"Not yet," Marcum said. "But she's hired Ed Grayson."

"Master of Darkness," the CJ said and they both laughed.

"Yes, him," Marcum said. "They're working out a settlement as we speak. She'll make out alright. Not the whole thing, but she never wanted or expected that. Laurence's sister, Jeanne, will still get the bulk of it. So she's happy."

"What's going on with the life insurance?"

"Bastards are fighting it for now," Marcum said. "Calling it suspicious, but she knows what they mean. Grayson's fighting that front as well. Another decent settlement. Half a mil isn't too shabby."

"Sounds like you know way too much, Sam," the CJ said. "Mind what I say. I were you, I'd stay away from her. For now, anyway. Give it a frigging year. Let the dust settle. Plus, consider your wife. She's a good gal."

Marcum smirked, nodded. The CJ knew that Marcum's loyal, fat old wife was no substitute for Susie Hines.

After a moment, the CJ looked back at Gunther and Margo.

"I think old Gunther will make a decent DA," he said. "And perhaps a better US Attorney."

Marcum laughed. "Look at you," he said. "Already figuring how that'll help you get up to SCOTUS."

"Scotus?" the CJ said. "Not just Scotus. The Chief Justice."

Marcum raised his glass and toasted the CJ, then drank, just as Gunther walked over.

"I have to get back," he told the CJ. "I'm meeting with Dean Alessi."

"You haven't figured out a way to get rid of that guy?" Marcum asked. "Following me like that, and maybe still following me."

"Yes, it is troubling," the CJ told Marcum, answering for Gunther. "But our rules make it difficult to fire people. After all, he's been with the LDO for what, sixteen years?"

"Well, let's just say," Gunther told them both, "I'm building a case."

"You know," the CJ said and smiled, "sometimes it's good having guys like Dean Alessi around to keep us on our toes, if not completely honest."

They laughed at that and the CJ held up what was left in his champagne glass for a final toast as Gunther and Marcum raised their glasses as well. Margo saw what was going on and she came over and raised her glass.

"To Dean Alessi," the CJ said.

"Here, here," they said and drank their champagne.

Chapter Twenty-Five
Foley's Unofficial Investigation: Part I

At around eleven on a blistery cold Monday night in early January about a month later, just after all the buzz and cheer had fizzled out of the holidays, Dean was awakened by someone ringing his front doorbell, then banging at the door. He had fallen asleep on the couch watching a west coast hockey game after putting Laura to bed.

He pushed himself off the couch with a groan and wobbled over to the front door. Peeking out of the curtains along the long side window of the door, he saw Stu Foley shivering out there with his back to him.

"What the?" Dean mumbled to himself. He switched on the front porch light and opened the door to the smell of winter and a gust of icy wind.

"Stuey? What the hell?"

Foley turned around and the light focusing upon him showed that he was not only cold and shivering but really banged up. There was a red welt on his left cheekbone and one along the bridge of his left eye. A fresh cut with blood still oozing was open across his forehead. Under his left eye, a definite red and purple bruise was growing.

"What the hell happened to you?"

"That bastard Stan Mazurka happened to me, that's what," Foley said. "You gonna let me in or let me freeze to death out here."

"Yeah, sure," Dean said. "Come on in."

A cold gust blew a sheet of icy snow particles off the surface of the front lawn up onto and across the porch as Dean stepped outside momentarily and helped Foley into his warm foyer. He led him into the kitchen and sat him down at the kitchen table. Then, Dean got a plastic sandwich bag out of a drawer and stuffed it with ice cubes from the fridge. He handed it to Foley and watched him wince as he placed it flush against the left side of his face.

"You want some coffee?" Dean asked. "Whiskey?"

"Whiskey," Foley said.

Dean went over to the pantry and grabbed a bottle of bourbon. He pulled some glasses out of the cupboard and poured himself and Foley three knuckles worth.

"So what the hell happened?" Dean asked as he handed Foley the glass and sat down next to him at the table.

"Bastard cold-cocked me," Foley said.

Foley took a sip of the bourbon and winced again.

"What bastard? Mazurka?"

"Yeah, that bastard."

"Why? Where were you?" Dean asked, taking a short sip from his glass followed by a wince of his own.

"Following his boss," Foley said. "I slipped up again tonight, I guess, didn't notice him. I was in the parking lot of the Marriot over on Maple Road, the one in Amherst, using my cell phone to take a picture of the license plate of Marcum's Lexus.

"Fifteen minutes before that, I had followed Marcum driving the Lexus into the lot. He parked in a spot a few down from that slut, Susie Hines, who was already there, waiting for him with her car idling to keep warm from the cold. When Marcum arrived, she turned off the car and got out. Without even acknowledging him, she walked straight ahead into the hotel lobby. He followed a few paces behind, and I followed a few paces behind him. Once inside the lobby, I saw Marcum go up to the desk clerk and get a room. Then, after getting the room, he strolled to the elevators where Susie Hines was waiting. They got in and rode up. What room they shared, I have no idea. But I'm certain they shared a room."

Foley sighed, grimacing as he pressed the makeshift ice bag against the left side of his face, and took another sip from his glass.

"There was no use waiting there in the hotel lobby," Foley went on, "so I went back to the parking lot and started snapping pictures of their cars and license plates. While I was taking a picture of Marcum's, Mazurka must've snuck up behind me and, as I was checking out the pics I had just taken, blasted me with a right hook from out of nowhere across the left side of my face. I went down like a sack of potatoes. I thought I was back in the ring from my glass jaw days boxing in the Marine Corps. Anyway, by the time I got my senses back, Mazurka had lifted my cell phone and taken off."

"You're sure it was him?" Dean asked. "Mazurka? You saw him?"

"Not exactly," Foley said. "I mean, like I said, he snuck up behind me and co-cocked me. And the parking lot was dark."

"But you saw Marcum and Susan Hines," Dean said. "You're sure of that."

"Yes," Foley said. "Them, I saw. Sure as the day is long."

"And then what?"

"And then what, what?" Foley asked.

"What did you see after getting punched?" Dean asked. "Did you see Marcum and Susie Hines come out together? Get back in their cars?"

"No," he said. "Their cars stayed put. They had just gone up to the room. It was going to be a quickie, no doubt, but not that quick. I wasn't feeling so good after just getting smacked, if you can understand that, so I came here." He sighed and sipped some more of his drink. "I almost passed out on the way. Plus, it had started snowing again. I'm so fucking sick of this shit-ass cold weather. I should buy me a condo on the beach in Florida, is what I should do."

"Jesus, Stuey," Dean said. "What the hell you following them for anyway?"

Foley sighed.

"Couple reasons," he said. "First, because I'm getting paid to do it. Second, boss, you may have closed your unofficial case against the DA, but I haven't. And I don't have to. And the next time Stan Mazurka co-cocks me will be the last time that mother-fucker does anything."

"You're getting paid to do what?" Dean asked. "Who's paying you?"

213

"Jeanne Forster," he said. "Kent Laurence's sister."

"What? How the hell did that happen?"

Foley lowered the ice pack, closed his eyes and cursed. Dean noticed the welt under his left eye, that it was getting purplish already.

Then, Foley took a breath and continued the story.

"Well, I contacted the sister a few weeks back," he said. "I mean, I was always curious why the family didn't make more of a fuss about the botched prosecution of Susie Hines. What I found out, first of all, was that Kent Laurence didn't have much of a family. His older brothers, who actually started the family real estate business with their father, were dead. All he had left was a sister, Jeanne, a couple years younger than him.

"And according to her, she and Kent had never been close. Kent was a fun-loving kind of guy, easy going, shiftless, I think she called him. She said he went through the motions of helping her and his brothers run the family business, but his heart was never into it. He was doing it for the money and that's about it. So when their brothers died, about five or so years ago, he told her he had no interest in keeping the business running. He'd take his one-half share of whatever it was worth, at least ten million by then, and she could do with her half what she wanted. That pissed her off, his lack of loyalty to the family name, to what their father and his brothers had built. So after that, she didn't want much to so with him.

"And when he married Susie Hines, she laughed in his face. She told him flat out that it was another of a long string of stupid things he did while going through a long, drawn out mid-life crises. Sister Jeanne remains convinced that Susie Hines never loved him, and worse than that, probably killed him to get out of the marriage and get her hands on his money.

"In their one and only face-to-face meeting a couple days after the shooting, Susie cried and begged the sister to believe that Kent's shooting had been a terrible accident. She even implied that it had been mostly Kent's fault. He had handed her the pistol after a couple or three too many glasses of wine (even though the toxicology report could find no evidence of alcohol in his bloodstream), and during the exchange, it went off, striking him square on the left side of the chest, severing the aortic artery, killing him instantly.

"Through her tears, or 'alligator tears,' the sister called them, Susie had told Jeanne Forster that she had never fired a gun in all her life before that night and that Kent should never have handed it to her so carelessly, joking around like that, half-drunk, with the safety off. It just went off and afterward dropped to the floor where the police found it. She even had the nerve to tell the sister that she could have been the one to have gotten shot and killed."

"And the sister doesn't believe any of it," Dean broke in, "that it was a tragic accident."

"Not a word," Foley said. "She thinks it was cold-blooded murder. And she further thinks Sam Marcum's involved in it."

"So why didn't she pursue anything?" Dean asked. "Raise a stink."

"Because she saw the writing on the wall," Foley said. "She saw that fighting city hall was a losing proposition. And, she had personal, political reasons of her own to keep quiet.

"Plus, Susie was smart and didn't get greedy going after Kent Laurence's estate," Foley continued. "Susie's lawyers were not all that aggressive in seeking what she was legally due from Kent Laurence's estate. Still, she ended up with a pretty penny, three and a quarter million dollars, from what Jeanne Forster told me, setting her up on easy street for the rest of her life, a damned good nest egg. But sister Jeanne got the bulk of her brother's estate, something like nine million. That took the edge off the botched prosecution, I guess."

Foley raised the ice pack to the left side of his face and winced again.

"Jesus, that smarts," he said.

"But you said something else had to do with it as well," Dean said. "The sister's lack of interest. Something personal. Political reasons. What's that about?"

"Well," Foley said, "it seems that Jeanne Forster has a son, Brett. It seems that Brett finished law school a couple years back and, after flunking the bar exam a couple times, he was in desperate need of a friend in high places who might have some influence on the Council of Bar Examiners."

"Marcum did that? He pulled some strings?"

"Not Marcum," Foley said. "The CJ."

"Krane?" Dean was frowning. "Why…?"

"Why do you think why? To help out his old buddy and now sworn ally, Sam Marcum. Despite this mess, he got Marcum on the Supreme Court, to become another of his minions, and now is in the process in getting Herr Gunther appointed as the new DA."

"That's really happening?" Dean asked. "I heard that

rumor, too."

"It's no rumor, from what I understand," Foley said, "And it should happen in short order, a few weeks. That should be good news for you, no? Herr Gunther will finally be off your back."

"I may not last until he's gone," Dean said, "which won't be until March from what I'm hearing. That's a plum job, and several factions have come out pushing their own boys. And you know how the Governor's office obsesses over such things."

Dean sighed.

"Anyway, at the office, every day is a different crisis," Dean went on. "Another claimed lack of judgment on my part, another one-sided, high tension meeting between Gunther and me, during which I have to do everything in my power to stop myself from slugging him. In short, with each passing day, I am another step closer out the door."

"Wish there was something I could do about that, boss," he said.

Dean finished off his glass of bourbon and shrugged as he clinked the ice around the bottom of the glass.

"Me, too," Dean said.

Foley put the ice pack down on the kitchen table and sighed. Both he and Dean thought about things for a while.

"But I still don't see what you're talking with Kent Laurence's sister has to do with you being in the parking lot of the Marriot," Dean said, "taking photos of Sam Marcum's Lexus."

"Well, I told you," Foley said, "I'm getting paid to do it – by Kent Laurence's sister. Not out her love for Kent, but out of her own self-interest.

"During my call with her a few weeks back, I happened to mention that I was retired from my government job but still doing part-time PI work. At some point during the call, literally from out of the blue, she asked if I'd like to take on a new client – her. And the job she hired me for was to try and make a civil case of murder against Sam Marcum and Susie Hines.

"Susie Hines has immunity and so is untouchable criminally. But Marcum isn't, so there was that. But, the larger reward for her was getting back the three point five million dollars that Susie Hines got from her brother's estate. And, of course, some justice for her brother, despite his shortcomings. To do that, I need to somehow prove that Marcum and Susie Hines plotted to murder Kent, pulled it off, and then plotted so that she would gain immunity from prosecution for it."

"So how have you earned your retainer from Jeanne Forster so far?" Dean asked. "Other than taking a fist to the side of your face, that is? What have you proved except that Sam Marcum is screwing Susie Hines on a regular basis using a room at the Marriot Hotel on Maple Street? Or stated another way, what proof have you uncovered, Stuey, that Marcum and Susie Hines conspired to murder Kent Laurence, pulled it off, and then, covered it up?"

Foley shrugged defensively, then, after putting the ice pack, now greatly melted back against the left side of his forehead, he hardened his gaze.

"Well, I admit, not much," he said. "I mean, except for confirming tonight, and on a few other nights before this, what we already know, that Marcum and Susie Hines are having an affair. And from what Parlatto told us, that the affair has been ongoing for quite some time, even before Kent Laurence was murdered."

"Sounds like you're no further along than you were during your unofficial investigation for the LDO," Dean said. He thought a moment, then asked, "You really believe that Susie Hines murdered Kent Laurence and that Marcum was involved in it?"

Foley looked across at Dean with an intent frown.

"Yes," he said, "that's exactly what I believe. Susie Hines murdered her husband, and Marcum was part of it right from the start. I mean, look what Parlatto told us, he and Susie were lovers going back at least a couple years before the shooting. You don't think in all their secret trysts in dark, steamy cheap motel rooms, or in some nook in Randolph Park, they didn't talk about being together without Kent Laurence hovering over everything they did, making them have to sneak around? Not to mention all that money he had, and getting their hands on at least a part of his fortune."

Foley sighed, felt his left eye and winced.

"Of course they talked about it," Foley continued. "And somewhere along the way, all that talk morphed into a plan. And then, the plan became reality. Maybe, not as they originally drew it up. She'd shoot Kent Laurence, and then her lover, the DA, would simply tell the world that there was no proof that it was murder. He'd close the file based on a nothing investigation and nobody would ever be the wiser. The public would forgot about whatever controversy it caused in the next news cycle.

"But to his surprise, people didn't forget and the whispers didn't go away. And then, the following week, there was even a Buffalo News editorial questioning why the investigation had been closed.

"But his ole pal Brad Gunther gave our former DA a way out of any disciplinary, and more importantly, criminal scrutiny. That was during the meeting I followed the DA to, that meeting at The Pub the night before Gunther's first day on the job as LDO Director.

"And, as we both now know," Foley went on, "that way out involved putting a case against Susie Hines before a grand jury. But instead of getting a no bill, as might have been expected, Marcum took even more of the heat off himself by having his crony, Larry Donnelly, get the grand jury to indict his former first assistant for manslaughter.

"But, as our story further goes, or at least as mine does," Foley said, "Marcum persuaded Larry Donnelly to intentionally botch the waiver of indictment procedure so that Susie would end up being immunized, accidentally on purpose, sort of speak, and thus go scot-free. And the persuasion involved a promise that once he became a Supreme Court Associate Justice, good old Larry would become his confidential law clerk, a cushy little lifetime appointment, with a decent pay and plenty of lifetime perks.

"So now, Susie Hines had become forever untouchable, as far as being prosecuted for the shooting death of her dearly departed husband, Kent Laurence."

Dean took a sip of his bourbon and, after a laugh, said, "So you think you got it all figured out, do you? That's quite a neat theory you've come up with, you know that, Stuey?"

"Yeah, I do, except it's not a theory," Foley said. "It's the truth. Like Sun Tzu said…"

"And I said, no more Sun Tzu bullshit," Dean said. "And no, it's not a fact. Right now, all you got is a plot in a crime novel, even a good crime novel maybe. Fiction. When you get some proof, then it becomes a fact."

Foley shrugged. He grimaced again as he stuck the watered down ice pack to his face.

"Yeah, you're right, boss," he said. "And as is the way of the world, where justice never wins out, that's probably all I'll ever have. Fiction. The basis for a good novel."

Dean shrugged, but then, after a moment, he gave Foley a hopeful look.

"Or maybe for once in your life," he said. "It'll come around."

Foley shrugged unenthusiastically and, holding the ice pack firmly to his face, muttered, "Bastards."

Chapter Twenty-Six
Foley's Unofficial Investigation: Part II

A week later, Foley called Dean at work and asked if he'd meet him out for dinner at Scianno's. He had more to tell him about his now "former" DA Sam Marcum investigation. "A new development," he claimed.

It was Tuesday evening so Scianno's wasn't all that busy and even Enrico Scianno had taken the night off. The hostess settled them into a quiet corner table and a server brought them hot Italian bread and rolls and a plate of garlic infused olive oil to spread on them. She also brought them a carafe of the house Chianti.

"So what's your news?" Dean asked as he dipped a hunk of bread into the olive oil.

"Monday, I interviewed Detective Jack Miller of the Manchester PD."

Dean shrugged as he chewed with his head bent over the plate of olive oil.

"He headed their homicide division," Foley explained. "He retired around the same time as me."

Dean shrugged and as he dipped another hunk of bread into the olive oil, said, "So?"

"So he handled the Laurence shooting," Foley said.

Dean looked up, his mouth open.

"Oh," he said, then shrugged before shoving more olive oil dipped crusty bread into his mouth. "And?"

"Well," Foley said, "let me tell it to you."

Dean sat back and waited.

"Anyway," Foley continued, "Last week, I finally got ahold of a copy of the Manchester PD police report of the Laurence shooting after putting in the request just after his sister hired me. Jack Miller personally prepared it, not one of the junior detectives under him. The report didn't say much we didn't already know. Frantic 911 call from Susie Hines around nine at night. Says someone's been shot. She's hysterical. A squad car races out to the Laurence mansion. She greets them at the front door, still hysterical, jabbering on about how it was an accident. Blood, still wet, was noted on the front of her blouse and at first, the patrol officers thought she was the one who was shot.

"But after showing them otherwise, she leads them upstairs and they find Kent Laurence sprawled out on the master bedroom floor. He's in his boxers, no shirt. The gun, a Ruger SP101 double action revolver, is on the floor a couple feet from the body. The officers note a gaping gunshot wound to the chest. They take his pulse, find nothing, just as an ambulance is pulling up to the house. All the while, Susie Hines is crying and blabbering on off to the side that he was showing her the gun when it went off. That he'd been drinking. That he was screwing around. That it was an accident.

"The EMTs rush in and take the body to the hospital, and as we know, poor Kent Laurence is DOA. More cops arrive, as did Detective Miller. They spread some yellow tape around the master bedroom and lock down the scene until their forensic guys arrive and start taking samples of this and that, measurements, photographs, all the usual.

"Susie is taken downstairs, to the front living room and Miller gives her her rights. But she keeps talking, telling him it was an accident. That Kent had handed her the gun, that she hated guns, that it went off. She even kept talking when Miller started tape-recording her. Somewhere along the way, he figures out who she is, the first assistant district attorney, and notes that in the report.

"And that was pretty much it," Foley said. "At least, according to the report."

Foley stared off and shrugged.

"What, Stuey?"

"I don't know," he said. "That report, it just seems like there was something missing. It just kind of trails off. Susie Hines gives her statement, sticking to the accidental shooting story, Miller confers with the Chief of Police, the Chief of Police calls the DA, and they decide not to make an arrest. They buy her story for the time being until the forensic guys finish their analysis of the crime scene. See if they find something inconsistent, that sort of thing. She's allowed to go back up into the bedroom and pack some things, under the watchful eye of Detective Miller, of course. And then she heads off to a hotel for the night.

"I also got the forensic report, the one Donnelly must

have used to get her indicted. Some junior medical examiner from the County crime lab opined that the bullet wound, you know, the trajectory and all that, plus the blood splatter evidence, didn't jibe with Susie Hines' story. The opinion was overlaid with a lot of probables, nothing all that definite. But Donnelly must have played that up big in the grand jury to get them to indict."

"Well, like they say," Dean said, "you can indict a ham sandwich in the grand jury."

Their server returned to take their orders interrupting Foley for the moment. He ordered his favorite, chicken parm, and Dean asked for the spaghetti plate, regular house sauce, and two meatballs. He loved Scianno's sauce and meatballs.

"So was the hotel she went to the same Marriot where you got bopped by Mazurka," Dean said. "By the way, you're looking a lot better than the other night."

Foley shrugged and continued, "Yeah, a lot better. But I still owe that Mazurka a punch in the nose. Or worse."

"If it was him," Dean said. "Maybe it was a mugger."

"And he took only my shit-ass cell phone I'd been using to take pictures of the DA's car? I had a hundred dollars in my wallet."

It was Dean's turn to shrug.

"So was it?" Dean asked. "The same hotel? The Marriot?"

"I have no idea," he said. "Mrs. Hines-Laurence packs and leaves the house, goes to a hotel. End of report."

"And the rest is history," Dean said with a shrug. "No justice in the world."

"You got that right."

"So you started by saying you interviewed Detective Miller," Dean said. "How did that come about?"

"I called him up," he said. "He was crabby about it but agreed to meet me at a Denny's near his house. I bought him breakfast and we chatted. Well, I'll bill the breakfast to Jeanne Forbes."

"You're still on her payroll, then," Dean said.

"Why not?" Foley said. "She's got nothing to lose paying me a few bucks to sniff around and a whole lot to gain."

"So you get anything from your chat with Detective Miller?" Dean asked.

"Other than an impression?" Foley said. "No."

"An impression of what?" Dean asked.

"An impression that the end of the police report is missing something," he said. "And that Miller is bothered by whatever it's missing."

"And what gave you that impression?"

"Miller," he said. "Not what he said, but how he said it. The way he looked, or couldn't look at me. Actually, he looked like hell. His hair uncombed, stubble on his chin, barely out of the bathrobe kind of look to him."

"Isn't that the way all retired guys look, Stuey?" Dean asked, dipping another hunk of bread in the olive oil spread. "Look at you."

Foley dipped his own bread and smirked.

"Funny," he said.

Then, Dean asked, "Why would Miller lie?"

"You have to ask?" Foley said. "Money, politics."

"I thought you had new developments?' Dean said.

"Looks like another dead end to me. And it looks like you're paid for investigation is going just about as good as the LDO's unofficial investigation."

"Looks like," Foley said. "Unless…"

He trailed off and bit into his hunk of bread dripping with the olive spread.

"Unless what?" Dean asked.

Finally, Foley looked up at him.

"Unless Miller has a conscience," he said.

Chapter Twenty-Seven
Falling Down

A week later, Dean came home from work to find Laura sprawled out sideways at the bottom of the basement stairs. She had been doing laundry drunk and had slipped and fallen carrying a basket full of clothes smacking the side of her head on the cement floor. Dean had no idea how many stairs she had fallen down. The laundry basket had been launched as she fell with the dirty shirts and jeans and shorts and underwear scattered under and around her.

She was still unconscious when Dean lifted her off the floor and secured her one hundred ten pound frame in his arms. Laura remained out as Dean carried her upstairs and out the side door and into his car. Ten minutes later, he pulled into the ER ramp of Sisters of Mercy Hospital and an orderly helped pull Laura out of the backseat and into a wheelchair. A young doctor and several nurses worked on her almost immediately after she was placed on a gurney in one of the ER cubicles.

"What happened?" the ER doc asked Dean as he

focused a light into her eyes. One of the nurses was cleaning a scrape on her forehead.

"She fell down the cellar stairs," Dean said.

"Really?" the doc said as he switched off the light and looked back at Dean.

Dean didn't like the implication of that, as if he was a wife-beater.

"Look, she's an alcoholic," he told the doctor. "She was washing clothes. She fell down the fucking stairs."

After a moment, the doctor nodded.

"We'll have to x-ray her," he said. "Rule out a fracture."

After a few minutes, they took her up to radiology while Dean waited in her ER cubicle. Half an hour later, they wheeled her back. The ER doc came back and told him there was no fracture, just a bad bruise to the head. The fall had knocked her out, given her a concussion.

Dean nodded, relieved. But he was also ashamed of himself for the hopeful thought that had passed through his mind when he first saw her sprawled on the cellar floor at the bottom of the cellar stairs that maybe she was dead.

The ER doc told Dean that her injuries were bad enough to admit her for the night. He also talked to Dean about her drinking. It was now clear to him, after working on Laura, that she had consumed quite a few drinks throughout that day before falling down the stairs.

"This may be the time to get her into rehab," he said.

"She's already been through that," Dean said. "As you can see, it didn't work."

"Maybe this time, it will."

Dean knew the spiel by heart. Alcoholism was a bad

disease and it often took several times before the person hit rock bottom worse than the time before for a person to gather the will and strength to beat it if it didn't kill him or her first. He also knew that spiel from the Lawyers' Helping Lawyers bar association group that sometimes got involved with one of the many alcoholic lawyers who started neglecting clients' cases or showing up to court drunk and decided it was better getting help than losing their law license. But he was tired of such talk right now. It demonstrated a weakness he didn't feel like tolerating.

"And maybe it won't," he said.

It took a couple hours to get Laura a bed. By then, Dean had called Laura's older sister, Cindy, and she finally made it to the hospital. Cindy blamed Dean for Laura's "downfall," as she called it, as if it had nothing to do with the death of Steven. Perhaps, she blamed Dean for Steven's death as well. Bad genetics or something. Cindy certainly blamed him for allowing Laura to have fallen down so deep into depression that she tried to drive it away through drink.

Cindy coldly greeted Dean in the waiting area off the main lobby and they went upstairs to Laura's room without saying a word to each other. Laura had been secured into her bed with vinyl straps. Her face was swollen and bruised and there was an IV pricked into her right arm. Cindy started crying as she stood staring down at her sister. Finally, as she bent down at her bed and kissed Laura, she gave Dean a hurtful, sideways glance. He ignored it.

Laura was out of it, snoring gently now.

"What are you going to do?" Cindy asked.

"They suggested Lakeview Manor again," he said.

"Another thirty-day program."

"Think she'll go?"

Dean shrugged. Maybe the fall would convince her she needed help. Maybe it wouldn't.

They stayed another half hour and then left together. By then, it was nine o'clock. Cindy offered a curt goodbye in the lobby and told him to call her if anything changed and keep her informed as to Laura's rehab. He said he would and watched her walk away.

He sighed and thought the last place he wanted to go was back home. There was a mess of clothes strewn along the cellar floor that needed to be picked up, and perhaps some of Laura's blood as well that needed to be scrubbed. But that would have to wait.

He dug into the pocket of his suit pants and found his cell phone. He clicked to the contacts list and found Kat's number. Then, after an indeterminable time, trembling, he pressed the call button.

An hour later, he was naked under the covers of Kat's bed. She lay next to him.

"I can't believe I let this happen," Kat said after a time.

"I did too," Dean said, and let go of short, mirthless laugh.

"It's not funny, Dean," she said. "This is wrong on so many levels."

"I'm not laughing," he said. "I appreciate how wrong it is."

But still, right then, it felt right.

"This cannot happen again," Kat said in a determined

way that somehow lacked confidence. "You're married. Your wife is sick."

"She's beyond sick," Dean said. "She's killing herself."

"Well, this certainly won't help with that."

"It's helping me," he said and turned to her. "It's helping me."

She turned to him and stared into his eyes.

"It's helping me, too," she finally said with a wisp of a breath leaving her lips.

They leaned forward into each other and kissed for a time.

"I'm falling in love with you, Kat," Dean said. "I – I am in love with you."

Kat said nothing.

"Kat?"

"It's not right, Dean," she said. That stubborn wall had risen again. "Bad timing or something. This should never have happened between us. What's worse, we can't take it back."

After a time, she fell onto her back.

"You should go," she said.

He let out a frustrated groan, lifted himself up and out of the bed. He quickly dressed and was on his way out of Kat's bedroom as he plucked his cell phone out of this pants and looked down at it to see if anyone had called. There was one missed call, but not from the hospital, or Cindy, thank God, or Stu Foley. It was from his father's nursing home. There was no message.

Dean frowned. That was all he needed to complete this rotten day. His father sick, depressed, whatever. He pressed the call-back button and waited. Finally, after several rings, the night receptionist answered. Dean introduced himself. She sounded funny as she repeated his name, "Yes, Mister Alessi," and then quickly said she that the head nurse needed to talk to him.

"Is something wrong with my father?"

Moments later, the head nurse was on the phone.

After a moment, she told him in an even, stark voice: "Your father passed away."

He had died in his sleep sometime in the early evening, sometime after dinner. Upright, in his wheelchair, with the TV blaring Jeopardy. It had been a peaceful death, the nurse added as if that mattered. He could come in any time that evening to see the body. However, at some point, it would have to be delivered to the morgue. Of course, he'd have to make funeral arrangements.

"Dean?" Kat asked.

She had put on a bathrobe and was now herself out of bed, standing behind him. He turned around in the middle of the bedroom and gave her a sad, shocked look.

"It's my father," he said. A moment later, he started crying. "He's dead."

Kat stepped forward and took him into her arms. After a time, he settled down and told her the details. That he had died in his sleep. In his wheelchair. Then, he laughed and thought, watching Jeopardy.

Dean bowed his head, fell into Kat's left shoulder, and let her hold him.

After a time, she whispered, "Dean?"

He looked up at her.

"I think I love you, too," she told him.

Chapter Twenty-Eight
Foley's Unofficial Investigation: Part III

Two days after the funeral for Dean's father, Foley called.

"How you doing, boss?"

"I'm okay," Dean said. "Going back to work tomorrow. I guess even Herr Gunther will have to be nice to me for a few days before he starts up with his bullshit again."

"Any word on that job thing you mentioned at the wake?" Foley said.

"Not yet," Dean said.

"With the tax department or something, you said, right?"

"Yeah. The tax department," Dean said. "They need an investigative attorney. You know, to chase tax cheats. Only thing is, the job pays ten grand less than the LDO."

"Geez." Foley sighed. "So how's Laura doing?"

"Initial reports, fine," Dean said. "Adjusting, doing what's required. The usual drill, I guess. I'm going down to see her Saturday."

"Well, tell her hello from me," Foley said.

"Sure, thing, Stuey," Dean said. "Well, thanks for calling. Appreciate it."

"Hold on," he said. "There's something else. A possible break in my DA investigation."

"Geez, Stu," Dean said, "I thought it was a dead end. Justice lost."

"No, listen," he said. "This may be the break we've been waiting for."

"We've?" Dean said. "You've. It's the break you've been waiting for. I want nothing to do with it."

"But listen, that Detective Miller called me late last night," Foley said.

"He did?"

"Yeah, around midnight, in fact. He sounded a bit tipsy. Said he's been thinking about our talk about the Laurence shooting, that he needs to get something off his chest."

"Really," Dean said.

"Yeah, really," Foley continued. "I told you I had a feeling about him. That he was holding something back and it was screwing up his mind. He wants to meet with me this evening, around six or so. Said he's got a cabin down in Alleghany County, near the town of Bliss, wherever the hell that is. I asked if it was alright if you came along with me."

"Bliss?" Dean asked. "That's like an hour and a half drive, isn't it? Up in the hills, and in this weather...'

"Yes, but..."

"To find out what?"

"I don't know," Foley said. "But I'm telling you the guy sounded weird."

Dean sighed. Bliss.

"Alright," he said. "But just make sure that Mazurka's not following you. That would be the straw that broke the camel's back for sure if Herr Gunther got wind I was still sniffing around all that, especially now that Marcum's an associate justice of the Supreme Court."

"No, I'll take care of old Stanley," Foley said. "Although he does tail me from time to time. I'm gonna make it so that he can't do that tonight without me knowing about it."

"Look," Dean said, "I don't want to know. Just make sure…"

"Yeah, yeah," Foley said, "calm down, boss. I got it all under control. I'll pick you up around four-thirty sharp."

The cabin was a beat-up, old A-frame about a half mile off the state highway on ten acres of prime hunting land with a decent-sized creek splitting its north corner. It was long past dark by the time Dean and Foley got out there, deep in the silent dead of winter. Dean was even more apprehensive about driving out there that evening as the weather man had reported that there was likely to be snow flurries or possibly even squalls drifting down on them as the night wore on with the wind shifting to the southeast over Lake Erie. Lake effect, they called it, and there could be a couple feet of snow dropped in a narrow band once it lifted all that moisture off the warm lake into a cold mass of air moving over it. As it was, winter had come weeks ago to these hills inland from the lake and there were one or two-foot drifts in some spots along the hills.

On the ride down, Foley and Dean heard a curious report on the five o'clock news, "another twist," the anchor had called it, in the tragic Kent Laurence shooting. Former DA, now Supreme Court Associate Justice Sam Marcum, was divorcing his wife of thirty years and was rumored to be engaged to his former first assistant district attorney, Susan Hines, formerly, Susan Hines-Laurence. Of course, the anchor added that former Assistant District Attorney, Larry Donnelly, and now Judge Marcum's confidential law clerk, had botched the waiver of indictment procedure which not only led to the dismissal of the "murder" charge against Hines but also barred her from ever being prosecuted for it.

When the evening talk-show DJ, Buddy Roberts, came back from the report, he laughed and commented that it was odd, to say the least for Marcum to be marrying Hines.

"Makes one wonder, doesn't it?" the DJ asked. "What role did our former DA play in all this?"

"Well, he's a judge now," the DJ's sidekick. Joey Botts, chimed in, "so that makes him untouchable, doesn't it?"

"I guess so," the DJ said. "I always heard that Judges get away with murder."

"Wow," Dean said under his breath as he stared out into the gloom and darkness, "that comes close to being defamatory."

"Isn't truth a defense?" Foley asked.

"Yes, it sure is," Dean said as he looked over at Foley and laughed. "It sure is."

After they had driven a while farther, Dean asked, "So how are you so sure that Mazurka isn't behind us?"

"I told you," he said. "I took care of that."

"Wanna tell me how?"

"Thought you didn't want to know."

"Well, I do now," Dean said.

Foley shrugged.

"This guy owed me a favor," he said. "So I asked him to stake-out old Stanley tonight. If he took off from his house, he'd tail him and let me know what Stanley was up to, especially if old Stanley was up to tailing me."

"And so far, that isn't the case," Dean said.

"Which means," Foley said. "Old Stanley took this cold night off, stayed home."

"And maybe that means Mazurka doesn't need to follow you anymore," Dean said.

"What do you mean? Why?"

"Maybe his boss thinks that they're in the clear," Dean said. "That he and his lover pulled off the perfect crime. Got away with murder."

"Maybe they did," Foley said, sighed, then added, "Well, let's see what Detective Miller has to say about that."

Jack Miller greeted Foley and Dean at the front door of his rickety cabin with a sour expression. Miller looked as if he hadn't been taking very good care of himself lately. He was a tall, frumpy man with a big pouch of a belly and back problems, so he hunched forward and sideways a bit. His eyes were hollow orbs with dark circles under them and his skin was grayish, pasty and slack. His gray hair was stringy and unkempt, in need of trimming, and there was a three day, gray stubble on his chin. Of course, he gave off a vague hint of sour body odor.

"Come in," he said gruffly, turned and waved behind his back for them to join him.

His old A-frame consisted of a large living room/kitchen combo with a stove and fridge and sink against one wall and some cupboards for pots and pans and utensils hanging along another wall. In the middle, there was a small table and a cutting block. A short hallway led from the kitchen to the couple small bedrooms and a narrow bathroom. There was a makeshift propane furnace in the corner that was grinding away keeping the cabin warm.

Miller pointed out chairs at the kitchen table and after they sat down, he joined them. There was a half-empty bottle of bourbon and an empty glass on the table in front of him. After sitting down, Miller picked up the bottle and poured about half-way up the glass.

"Join me, gentlemen?" he asked. "I'm celebrating."

"Celebrating? Celebrating what, Detective?" Foley asked.

"A clear conscience," he said.

"I'll drink to that," Foley said and looked at Dean.

"Me, too, I guess," Dean said.

Miller lumbered over and fetched two reasonably clean glasses from the cupboard and carried them between his fingers over to the kitchen table and set them down. He poured the bourbon half-way into each glass, then pushed one to Foley and the other to Dean.

Miller raised his glass and waited for them to raise theirs.

"To a clear conscience," he said, then threw back his head and swallowed down a good portion of what was in the glass.

As he did so, Foley and Dean lifted their glasses, took short sips and winced.

"So what is this about, Detective?" Foley asked. "Why'd you want to see us?"

"Call me Jack," Miller said. He leaned forward and glared at Foley across the table. "What is this about? The bullshit I told you the other day."

Foley flashed Dean an I-told-you-so look.

"Yeah, like what about it was bullshit?"

Miller picked up his glass of bourbon and took a drink, winced, smiled, then winked at Foley.

"Well," Miller said. "Let's just say I left out some important details. Like the detail about the DA being at the scene of the crime."

"At the scene?" Foley asked. "You mean he went out there that night?"

"Yeah," Miller said. "He came out to the house. He was there. And he interviewed the suspect. Alone. In the guest bedroom."

"Who told you to keep that out of the final report?" Foley asked.

"Who do you think? My Chief," Miller said. "Marcum helped him win the election or got him out of some trouble or some shit. I don't know what the payback was for. All I know is that the Chief owed him payback. And that night, he paid it."

"But why leave that out of the report?" Dean asked and took a sip of his drink. He shrugged. "It's not so odd to have the DA show up especially with a close deputy involved."

"Wait, there's more," Miller said. "A lot more. See, after we, well, they, the Chief and Marcum, let Mrs. Hines-Laurence pack some things and leave the house, I followed her. I didn't tell the Chief what I was doing. I told him, and Marcum, I was heading back to the station, you know, to file the report. Call it a hunch, but I didn't do that. Like I said, I followed her instead.

"And at first, there was nothing to see. She drove to that Marriot on Maple Road, went into the lobby, got a room, I guess. But then, just as I was about to drive out of there and go back to headquarters, file my report, guess who I see drive in and find a parking space?" He held up the glass and took another swallow. "The DA."

"This still isn't proving anything," Dean said, "except what we expected, that the DA and Susie Hines were lovers back before the shooting. I wish we'd known this six months ago. It backs up everything Parlatto told us."

"And then some," added Foley.

"There's more gentlemen," Miller said. "Much more."

Dean and Foley turned to Miller as he took another sip of his bourbon and leaned forward as if he was about to tell a ghost story around a campfire.

"I followed Marcum inside the hotel," Miller said. "He headed straight for the elevator like he knew where he was going. Once he got inside, he went up to wherever he was going – her room, I figured. I went up to the desk clerk and flashed my badge, demanding to know what room Susan Hines-Laurence had checked into. He was a pimply kid, fresh out of college. He looked it up on his computer and told me, Room 411. I hustled to the stairwell and ran up there. I didn't know what I was doing, or what I was going to find. I figured I'd sneak onto the hallway and put my ear to the door of Room 411, see if I could hear voices." He laughed. "But, shit, instead I learned a whole lot more than I ever bargained for.

"As it turned out, 411 was only a couple of rooms down from the stairwell and, as I opened the door, I almost ran into them. I closed the door just in the nick of time without being seen. The DA was already half out of the room, but he was looking back in so he didn't see me. At first, I figured, well, no big deal. She works for him, they were probably close friends. Not so unusual that he'd want to take care of her, like a daughter or something. See if she was alright after what had just happened.

"But as he came out of the room all the way out into the hall, she came out after him and hugged him out there. Not like a friend, or father figure, you know. It was a helluva lot more than that.

"Anyway, I kept watching them through a crack in the stairwell door, and I was close enough to even hear what they were saying. And suddenly, I thought of my smartphone." He laughed. "One of the new detectives had just shown me a few days earlier how to use the video record feature. So, I said, what the hell. Let me try it. Tape this little scene, at least record what they were saying to each other. So I held the phone to the crack in the stairwell door and by some miracle, it videoed them out there, in living color and recorded every damn word they said, word for word, clear as a bell."

Miller shook his head and laughed at the marvel of that.

"Recorded it all on my cell phone," he said. "The fucking modern age."

Miller stood and went over to a coat rack near the front door. He reached inside the pocket of a jacket hanging on it and pulled out his smartphone.

"Want to watch it?" he asked. "What I recorded that night?"

Foley and Dean looked at each other, their eyes widening with the wonder of what was being offered. Then, they turned back to Miller.

"Sure," Foley said. "Of course."

Miller brought the smartphone to the table, tapped some keys and found the video playback button.

"Here goes," he said and sat back.

The picture was a bit choppy with Miller sticking the top part of the smartphone, as he explained it, just out of the open crack of the stairwell door. But the DA and Susie Hines were clearly out there, holding each other. And what they had to say was picked up, as Miller had claimed, clear as a bell.

Foley and Dean leaned forward, squinting, watched and listened.

The DA: *You gonna be alright, Susie?*

Her: *Yeah, Sam.*

She sighs hugs tightly onto his waist.

Her: *I can't believe it, Sam.*

Him, stroking her hair: *What?*

Then, she edges back, looks up at him. After a moment, they kiss, then back away, still holding each other.

Her: *We did it.*

Another kiss.

Her: *Sure you can't stay. Be with me. I don't...I don't know if I can sleep.*

Him: *No, she'll be wondering. We got lay low for a while. You know that. We talked about that.*

Her: *We've been laying low for two years. But now...he's out of our lives.*

A long sigh. They hold each other again.

Him: *I still feel bad about it. The whole evening, I kept thinking of calling you, of calling it off.*

Her: *Well, it's too late for that now. It's done.*

They hold each other for a time, then back away.

Him: *I gotta go.*

Her: *I love you.*

Him: *Love you, too.*

Her: *Bye.*

And with that, he bolts and walks briskly down the hall until he finally turns right into the foyer at the elevators.

And that was it. Miller said he pulled his smartphone back into the stairwell as Susie Hines went back into her room, careful not the let the stairwell door slam shut.

Foley asked Miller to play the video again and they watched and listened more closely this time, getting every word.

"It's a damned confession," Dean said.

"Or pretty damn close," Foley said.

"So what happened?" Dean asked. "Why didn't all that end up in the report?"

"When I got back to headquarters, I told the Chief all about it, what I saw, what I heard," Miller said. "I played the cell phone recording and he watched it three, four times.

"Then the Chief got silent for awhile, mulling things over. Finally, he looked at me and said, 'Fuck it.'" Miller laughed. "That's exactly what he said. Fuck it. He gave me this hard look and told me the recording was bullshit. That it was all still an ambiguous nothing. That I was dreaming if I thought we could charge The DA and Mrs. Laurence on the basis of that. All he knew, Sam Marcum was a good and decent man. And he wasn't going to ruin the reputation of a man like that on speculation and an ambiguous conversation, taped or not." Miller's face cringed up and he looked away. "He turned to me and ordered me to end my report right where it was – with Mrs. Laurence going off to the hotel. Forgot about that I had followed her out there, what I'd seen. It was going to end right where it was."

Miller took a deep breath.

"And as you know," he said. "I did exactly what the Chief said."

"I just don't get it," Foley said after a time. "Why'd you go along with something like that, Chief or no Chief? It was pretty damning stuff what you found, Detective." Foley looked at Dean. "Right, Dean?"

"Proof beyond a reasonable doubt," Dean said. "Seems to me."

Foley turned back to Miller and asked, "So why'd you do it? Listen to him? Why didn't you walk out of there and go to someone else with it?"

Miller stared at the floor. Dean scowled at Foley and shrugged, questioning the hard approach.

After a time, Miller looked up at Foley.

"Well, let's just say this," he said, "the Chief had me over a kind of barrel."

"Yeah? What kind of barrel?" Foley asked.

Miller sighed, looked away.

"An infidelity kind of barrel," he said. "And a retirement kind of barrel."

After a few moments, he looked back at them.

"See, there was this dispatcher got hired a couple years back," he said. "She's forty, forty-one. Brenda. Divorcee. Blonde, smoke-skinny type. Anyway, when Brenda first started, we used to talk about things, chit-chat, you know. We had some laughs, became friends. Then, one day we went out after a shift to a bar near the headquarters. We had a few too many beers and ended up in her car making out. Next thing I know, I get us a room at a nearby motel, do whatever. We were on the way back to the bar to get my wheels when she rear-ended another car stopped at a red light. Luckily, no one was hurt bad, just some bumps and bruises. But the county sheriff's patrol who responded had to charge her. There were too many witnesses, she was too drunk.

"Anyway, the story got back to the Chief that I was in the car with her and he agreed to let it go, bury it. So, you know, now he had something pretty powerful hanging over my head. It was either bury the story about the so-called ambiguous meeting between the DA and Susan Hines-Laurence after the shooting, or he'd exhume the story about me and the now terminated, drunken dispatcher. And something like that could affect my retirement. Thirty years down the drain. Not to mention my thirty-five-year marriage."

"Bottom line, no matter the reason," Foley said, "you went along with the cover-up. And now you got a guilty conscience."

"Let's just say," Miller said, "I haven't slept so good since then."

He smirked, shrugged.

"Deep inside," he went on, "I keep thinking I'm helping two people get away with murder. It's not easy living with that on your mind day-in-and-day-out, let alone getting a good night's sleep. So I started drinking even more than I used to, but passing out every other night drunk is no way to get some sleep."

He took a deep breath. His eyes were dark, tired. Worried. At last, he looked at Foley.

"Then you came around couple weeks ago and woke my conscience up, I guess," he said. He finished what was in his glass. "I know I should have reported the truth from day one and told the Chief to fuck off. It was the one time I caved to politics. It was the one time I failed to report the truth."

"Well, you just came clean," said Foley. "And like they say, better late than never." Foley reached over and patted Miller's right forearm. "When do you wanna come in and report this to a cop? Make it official?"

Miller frowned.

"What cop?" he asked. "Who can we trust?"

Foley nodded. Miller had a point. Who could they trust? Not the Manchester PD, and not even the interim DA, Fred Carpenter, who was good friends and a political ally of Marcum.

"Let me sleep on that," he told Miller. "Who to go to with what you got."

He picked up Miller's smartphone and examined it for a time.

"I am wondering if there's a way to make a copy of what you recorded," he said, then looked at Dean. "There a way to do that?"

There was, of course, and Dean showed them how. He transferred the video from Miller's smartphone to Foley's brand new one.

On the way home, Dean asked Foley, "You think he'll be alright?"

"Yeah," Foley said. "He'll sleep like a baby, tonight at least, now that's off his chest."

"Maybe you'll be wrong this time," Dean said after a time. "Maybe it's come around for once."

"We'll see," Foley said. "We got a long way to go before that."

Chapter Twenty-Nine
A Change of Plans

It was almost nine by the time Foley dropped Dean at his house and drove off. As Dean slowly strolled up the driveway to the side entrance door, a shadow of someone moved out from behind the house. Dean gasped and almost dropped his keys.

"Dean." It was woman's voice.

Dean frowned and focused on the dark figure standing before him who had stated his name. After a moment, he relaxed. It was Kat.

She walked up to him and fell into his arms.

"Kat?"

Dean looked around as they embraced. He had neighbors and he was a married man but even thinking that seemed ridiculous. He was holding the woman he was falling in love with, or had fallen in love with. And then, of course, he thought of Laura.

"I'm so sorry about your father," she said. "I just couldn't go to the funeral."

She backed away from him.

"After what we did," she said. "What happened between us. And you being at my house when you got the call. I just couldn't face you. You understand, don't you?"

"Look," Dean said, "let's talk about this inside."

As he turned and opened the side door, he added, "I have something to tell you." Before stepping inside, he turned to her. "There's been a break in the unofficial DA case. That's where I was tonight. With Foley."

They sat at the kitchen table and he brought her a glass of wine. He took out a beer and sat down next to her.

"How are you?" she asked.

"I'm okay," he said. "I'm coming in tomorrow. Time to get back to the harassment of Herr Gunther and his fraus, Hartman, and Smith."

Kat laughed. He had confided his pet names for his office foes some time ago.

"So what's the break in the DA case?"

He told her about the meeting with Detective Miller and Foley that evening, and what Miller saw and heard and of course, the video recording on his cell phone.

"We transferred the video to Foley's phone," Dean said. "He's going to upload to his laptop."

Kat thought for a bit.

"And it incriminated them?" Kat asked. "You're sure of that?"

Dean tried to tell her verbatim what Marcum and Susie Hines said in the video.

"Yeah," she said and laughed, "sounds pretty damning."

"What else could it mean?" Dean said with a shrug. "We

did it. It's done. Did what? Murdered Kent Laurence, that's what."

Kat thought another long moment, then nodded.

"What are you going to do with it?" Kat asked. "Shouldn't you be telling the police?"

"Foley wants to sleep on our next move," Dean said. "Take it to the right people. Definitely, not the Manchester PD. They are tainted by whatever the Chief has on his conscience. Why he let the DA get away with it. And the present, interim DA, Carpenter, is an ally of Marcum. He was hired by Marcum and Foley wonders where his loyalties are gonna lie. Plus, he's bucking to be appointed to the job and might feel he'll need Marcum's support and the help of his allies to get it. He might scuttle it somehow. Say it's ambiguous, and just like Marcum, refuse to appoint a special prosecutor."

"So where do you take it, then?" Kat asked.

"That's what Foley needs to sleep on," he said with a shrug. "Figure out the next move. Make sure it's the right one."

"So what happens next?" Kat asked. "Say you find a prosecutor or a cop willing to listen."

"Well, Susie's free and clear, we already know that," Dean said. "The only thing she can be prosecuted for is perjury for her testimony before the grand jury. But Marcum, he can be prosecuted as an accomplice to murder. Kent Laurence's murder."

Kat sipped her wine and brooded over all this for a time. Finally, she looked at Dean.

"There's Detective Miller, his testimony, and his

recording, of course," Kat said, then asked, "And you think that's enough? Oh, and the forensic bullet trajectory stuff. You mentioned that."

"Yeah, that, and Marcum's affair with the dead guy's wife," Dean added and sighed. "Now it is sounding like a cheap crime novel. Something by Dashiell Hammett."

"Sounds like a close case," Kat said after a time. She sighed, took a sip of wine. "Whether it's proof beyond a reasonable doubt, well... one thing I do know, you need to be careful with this, Dean."

"Careful?"

"Sure," Kat said. "I mean, what you're talking about here is a lot more serious than a conflict of interest disciplinary investigation. What you're talking is a murder case against a former, much-respected DA, who is now an appellate judge, one of the leading jurists in the state. I mean, and don't take offense, Dean, but it seems you're in way over your head on this one. And Foley, too."

"Don't you think I know that," Dean said. "Anyway, Foley said he wants to sleep on it. And I see no harm in that. No one knows Detective Miller is wallowing in guilt, ready to spill what he knows about Marcum's meeting with Susie Hines right after the shooting – or murder, I should say. And that he's got a video recording to back up what he saw. That alone is going to create a scandal that'll probably take Justice Marcum down – and maybe some other people with him along the way."

"You are definitely in way over your head, Dean," Kat said. "Way over."

They sat in silence for a time sipping their drinks.

Finally, Kat asked how Laura was doing.

Dean looked over at her and shrugged.

"She seems to be doing alright," he said. "She's getting through it, I guess. There's always this sadness about her."

He reached out his hand to Kat, and she held it.

"I've been doing a lot of thinking," he said. "About us."

Kat looked at him. After a moment, she pulled her hand away.

"Me, too," she said and sighed. "We have to stop this, Dean."

"Stop?"

"Yes," she said. "We have to stop seeing each other."

"That wasn't exactly my plan," Dean said.

"What was it then? Your plan?" she asked. "You leave her for me? I can just imagine that scene. The day you drive her home from rehab, you tell her, oh, by the way, honey, I'm leaving you for Kat Franklin." She laughed and pointed across the room. "Straight for the liquor cabinet and her favorite bottle of booze she goes, and you'd hate yourself for the rest of your life. And I'd hate myself, too."

He sighed. She had a point. At last, he looked at her.

"Well, I wouldn't tell her right away," he said. "I mean not the day she comes home."

Kat looked away.

"I can't live with any of it, Dean," she said.

"Jesus," he said. "You love me, right."

She sighed and turned to him.

"Yes, I think I do," Kat said. "I mean, I think about you all the time. But I like to believe I have morals, Dean. That I respect vows. And you made a vow to her. And if she beats this drinking thing, you should live up to that vow."

Dean looked away, seething now. How could he have allowed this to happen? He took a long swallow of beer. After a sigh, he stood and walked over and knelt down before Kat. He pulled her to him and fell into her bosom.

"I am in love with you," he told her. "That's all I know."

He lifted his head from her, and despite what Kat had just said about his vow, she kissed him.

But then Dean's cell phone rang. After a sigh, still kneeling before Kat, Dean lifted it out of his pants pocket and checked the number. It was Foley. After a third ring, Dean answered it

"What's up, Stuey?" Dean asked.

He stood and began to pace the kitchen. Kat had pushed away her glass of wine and stood as well, looking ready to leave. Whatever magic had passed between them, despite her sermon about morality, had worn off. She was getting ready to leave.

"I got an itch," Foley said.

"What?"

"An itch," he said.

"You drunk or what?"

"I think Mazurka followed me home just now."

"But like you said, your buddy didn't call," Dean said. "The one you told me about. The guy who was supposed to be keeping tabs on him."

"My buddy isn't answering his cell phone," Foley said. "I called him to see what's what, and nada. No answer."

Dean shrugged. Kat was on her way out when Dean grabbed her arm.

"No, wait," Dean whispered to her. "We're not done."

But she pulled out of his grasp and hurried out the side door.

"Shit."

"What?" Foley asked. "Who's with you?"

"Never mind," Dean said.

"I'm just worried about Miller," Foley said. "If Mazurka somehow slipped my guy's tail, and followed us out there."

"Then our goose is cooked," Dean said.

"And maybe Miller's too," Foley said. "For real."

Dean went to the front window of his living room and looked just in time to see Kat driving off in a snow squall.

"Whoa!" he said to Foley. "Where did all that snow come from?"

"Yeah, a blizzard here, too," Foley said. "No way to drive back down to Bliss in this. I just checked the weather. It's worse down there. They're expecting at least a couple feet."

Foley sighed.

"You try and call him?" Dean asked.

"Miller? Yeah," Foley said. "He didn't answer." He sighed again. "I am really worried about him. We never should have left him alone out there."

"Who do you think these guys are?" Dean asked. "The Mafia?"

"No," Foley said. "Worse."

Chapter Thirty
Herr Gunther

At ten minutes after nine the next morning, Dean got buzzed by Kathy Barnes.

"He wants to see you," she told him

Dean sighed. It was never a good thing being summoned out of the blue to Herr Gunther's office. Dean wondered if perhaps his visit yesterday to interview Jack Miller with Stu Foley may be coming home to roost. Maybe Foley had been right, Stan Mazurka had followed them down to Bliss.

Dean found the door to the Director's office closed and as he approached, he heard voices from inside. One of the voices was Liza Hartman's. He took a breath before knocking.

"C'min," Gunther called out and was laughing at some private joke between him and Liza as Dean opened the door.

Liza scowled at Dean as she got up from one of two chairs facing Gunther's long desk. She brushed some lint off her short, black skirt and, without even bothering to acknowledge Dean, turned to Gunther and promised she'd have her report on some case she was handling on his desk by the end of the morning. Then she strode out. Despite her obvious dislike for him and her cold-hearted attitude toward most men, Dean could not suppress a twinge of physical desire for her. Her long, bare legs, revealed all the better by knee-length skirt, and her dominant attitude always brought that on.

"Have a seat, Dean," Gunther said.

Dean sat down and crossed his legs, waiting for Herr Gunther next volley of chastisement. But he started off easy, asking Dean how he was dealing with everything, with his Dad's passing and Laura still in rehab.

"I'm hanging in there, I guess," Dean said. "Taking it day by day."

"Well, what you must be going through somehow didn't stop you from taking a drive with your old pal, Stu Foley, all the way out to the country yesterday evening," Gunther said.

"How do you know about that?" Dean asked.

"You deny it?"

"No, of course not," Dean said. "I took a drive out to the country with Stu Foley, yes. On my own time. I was still on bereavement leave."

"And what was the purpose of the trip?"

There he goes, Dean thought. Herr Gunther in cross-examination mode again. It was going to be a long, disturbing meeting, from his perspective anyway.

"We were meeting Detective Jack Miller," Dean admitted. No use denying it. He knew that Gunther knew the first rule of any cross-examination is never ask a question to which you didn't know the answer. "He retired from the Manchester Police Department a few months back and was staying down at his hunting cabin in Bliss, way out there in Alleghany County."

"And what was the purpose of the meeting?" Gunther asked.

"Well," Dean said. He thought a moment and decided there was no use holding anything back. "Stuey had talked to Miller a few weeks back about his investigation into the Laurence shooting and Miller seemed not to have been completely honest. Stuey felt he was holding something back."

Dean looked at Gunther, who shrugged and said, "Go on."

"Anyway, Miller called Stu out of the blue yesterday morning and asked him to take a ride out to his cabin. Stu asked me if I'd mind riding along with him out there. Get my mind off things."

"And did it?" Gunther asked. "Get your mind off things."

"Not really," Dean said.

"So what did Miller tell you and Foley?" Gunther asked. "What was on his mind?"

"He didn't tell us anything," Dean lied. "The only thing we found out is that Detective Miller's an old drunk with delusions of grandeur."

Gunther put his fingers to his mouth and nodded. He looked concerned, as if he suspected that Dean wasn't being totally honest with him.

"And did your tagging along with Foley," Gunther

asked after a time, "have something to do with your concerns about the former DA, Sam Marcum?"

"Well, more Foley's concerns, I guess, than mine," Dean said. "Stu, well, he still wonders what happened. Justice Marcum's role in all of that." Dean sighed. "Stu's a persistent kind of guy and he has this idea that maybe our former DA was involved in something he shouldn't have been."

"Did I not tell you to stay away from that?" Gunther asked. "Is that not something we talked about on several occasions?"

Gunther paused until Dean realized that he was expecting an answer.

"Yes, we have."

"And did we also not discuss what an embarrassment it would be for this office," Gunther went on, "and how it would negatively affect its credibility if it ever got out that we were investigating Justice Marcum. Even on your own time, Dean, it would look bad for the office. Real bad."

Dean shrugged. He was about to say, even if we proved that the former DA, now judge, had directed Donnelly to intentionally botch the waiver of indictment procedure and, even better than that, if we proved that the DA was an accomplice in a sinister plot with his paramour, Susie Hines, to murder her husband.

But Dean didn't say any of that. What was the point? Gunther had his agenda and it did not involve rocking the boat or pissing off Sam Marcum.

"No matter," Gunther said. "What really concerns me is that once again, this shows a complete lack of judgment on your part, as we have discussed time and time again, Dean,"

"Well, I've just been going through a tough time," Dean said, "as you might imagine."

"That's an empty excuse," Gunther said. "I find this to be a serious act of insubordination. I'm afraid I intend to formalize it in writing and enter it into your personnel file. I also intend to speak with the Chief Justice about your continued employment here. Maybe, a transfer to Mental Hygiene can be arranged. I don't know. They are fully staffed."

Dean nodded. He knew he was one step closer to being out the door and out of a job. He made a mental note to call his contact at the Tax Department to see what was going on with the job supposedly waiting for him over there.

"Anything else?" Dean asked.

Gunther shook his head.

"No," he said. "You can go."

Dean nodded, got up and walked out. It had been a relatively tame session.

A moment after Dean left the office, Gunther was on the phone with the Chief Justice. The CJ had called him at home the previous night and told him that Marcum's bodyguard, Stan Mazurka, had followed Foley earlier in the evening to the cabin of former Detective Jack Miller down in Bliss and that Dean Alessi had been with him. Marcum, and now the CJ, were livid that Foley and Dean were apparently still looking into the Laurence shooting. And Marcum was wondering if Gunther may be behind it and was threatening to withdraw his recommendation for his appointment as DA. After Gunther had assured the CJ that he wasn't behind anything, that Foley and Alessi were acting on their own, he said he'd get to the bottom of it by meeting with Alessi the following morning.

"Alessi said Detective Miller didn't tell them anything," Gunther said. "Said he's just an old drunk with delusions of grandeur."

"What the hell does that mean?" the CJ asked. "When you going to fire that guy?"

"Alessi?"

"Well, you can't fire Foley," the CJ said.

"I can't just fire him, your Honor," Gunther said. "The IG's office would crucify us. He's worked here sixteen going on seventeen years and gotten exemplary performance evaluations for every single one of them. And his visit out to see Miller was on his own time."

"Well, his performance eval for this period better not be exemplary," the CJ said.

"Well, it won't be," Gunther said, "but it's not due until the end of February. I just told him that I would be speaking about this with you and that at very least, a transfer might be in order."

The CJ said nothing for a time.

"I just don't know what else can be done," Gunther said.

"Fire him," the CJ snapped. "Just fire him. On my authority. I'm tired of pussy-footing around with that guy. Fire him."

"Y-yes, your Honor," Gunther said.

After a time, the CJ said, "And I think Miller said a lot more than what Alessi told you."

"Really?" Gunther asked. "Something that implicates Justice Marcum ..."

"Sh!" the CJ said. "All I know is that Sam is plenty worried. He spent the morning pacing in front of my desk, not saying much."

Gunther waited as the CJ thought things through.

"Well, it'll play out one way or another, I guess," the CJ finally said. "You know what they say – what goes around, comes around."

Chapter Thirty-One
Miller's Time

Dean spent the rest of that morning, lunch and into the early afternoon trying to forget his meeting with Gunther and the ominous prospect that he was about to lose his job. Little did he know that during that time, Gunther was on the phone with Margo Anson-Clarke and Jenny Ziniski from HR getting the paperwork necessary to terminate him that very day pursuant to the CJ's direct order. The plan was for Gunther to call him into his office just before five and break the news.

Just before going out to lunch, Dean called Laura at the rehab facility. She seemed in relatively good spirits, ending the call with, "I love you, Dean."

He told Laura he loved her, too, but then he thought of Kat, knowing that his budding romance with her could only end up badly. Still, he wished she'd finish her sworn examination of an attorney for borrowing thousands of dollar from a client, a serious conflict of interest, so he could tell her about the latest of his disagreeable meetings with Gunther and the bad feeling he had about his employment status.

But before he could do that, at just before two, Foley called him.

"Hi, Stuey? What's up?"

"He's dead," Foley told him.

"What? Who's dead?"

"Miller."

"What?"

"Yeah," Foley said, "I just heard it on the radio. His brother went out to the cabin this morning. He hadn't seen him in a week and he was worried. He found Miller's body. They're calling it a suicide. Supposedly, he put a shotgun to his mouth and pulled the trigger."

"That's nuts," Dean said. "We just saw him. He was not suicidal."

"I should have gotten him out of there," Foley said. "I should never have left him alone like that. And blizzard or no blizzard, I should have driven down there last night to warn him. To help the man. I feel half-way responsible he's dead."

"So you're telling me it wasn't suicide?" Dean asked. "Is that what you're saying? That it was mur…"

"Yeah, murder. Why not?" Foley asked. "There's a lot at stake here for some people if Miller had come out of the closet with what he saw going on between Marcum and Susie Hines the night Kent Laurence was shot, or murdered, I should say, and then backed it up with the video. Marcum certainly knew it might mean spending the rest of his life in jail, losing everything. They'd all lose everything. Even dear, sweet Susie Hines could go to jail if they could make a perjury charge stick based upon her false testimony in the grand jury — that she didn't kill her husband. She's not immunized from that, lying under oath, right?"

"No," Dean said. "Only for his murder."

"At very least, Marcum could lose his spot on the Supreme Court if what Miller saw comes out," Foley continued, "and his reputation will certainly be reduced to shit, tarnished beyond repair. And as far as the CJ goes, he's the one who pushed Marcum for the Supreme Court in the first place, from what I understand. Being connected to Marcum for that would certainly be a blemish on his reputation. Maybe a bad blemish, bad enough that it could scuttle whatever plans he has for his judicial career that includes, so I hear, a spot on the US Supreme Court."

"But this all sounds a bit far-fetched, Stuey," Dean said. "Unreal. Something out of an Elmore Leonard novel."

"I'm telling you," Foley went on, "we should have gotten Miller out of that damned cabin. To the police. Had him make a statement. Start the process. Instead, all we have is a dead man. And dead men really do tell no tales, or whatever the hell the saying is." Foley sighed and Dean could imagine him shaking his head. "I should have driven out there last night, snow or no snow."

"What about Miller's cell phone?" Dean asked. "The recording he made. We still got that."

"I'm sure they grabbed it," Foley said.

"Who?" Dean asked. "The cops, paramedics?"

"No," Foley said, growing annoyed that Dean was being so dense, "whoever killed him. Marcum, Stan Mazurka. I already told you what I think happened. Marcum certainly had a motive to shut Miller up, to save his ass from jail. And Mazurka got paid to do it. What else is there to know?"

"But we don't know that happened," Dean said. "That's you talking. That's your conspiracy theory."

"Think about it, Dean," Foley said. "Really think about it."

"I don't know what to think."

"And I'm telling you Marcum paid Mazurka to kill Jack Miller and make it look like a suicide," Foley said. "And that's exactly what he did."

Dean thought for a time.

"Well, doesn't that put us in danger, too," he said. "I mean, Mazurka followed us out there last night. Right?

"Yes," Foley said. "He must have."

"So they know we were out there," Dean said. "And if they were worried enough to kill Miller..."

"Yeah, I realize that," Foley said. "But they have no idea what Miller told us. I mean, they might feel safe now that he's dead and they have what he recorded on the cell phone." But after a sigh, Foley added, "Or you're right, and they might want to be extra careful."

"This certainly has gotten way beyond what I first thought this case was about," Dean said and let out a breath. "Kat's right – we're in way over our heads. I think it's time we went to the police, put our cards on the table. Show them that cell phone video Miller made. That way, at least, we're safe."

"Yeah, I agree," Foley said. "That appears to be our only option right this minute. To make sure we stay healthy, that is. In hindsight, it's what we should have done yesterday. Maybe, had we, Miller would still be alive."

"So what's our options?" Dean asked. "Who do we

report this to?"

"There's an investigator for the State Police," Foley said. "He's the nephew of Pete Lassiter, my old partner. Supposed to be a good guy. He's in the Bureau of Criminal Investigation, BCI, over there. You know, they investigate major crimes, felonies, murders.

"That's who I came up with after banging my brain all last night – I remembered Pete's nephew worked over there. In fact, I even called Pete about him just a few minutes ago and he confirmed he was a good kid. Honest as the day is long. According to Pete, his nephew's got no political ties. Just does his job. "

"Sounds like a plan," Dean said.

"I called the kid – well, he's around forty – right after I got off the phone with Pete," Foley said. "I didn't tell him anything about what we had, just who I was. He seemed interested enough. I set up a meeting for three this afternoon."

"Where's he at?" Dean asked.

"Works out perfect," Foley said. "He's got something going on at the sub-stations just off the thruway," Foley said. "About a twenty-minute ride from downtown. You know where I'm talking about?"

"Yeah, right off the Thruway," Dean said, "Off the Kensington Expressway exit."

"Yeah, that's the one," Foley said. "See you there in twenty, twenty-five minutes."

"Will do," Dean said, then added, "Hey, maybe things'll coming around for a change. Big time."

"Yeah, maybe," Foley said with his usual wariness. "But

I wouldn't count my chickens just yet."

Chapter Thirty-Two
Kat's Story

The moment Dean ended the call with Foley, there was a knock at his door. Dean lost a heartbeat wondering who it could be.

"C'mon in," he called out.

It was Kat Franklin and he was glad for that. The last person he needed to see now was Gunther.

Dean stood up from behind his desk as Kat stepped into his office.

"I'm on my way out, Kat," he said. "What's up?"

"Where you going?"

"State police," he said. "I'm meeting Foley. We're doing what we should have done yesterday. Time to put our cards out on the table see if we can help make a case against Marcum."

"I heard about Detective Miller," Kat said. "They're calling it a suicide?"

"Yeah, suicide," Dean said. "But Foley doesn't think so, and neither do I."

"Count me in, too," Kat said. "But I think you should hear this before you go."

"Hear what?"

"I was witness to something today," she said. "At lunch. Something disturbing."

"Okay," Dean said and checked his watch. "But make it fast."

Kat told him that as she was walking out of the building on her way to the food court in the downtown shopping mall to grab something quick for lunch, she spotted Justice Marcum walking briskly, heading north, eyes forward and intense, deep in thought. She thought that odd, him on the street alone, obviously anxious to get someplace, so she decided to follow him.

Marcum strode another five blocks up Main Street, distracted like that until he made a hard left onto Houser Lane. After another couple of blocks up Houser, he entered a little Irish pub, Madigan's Olde Eire. The place has a small lunch menu, the usual Irish fare, bangers and mash, pot pie, served with dark, frothy pints of Guinness. Kat waited a couple minutes after he entered the tavern to follow him inside.

"And guess who I saw him sitting with?" she asked.

Dean shrugged.

"Stan Mazurka," she said.

"You know Mazurka?"

"No, not at the time," Kat said. "But soon enough, I figured it out. He looked like somebody named Stan Mazurka."

"When was that?" Dean asked.

"Around twelve-thirty," she said. "Anyway, I finagled my way to a booth right next to where they were sitting. The place wasn't crowded, only a couple other tables occupied, some guys at the bar watching ESPN or Fox News on the TVs behind the bar."

"Marcum didn't recognize you?"

"No," she said. "Why would he? He's not been on any panels for cases I argued up there."

Dean nodded. That was true.

"So what happened?"

Kat told him that she edged sideways in the booth with her face away from them, laid out the morning newspaper on the table to her left and pretended to be reading it. In truth, she was straining to listen to what they were talking about.

"What did you hear?" Dean asked.

"Not much," she said. "As you might expect, the noise level of even that quiet bar masked a lot of what they were saying. But during a lull in the clatter, I did hear Marcum tell Mazurka, quote, Foley must know, end-quote. And not long after that, I heard Marcum say, quote, and what if he made a copy, Stan, end-quote. That's how I was certain the guy with him was Mazurka. Worst of all, after a few seconds lull, Mazurka said, and I'm quoting again, Well, I guess I better take care of it."

"You heard that," Dean said. Again, he checked his watch. He was supposed to be meeting Foley in fifteen minutes. "I better take care of it?"

"Yes," Kat said. "His exact words. Marcum nodded, and said, again I'm quoting, yeah, you better.

"At that point, I took out my pen and, pretending to be

doing a cross-word puzzle, jotted down what they just said on my paper." She lifted up the section of the newspaper that Dean realized she had brought in with her. Kat looked down and read what she had written. "Foley must know. And, what if he made a copy. That was Marcum, and then Mazurka saying, Well, I guess I better take care of it. And, Marcum, Yeah, you better. That's it, word for word."

Dean took out his cell phone, found Foley's name in his contact list and pressed the call button. After four rings, his voice mail message came on. But Dean did not leave an answer.

"Look, I gotta get out to the state trooper station, the one just off the Thruway, and meet Foley," he said. "Then, all this will come to a head. And hopefully, a happy ending."

"A comes around kind of ending?" Kat asked.

Dean thought a moment, then laughed.

"Yeah, a comes around ending," he said.

Dean walked out from behind his desk and approached Kat. He took her into his arms and they kissed.

"Want me to come with you?" she asked.

"No," he said. "I'll tell them what you heard at Madigan's, have them call you to confirm." After checking his watch again, he said, "I really do have to go. You know how Foley hates it when you're late."

Kat laughed as he edged away from her and walked out of his office. At the doorway, she called to him.

"Hey, Dean."

He stopped and turned to her.

"Please be careful," she said.

He nodded, smiled at her, then left.

Chapter Thirty-Three
Rescue Me

Dean arrived at the Thruway state police sub-station about forty minutes after Foley's call. The sub-station was an ugly tan, one-story rectangular building just off the entrance ramp of a busy stretch of the New York State Thruway just south of Buffalo. A small fleet of patrol cars, late model black, souped-up Dodge Chargers and Ford Mustangs, were parked in a lot adjacent to the building. The building consisted of a spacious room divided into cubicles for use by troopers from Troop "A" to prepare reports. Down a short hallway were several interrogation rooms, a booking space, and at the very end of the station, a cramped locker-room with a latrine and some showers. Down another short hallway from the main room was a ten by ten foot holding cell that was mostly used for the temporary custody of drunken DWI arrestees before they were transported downtown to the pre-arraignment lock-up in the county jail.

Dean hurried from his car in the small visitor's parking lot to the lobby. He was expecting to find Foley standing there sour-pussed and tapping his right foot for having to wait so long for his arrival. But the lobby was deserted. Frowning, Dean walked through the automatic entrance doors, approached the front desk officer and asked the bored, frowning young trooper sitting behind it if a Stuart Foley had been there. The trooper shook his head and gave Dean a flat no. Dean then asked the trooper if he might check back with – and, with some consternation, it occurred to him that Foley had not given him the name of Pete Lassiter's nephew, the BCI investigator – so he guessed simply, Lassiter. The desk officer informed Dean that there was no investigator by that name at the station.

"Well, any investigator," Dean said. "My acquaintance, Stu Foley, had an appointment with a BCI investigator, at this station. This investigator would have an uncle by the name of Pete Lassiter."

The young desk officer smirked, lifted the receiver and called back there, even mentioning the name, Pete Lassister. After a moment, Dean realized that he had struck pay dirt.

"Here," the desk officer handed him the phone.

"Hello," said a voice. "Inspector Tom Quinn here. How can I help you?"

"You're Pete Lassiter's nephew?" Dean asked.

Investigator Quinn said, "Yes, Mr. Lassiter is my uncle."

Dean told him that he and Foley were supposed to meet here and speak with him about evidence they had gathered that might be helpful solving a serious crime. Dean didn't want to reveal too much at that point. If he started telling him that it involved a potential murder charge against the former DA and now Supreme Court Justice, Sam Marcum, Dean worried that the Investigator Quinn might have serious concerns about his sanity.

"Mr. Foley didn't call you?"

"No, sir," Quinn said. Dean could tell from his voice that the investigator was wondering what kind of prank this was. "I have not heard from a Mr. Foley. Would you like to meet with me without him? Provide your information, see what you got?"

Dean thought about that. But all he had was a rather far-fetched story. Foley had the key piece of evidence proving it – a copy of Miller's cell phone video recording.

"No, I think both Mr. Foley and I need to speak with you about this together," Dean said. "Let me try to track him down and get back to you."

"Alright," said Quinn. "But I'm off duty at five."

Dean checked his watch. It was already quarter past three. Where the hell was Foley?

Immediately upon hanging up with Investigator Quinn, and still standing before the scowling desk officer, Dean took out his cell phone and called Foley. Again, there was no answer, only Foley's somewhat annoying voice mail message: "In the words of Sun Tzu, all war is deception. And hence, I may or may not be available to answer this call. But please do leave a message."

"Sun Tzu to you," Dean muttered to himself, still under the watchful eye of the desk officer, as he waited for Foley's voice message to finish, and the beep to sound, so he could leave his message.

Finally, there came the beep, and Dean said, "Hey, Stuey, I'm at the trooper station and you're not. Where are you? Please call me ASAP. Thanks."

Upon leaving the message, Dean asked the desk officer if he could wait there for a call back.

"Well, I'd prefer if you waited in the lobby," he said, "or better yet, back in your car."

The desk officer had concluded, Dean felt, that he was a nut.

Dean returned to his car and waited fifteen minutes for Foley to call. But no return call came. Dean then called Kat's cell phone and she didn't answer either so he left a voice mail message that Foley was a no-show and wondered if she had heard from him. She called Dean back moments later.

"Why would he call me?" she asked.

"I don't know," Dean said. "I'm just wondering where the hell he is."

"Why don't you go check his house?" Kat asked.

Dean shrugged, not sure why that didn't make logical sense. It still wouldn't explain why Foley hadn't shown up at the trooper station or answered or returned his call.

"I guess I'll have to," Dean said. "See what happened to that slug."

Twenty minutes later, Dean pulled into Foley's driveway. The house looked empty. Ginny was at work, and wouldn't be home until at least six.

The first thing Dean noticed after getting out of his car was the rumbling sound of a car motor coming from somewhere. Finally, after a time, he realized it was coming from Foley's attached garage. He went to the garage door and tried to lift it but it wouldn't budge. Frowning, he held an ear to the door. A car engine was definitely running inside the garage. He sniffed the air and decided in addition to hearing the car's motor, he could smell the sweet, heavy sick smell of its exhaust.

Frowning, Dean went to the side door of the house along the driveway. He'd been inside it enough to know that it opened to a short set of stairs to a foyer leading on the left to a small kitchen and to the right to a decent sized living room. Dean rang the doorbell, still wondering, and now starting to worry, about a car idling in the garage.

When no one answered, he backed away from the door and called out, "Hey, Stuey! Where the hell are you?"

Suddenly, the side door opened and a hulking figure stepped out a foot or so onto the driveway.

"Can I help you?"

Dean stepped back and was unable to speak. He decided that the guy in front of him must be none other than Stan Mazurka.

Finally, he cleared his throat.

"Where's Stu Foley?" he asked. "This is his house."

"Let's just say he's indisposed," Mazurka said.

"Who are you?"

Mazurka stepped toward Dean. He was a big man, well over six foot tall, heavy-set, with wide shoulders and a large, rough-hewn pockmarked face with small beady eyes that slanted downward in a perpetual scowl. Even when the man smiled, he scowled.

"I think you better come inside with me," Mazurka said.

In the next moment, he grabbed hold of Dean's shoulders and pulled him towards him.

"Hey!" Dean protested. "Get your hands…"

But Mazurka held firm and before Dean knew it, he had been pulled inside Foley's side door foyer, and up three steps into his kitchen.

"Get your fucking hands off me!" Dean shouted.

But by now, it was too late. Mazurka pushed him and Dean tumbled backward completely into the kitchen. By the time Dean recovered and gathered his balance at the side of the kitchen table, he saw that Mazurka was pointing a small, silver pistol at him.

"What's this?" Dean asked.

From somewhere down the hall from the kitchen leading to the attached garage, Dean heard the idling car engine.

"Wish you hadn't stumbled onto this, Mister Alessi," Mazurka said. "But having done so, you give me no choice."

"No choice for what?" Dean asked.

Dean's heart was beating fast now. All he felt was serious danger. The closest thing to this feeling was the time about three years ago when that idiot in the pickup truck had careened over into his lane on the Thruway and broadsided him. In the instant before the crash, he had felt death close by, riding on his shoulders as the saying goes, and that was what he was feeling now.

Mazurka roused him from that thought by thrusting the pistol at him.

"You know where the garage is?" he asked.

Dean shrugged dumbly. He could not think properly at that moment and had no idea what this man wanted.

"The – the garage?"

"Yeah, wake up and get your ass moving to it," Mazurka

said and pointed the gun that way.

Dean nodded feebly and turned. He started walking though his legs felt rubbery, useless.

"C'mon," Mazurka said, "get moving."

Dean finally made it to the door leading out to the garage and stopped. From out there, the car idling was even louder. And the sickeningly sweet smell of car exhaust fumes was worse here than it had been outside and made it difficult to breathe. Suddenly, it occurred to Dean exactly what was going on. Carbon monoxide poisoning. Foley must be in the vehicle idling out there in the garage, suffocating on the vehicle's exhaust.

"Open the fucking door," Mazurka barked as Dean stood before it.

Dean reached out, opened it, and confirmed his fear. The fumes nearly overwhelmed him and even Mazurka had to back off and cover his face with his right shoulder. Then, Dean saw Foley leaning forward against the steering wheel of his beloved Navy blue Blazer, his eyes closed, probably dead already.

Dean turned to Mazurka.

"What the fuck?" he pleaded.

Mazurka waved the pistol at him.

"You're gonna get in there with him," he said.

"You gonna make it look like a double suicide?" Dean asked.

"You got a better idea, counselor?" Mazurka asked. "Yeah, that's exactly what I'm gonna make it look like. All people gonna know is that both of you were found out in Foley's Blazer, asphyxiated. How it happened, and why, will be a subject of speculation. Maybe it was an accident, two idiots talking about old times overcome by the fumes. Or some other assholes may suggest it was a gay lovers' double suicide." Mazurka smiled. "But none of that will matter. Both of you will be dead, and that'll be that. No tales to tell and nothing more to worry about."

Dean looked at the short barrel of Mazurka's gun and tried to think what to do. Charge him? Would Mazurka shoot or would that botch the whole thing worse than it already was.

"Don't even think about it, counselor," Mazurka said. "Because I will shoot. Then we'll set it up as a gay lovers' murder-suicide or some bullshit."

"Well, I am not about to let you kill me."

"When I push you inside the garage," Mazurka said and flashed a toothy grin, "you'll have no choice in the matter."

"No man," Dean said, and heard himself whimpering now. In fact, through the whole thing, he was starting to feel disembodied. Not part of it, as if it was a movie and he was merely watching it.

Mazurka suddenly launched forward and grabbed hold of Dean while thrusting the pistol into his ribs. He was about to shove Dean into the garage, when a voice from the other end of the kitchen hall shouted, "Stop it! Take your hands off him!"

Mazurka turned around. But before he could say a word or do anything, a shot rang out like thunder in a small, tin shed. Dean's ears went numb, throbbing, and in the next instant, he saw Mazurka's face twist in pain. An instant later, his legs gave out and he went tumbling backward and fell to the kitchen floor. Without hesitation, Kat stepped forward and kicked Mazurka in the head.

Dean collapsed to his knees, overcome by the fumes and the aftermath of an adrenal rush. After a moment, he rolled to a sitting position and looked up at Kat, his ears still ringing. She was shouting something at him but the sound of her voice was muffled as if she was speaking underwater.

"Help Stuey!" she was shouting. "We have to help Stuey!"

Somehow, Dean managed to gather his wits about him and was up on his feet following Kat into the garage. Coughing, she had already opened the driver's door to the Blazer. Foley was limp, leaning to his left, his right wrist attached to the steering wheel by a set of handcuffs.

"Jesus!" Kat cried.

She reached over Foley's frame and turned off the Blazer's engine. Then, she turned around to Dean.

"Open the garage door!" she shouted at him. "Where's the damn opener switch!"

Chapter Thirty-Four
Foley's Revenge

As the garage door slowly rose up, a gust of cold wind filled the interior and out rushed the thick, killing cloud of carbon monoxide gas.

"Is he dead?" Dean asked. "Jesus."

Kat was shaking Foley, yelling at him to wake up. She bent an ear to his chest, tried to feel his pulse. Finally, she turned to Dean.

"We got to get him out of here," she said. "Go back inside and check if the keys to these handcuffs are on Mazurka. I'll call 911." She gestured toward the door leading to the kitchen. Mazurka was in there, bleeding from a gunshot wound to his right thigh. Then, she turned back to Foley and resumed shaking him, calling his name.

Dean trotted back into the kitchen. Mazurka lay sprawled against the stove, a red hole in his right thigh. He was moaning and seemed out of it, lapsing into shock, Dean supposed. Dean crouched down by his side and said, "Where's the fucking key?" But Mazurka only moaned. As

Dean patted Mazurka's clothes, searching for the key, and was about to reach into his front pants pocket, Mazurka's left arm reached out of nowhere and grabbed Dean by the ankle, pulling him down to the floor. Dean kicked frantically at Mazurka and finally caught the thigh wound and that was the end of that. Mazurka rolled up into a ball and cried out in pain, then seemed to have passed out.

Kat entered the kitchen just as Dean was moving back to Mazurka's body to search for the key. He told her what had happened and she went over to where Mazurka lay.

"How's Stuey?"

"I think he's alive, breathing," she said. "But still out of it."

As she went through Mazurka's pockets, Dean said, "Be careful."

"Here they are," she said, lifting out the keys.

She and Dean ran back to the garage, unlocked the handcuffs and pulled Foley out of the Blazer. As they dragged him outside into the fresh, frigid air, he started moaning. Within a minute, he was awake, sitting and coughing on the frozen driveway as the sun, a cold, white orb, was setting low in that darkening late afternoon sky.

"What happened?" Foley moaned. "Where is he?"

"Kat shot him," Dean said.

Foley looked at her and raised his eyebrows, very much impressed.

"You can shoot?"

Kat nodded. "Yeah, I can shoot."

"Jesus, the world never ceases to amaze," Foley said.

From the distance, the sirens blaring caused them to

look up.

"He alive?" Foley asked. He looked at Dean.

Dean nodded.

"She blasted a hole in his right thigh," he said. "He's in shock, I think."

Suddenly, Foley stood and started walking, wobbling actually, toward the open garage.

"Where you going?" Kat asked.

Foley stopped and looked at her.

"I got some unfinished business inside my house," he said.

"Stuey, no," Dean said.

But Foley wouldn't listen. He staggered forward and Dean and Kat were right behind him ready to catch him if he fell. They followed him back into the kitchen. From out there, the sirens were getting louder, a mere block or two away.

"Stuey," Dean said.

Mazurka was still a lump laying on his side on the kitchen floor. He could be dead. But after a good look at him, they saw his chest rise and fall. He was still breathing.

A woozy Foley stumbled across the kitchen to where Mazurka lay and looked down at him.

"What the hell you doing, Stuey?" Dean asked.

He and Kat were right behind him, still close enough to grab him. But they held back, waiting to see what Foley intended to do. Then, in the next moment, he pulled back his right foot, and after letting it hang there a moment, launched his it toward Mazurka's head.

"Jesus, Stuey," Dean said as he pulled Foley back.

"Alright, let go," Foley said. "Let me do one more

thing."

"Enough," Dean said. "You're gonna kill him."

"Just check and see if he has his cell phone on him."

"Why?"

"Just do it."

Dean reached down and dug his hands into Mazurka's pockets and found his cell phone. The big lug of a man moaned and stirred momentarily.

Dean stood and handed Foley the phone.

Foley found the contacts list, and Sam Marcum's name was there.

"Bingo," he said and turned to Dean. "Can I record a call on this?"

Dean nodded, now figuring out what Foley intended. He took the phone and found the audio record app.

"Now make your call," Dean said. "It should record it."

Foley tapped the call button for Marcum's cell number. On the second ring, Marcum answered.

"Is it done?" he asked, seeing the call number and thinking, of course, that he was talking to Mazurka.

"Yes," Foley said, making his voice deeper. "Foley's dead. Just like Miller."

"Good," Marcum said. "Well done."

Marcum appeared to hesitate a moment as the sirens were blaring now, right in front of Foley's house, a patrol car, an ambulance, and a fire engine. All three of them looked that way and Foley tried to cover the phone.

"What's that?" Marcum asked.

"An ambulance," Foley said, trying to mask his voice.

But Marcum had been scared off.

"Hello?" Foley said. There was no response.

But Foley was confident that Marcum had said enough. In the next moment, two police officers ran into the kitchen, weapons drawn. When they saw Foley, Dean and Kat standing there, and Mazurka's body on the floor, they told them to slowly get down onto their knees and bring their hands slowly over their heads. They obeyed as Dean quickly explained what had happened, adding that Foley needed immediate treatment for carbon monoxide poisoning.

As if on cue, Foley passed out.

Chapter Thirty-Five
A Meeting with the CJ

First thing on a Tuesday morning a month after Sam Marcum's arrest as an accomplice for the murders of Kent Laurence and Detective Jack Miller, Dean was called for a meeting with the CJ. As he entered the judge's chambers, a place Dean had never been, Chief Judge Krane stood and surprised Dean by raising his arms in a friendly greeting.

"Mister Alessi," he said expansively as if renewing an old friendship. "Come in!" He gestured to a chair before his wide desk. "Sit down."

"Thank you, your Honor," Dean said.

Dean sat down before the Chief Judge's desk, not really clear on what the man wanted from him that morning. He had been off from work for ten days after his near-murder at Foley's house. Stu Foley had spent a couple days in the hospital and upon his release, he, Dean, and Kat met with state police investigators and the special prosecutor, Dave Keller, the District Attorney from Monroe County, who had been appointed by an Erie County judge upon request of the interim Erie County DA.

Based upon their statements, the cell phone tape, and the copy of Detective Miller's cell phone video, felony complaints were drawn up charging Sam Marcum with the second-degree murders of Kent Laurence, as an accomplice with Susie Hines, and Detective Miller as Stan Mazurka's accomplice. Stan Mazurka was charged with murdering Miller and the attempted murders, felony assault and kidnapping of Foley and Dean. Last but certainly not least, Susie Hines was charged with perjury based upon her testimony before the grand jury that she had not murdered Laurence.

Larry Donnelly, the former ADA and Justice Marcum's confidential law clerk, was under criminal investigation for official misconduct and bribe receiving related to his botching of Susie Hines' waiver of immunity before the grand jury, thus making her immune from prosecution for Kent Laurence's murder. Arrest warrants were promptly obtained based upon the charges, and Marcum, Mazurka, and Hines were paraded into court under the glare of several cameras from the local TV news stations. Marcum, Susie Hines and Mazurka were finally able to post bail and after doing so, they went into seclusion as they worked with their respective high-priced defense lawyers to come up with a defense in what promised to be one hell of a media circus as the latest local trial of the century.

Upon Dean's return to work, he met briefly with Gunther. Dean's job now appeared safe – there was no way to fire one of the star witnesses who had brought to justice two, and maybe three, lawyers who had gone ridiculously bad, one of them the former DA and present Associate Justice of the state Supreme.

Gunther told Dean that investigative files had been opened against Marcum, Susie Hines, and Donnelly, but they had been transferred to the LDO's satellite office in Albany run by Don Asperante for obvious conflict of interest reasons. And anyway, the formal investigations would be held in abeyance pending the outcome of the criminal proceedings. If Marcum and Hines were found guilty, which appeared likely, they'd be disbarred by operation of a state law providing for the automatic disbarment of any lawyer convicted of a felony. And murder was the ultimate felony in any state.

The same would apply to Larry Donnelly, should the special prosecutor succeed in making a case against him, although that seemed some problematic unless Marcum admitted that he had instructed him to botch Susie Hines' grand jury waiver of immunity procedure and Donnelly agreed to do it.

"First of all," the CJ began the meeting that morning, "I want to congratulate you on your tenacity and perseverance." He sighed and turned up his hands in a gesture of defeat. "None of us, even those who knew Sam Marcum for a very long time, saw him for what he was – a cheat and a scoundrel and a murderer."

He looked at Dean for a reaction, got none, and so continued, "Well, it looks like Sam'll be giving up his seat on the bench for a seat in state prison." He gave a short laugh. "And, indeed, like his judicial seat, his seat in jail will likely be a lifetime appointment."

Finally, Dean said, "It does appear to be a strong case."

He sighed, looked down and, after thinking a few moments, decided he had a right to say something bold. "And if there was any real justice in the world, he'd be getting a seat in the electric chair."

The CJ laughed.

"Well, I suppose that's my fault," he said. "About six years ago, if you recall, I wrote the decision that outlawed the death penalty in this state."

Dean forced a smile and nodded, still wondering about the real reason for this meeting.

The CJ sighed and smirked for a time. Then, he leaned forward and gave Dean a determined look.

"You still have interest in the LDO Director job after all this?"

The question took Dean by surprise. He drew in a breath and frowned.

"What about Brad Gunther?" he asked.

"Well, it's looking like Brad will be appointed to the take Sam Marcum's spot on the Court," the CJ said. He leaned back and regarded Dean for a time, letting that news sink in. After a nod, he added, "And that appointment should come in short order as the Judicial Conduct Commission is moving expeditiously to remove Sam from judicial office."

The CJ sighed. Dean suspected that he was likely behind that as well, that is, the Judicial Conduct Commission's taking expeditious action. He was forever the puppet master guiding the strings of this or that person or politician, commission or agency, to get exactly what he wanted, usually another ally appointed to some important position, in this case, Brad Gunther, as a Supreme Court Justice, to replace the ally he had just lost. Gunther had some fairly decent political connections himself and his loyalty to the CJ would be even greater than Marcum's once his appointment as Associate Justice to the Supreme Court was made.

"However," the CJ went on, now leaning forward and clasping his hands together on top of his desk, "if a certain meeting comes to light while his application for that judicial office is vetted – that you may or may not be aware of, if it in fact actually occurred – a meeting with Sam Marcum that I am led to believe took place the night before Sam, then still DA, reversed himself and decided to prosecute his first assistant, Susie Hines, certain people may not think kindly of Mister Gunther's, well… qualifications for judicial office. As you might understand, that meeting, and what Brad may have told Sam, may taint him in some way."

Dean sighed. He now saw why he had been summoned to the CJ's chambers. A bribe in the CJ's world was not always paid with money. Dean spent a few moments suppressing an angry reaction to what the CJ was proposing – his silence for the LDO Director's job.

Around ten last night, Foley had called Dean and brought up the very meeting about which the CJ was now referring. Foley had, up to then, neglected to tell the police about it in light of the more immediate and relevant circumstances concerning his attack by Mazurka allegedly at Marcum's behest. But last night, the meeting between Marcum and Gunther had occurred to him and it suddenly seemed extremely relevant to the overall case being pursued against Marcum, Susie Hines, and Stan Mazurka, not to mention its significance to the case the special prosecutor was trying to build against Larry Donnelly.

Foley was certain that Gunther, probably with the complicity and guidance of the CJ, had helped Marcum get out from under the scrutiny of the press, the LDO, the legal community and the public, for that matter, for failing to vigorously pursue an investigation into Susie Hines's shooting of her husband. At very least, Foley decided that reporting that meeting to the police would likely embarrass Gunther and the CJ by linking them more directly with Marcum and his outrageous crimes while DA, and especially whatever plans he had concocted to protect Susie Hines in the aftermath of Kent Laurence's murder. Maybe the CJ and Gunther wouldn't be considered accessories-after-the-fact, *per se*, under the criminal law, but in the public mind, and even among their brethren in the bar and on the bench, their reputations might be tarnished beyond repair. In short, Foley believed that this information would have a serious negative impact on any professional career ambitions either or both of them might have. And that would result in a bit more justice, a *real* comes around moment.

So that afternoon, Foley told Dean, he had called the investigator handling the case for the special prosecutor, Mark Keller, and told him he had thought of some information that might be useful concerning a suspicious meeting between Marcum and Gunther. And, Dean now surmised, that this investigator, or the special prosecutor himself, who may each be indebted to the CJ in some way, had alerted him.

"Just to be clear, your Honor," Dean said, "if I keep quiet about this particular meeting if indeed it really took place, you'll think better of my qualifications for the Director position?"

"I never said that Mister Alessi," the CJ said, scowling suddenly, having swiftly assessed Dean's position. He sighed, unclasped his hands, and leaned back in his deep, thick leather swivel chair, looking relaxed and in control as the King of Siam. After a moment, he swung sideways a few inches and regarded Dean with a derisive grin.

"You know," the CJ said, "it's been said about you, Dean, that you're too honest for your own good. Too honest, in fact, if this makes any sense, for you to be the guardian of the ethical code governing lawyers in this state. I hear that all the time from a lot of people."

"Believe me, your Honor," Dean said, "I've heard it, too."

The CJ laughed and said, "Well, what you need to learn, Dean, is that sometimes it pays to be practical. Sometimes justice is better served, if you will, by exercising common-sense discretion."

Dean sighed.

"But it's just this, your Honor," Dean said, "I have a hard time being practical when a lawyer's gone bad. When a lawyer's broken his oath to honorably serve his clients, the public, and the legal profession, it gets under my skin and makes me want to do something about it, so something to right that wrong."

"That's what I'm talking about," the CJ responded. "That's it exactly. See, Dean, if the public sees that too many of our brethren have gone bad, they'll lose confidence in the rest of us, everyone who've followed the rules best we could.

They'll think the whole legal and justice system has gone bad when in reality it's the other way around.

"So, in my view," the CJ went on, "unless we have someone, say like Justice Marcum and Susie Hines, for instance, who've gone really, really off the deep end of bad, then public disciplinary action is an absolute necessity for the system to operate properly. We can address and fix those seriously bad problems to the full extent of the law, sure, but the lessor ones we can fix so that everyone goes home happy. Make it a win-win situation instead of a zero-sum game. What I mean is, in that situation, the lawyer can be treated in a more, let us say, judicious and charitable manner that keeps them, and the legal profession, out of public scorn. Anyway, that is the way I see it. That is my vision."

"Isn't that what's called sweeping things under the rug?" Dean asked.

"Now, there you go again, Dean," the CJ said and laughed mirthlessly. "No, we're not sweeping anything under the rug. What I'm talking about is getting rid of the dirt in a practical, safe way, without inflicting the death penalty every time and in the process besmirching the reputations of the rest of us, the good guys. And as the LDO's new director, I am hoping you'll keep these philosophical considerations in mind. Should you be hired, that is."

The CJ swiveled around and faced Dean straight on.

"You hearing what I'm saying, Mister Alessi?"

"I believe so, your Honor," he said.

The debate was over so there was no use adding another word to it.

"Talk to your friend, Foley," the CJ added. "Maybe you

can even talk him into returning to his job as Chief Investigator after you become LDO Director."

Dean shrugged. He doubted Foley would listen to such a proposal, knowing Foley.

"And one other thing that'll maybe sweeten the pot for you," the CJ said with a smile. "If Brad Gunther gets the spot on the Court, Liza Hartman will be coming with him as his confidential law clerk."

That figured, too. Was there no end to the CJ's machinations?

Immediately upon returning to his office, Dean called Foley and told him about his meeting with the CJ. Foley grunted and laughed at points along the way of Dean's narrative. When Dean had finished, Foley remained quiet for a time.

"So when are you going to meet with Keller's investigator?" Dean asked.

Foley sighed and Dean could hear something gurgling up from within him.

"I'm not," he finally said. "I'm calling it off."

"What? Why?"

"Because sometimes you gotta play the game by their rules," Foley said. "Or you lose the game."

"Is that Sun Tzu?" Dean asked.

"No, Stu Foley."

Chapter Thirty-Six
Comes Around

"I want to extend my congratulations."

Dean had stood the moment Kat Franklin walked into his new office – the one vacated by Brad Gunther a month ago upon his appointment as Associate Justice to the state Supreme Court.

"Shut the door," he said.

Kat looked back momentarily, then turned to Dean.

"No, Dean," she said.

They hadn't had an intimate moment since the afternoon when Stan Mazurka tried to kill Foley and Dean and she had saved them. That had been the last time he had held her, kissed her. Dean had called her at home several times and even come to her office after that day, closing the door behind him, to talk about what was going on between them, to tell her that he loved her, craved her. But, as always, her response had been the same – that their affair ("fling," as she called it) had been a mistake and that nothing more could come of it. She would not be responsible for ending his marriage.

"How's Laura?" Kat asked, as if to emphasize how adamant she had remained in her wish that nothing be rekindled between them.

"She's fine," he said. "Staying sober, if that's what you mean."

That was true. Laura had not had a drink in weeks. And she was even managing a job as a retail clerk in a clothing store in the mall. She had a master's degree in social work but she had agreed with her therapist that, for now anyway, it probably wasn't a good idea for a recovering alcoholic to devote her time to helping people deal with serious emotional and mental problems.

And the other part of the Kat's question, what she was really asking, perhaps, concerning the health of his relationship with Laura, was oddly the same. They were fine. They had intimate, romantic moments, regularly made love. Dean was beginning to wonder if he was in love with two women, though the logistics of that seemed well beyond his practical abilities.

Kat nodded, not wishing to probe further.

"Well, I just wanted to say, I couldn't be happier that you finally got the job," she said. "I know you're going to make a great Director."

Dean shrugged. He hoped so, although he could not escape the feeling that he had sold his soul to the Devil – in the guise of Chief Judge Krane – to get it. And he was still just a little bit angry at Foley for making his soul-selling possible.

"Thanks, Kat," he said. He looked down at the printout

on his desk, a list of current serious investigations.

"You're a bit overloaded with serious cases," he said, nodding to the list. "With Liza Hartman gone."

"Well, you've been interviewing for her job, right? Has a decision been reached?"

"Yes, with Margo Anson-Clarke," he said. "And yes, we've made a decision."

He shrugged and let out a disagreeable sigh.

"What? Who is it?" Kat asked.

Dean sighed again.

"Who is it, Dean?"

He smirked, then blurted, "Larry Donnelly."

"Larry Donnelly? That incompetent scumbag? How could you...?"

Dean said, "Proof again, I suppose, what goes around..."

"Does not come around," Stu Foley finished for him as he walked into the Director's office. Kat turned to him and Foley said, "Hi, Kat."

"Hi, Stu," she said and looked back at Dean. "Dean just told me that Larry Donnelly is going to replace Liza as our new dis-con."

"So I heard," Foley said. "Gives the term, dis-clown, a wholly new and enhanced meaning, don't you think?"

"Jesus, you're serious, aren't you, Dean?" Kat said.

"Comes from on high," he said. "Despite two or three better candidates, the CJ wants Donnelly."

"But what about what he did before the grand jury," Kat went on, "to help get Susie Hines a free pass for murder?"

"A tragic mistake was all that's ever been proved," Dean

said. "When the special prosecutor closed his investigation against old Larry, it opened the door to this."

"And it seems that Donnelly earned this job," Foley added, "as his reward for keeping his mouth shut about the whole thing. That, of course, helped keep both our former leader, Brad Gunther, and the CJ, out of harm's way."

"I suppose a suspicious mind might think that way," Dean said.

Foley's point didn't make Dean feel so good about what they had done – keeping quiet about Gunther's meeting with Sam Marcum in The Pub in exchange for the Director job.

"We closed out our case against him as well?" Kat asked.

"We must have," Dean said. "Asperante must have closed it."

"I wonder who told him to do that," Kat asked.

"Well, what's done is done," Dean said, "and we'll make the best of it. Hopefully, Mister Donnelly will prove a more competent dis-con than an ADA."

Kat sighed.

"Well, I'll let you two boys alone," she said. "Staff meeting's at ten right?"

"Yes," Dean said. "I'm re-introducing old Mr. Foley here as Chief Investigator."

"I am sure that Dawn Smith will be tickled pink," Kat said.

"See," Foley said, "what goes around sometimes does come around."

Kat smirked and turned to leave. She looked back at Dean as he sat down behind his wide desk, while Stu Foley sat heavily in the chair facing him.

"So where do we begin?" Dean asked his Chief Investigator.

As Kat stepped out of the new Director's office and closed the door behind her, she thought, yes, every so often, what goes around, does come around. But then, she thought of another saying:

Be careful what you wish for.

Copyright

About the Author

Vincent L. Scarsella is the author of speculative, fantasy, and crime fiction. His published books include the crime novels "The Anonymous Man" (2013) and "Lawyers Gone Bad" (2014), as well as the young adult fantasy, "Escape from the Psi Academy", Book 1 of the Psi Wars! Series released in May, 2015. Book 2 of the series, "Return to the Psi Academy", is slated for publication by IFWG Publishing in the summer of 2016.

Scarsella has also published numerous speculative fiction short stories in print magazines such as *The Leading Edge*, *Aethlon*, and *Fictitious Force*, various anthologies, and in several online zines. His short story, "The Cards of Unknown Players," was nominated for the Pushcart Prize and has been republished by *Digital Science Fiction*.

Scarsella's full-length play, "Hate Crime," about race relations in the context of a legal thriller, was performed in Buffalo on September 13, 2016 and is scheduled for a reprise in late May, 2016. "The Penitent," about the Catholic Church child molestation scandal, was a finalist in the June 2015 Watermelon One-Act Play Festival.

Scarsella has also published non-fiction works, most notably, "The Human Manifesto: A General Plan for Human Survival," which was favorably reviewed in September 2011 by the Ernest Becker Foundation.

79584253R00170

Made in the USA
Columbia, SC
05 November 2017